WHY WAS RACHEL MURDERED?

BILL PRENTICE

Why Was Rachel Murdered?

Copyright 2018 by Bill Prentice

All rights reserved under International and Pan-American copyright conventions. No part of this publication may be reproduced, scanned, stored in any retrieval system, transmitted or distributed in any printed or electronic format without the written permission of the publisher.

This book is a work of fiction. Names, characters, places and incidents are the product of the author's imagination or are used fictitiously. Any resemblance to actual events, locales, businesses, organizations or persons, living or dead, is coincidental.

Book cover design by ebooklaunch.com

Published in Canada in 2018 by Echo Road

Echoroad.ca

First published in ebook and paperback in November 2018

ISBN: 978-1-7753337-1-5 (ebook)

ISBN: 978-1-7753337-0-8 (paperback)

❧ Created with Vellum

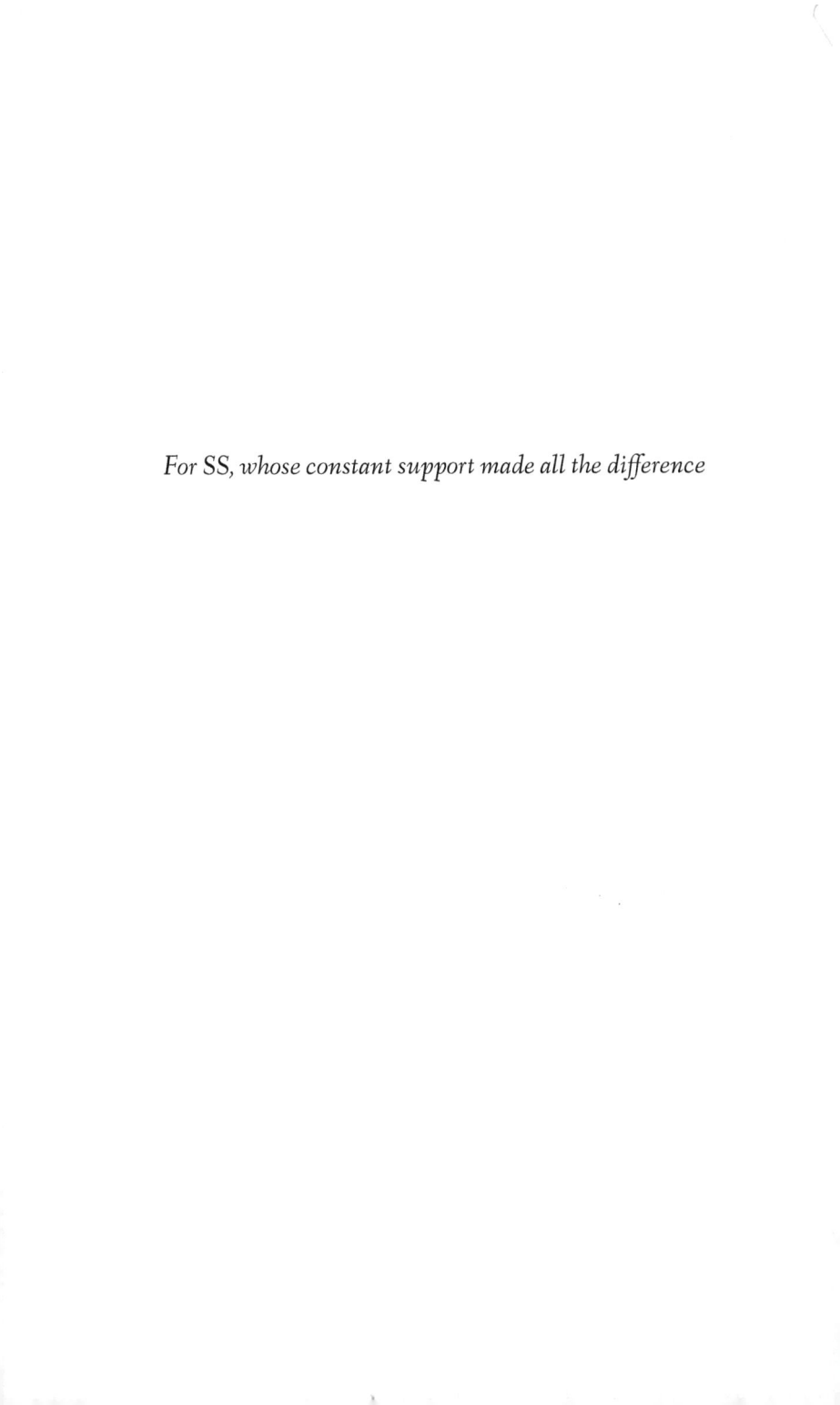

For SS, whose constant support made all the difference

1

Rachel Lisgar walked off the plane with a long list of tasks and not enough time.

She'd picked up a faint whiff of trouble in the back pages of a routine SEC filing by Hudson Ventures, an investment firm in midtown Manhattan. The hair on the back of her neck had risen. She followed the trail as far as she could in the official sources, then continued the hunt through a series of ever-more obscure online data banks. Now she had an ugly problem.

Devising the right solution preoccupied her while she cleared customs at Toronto's Billy Bishop Airport. The terminal's glass doors slid closed behind her as she finished a phone call with a grunt of satisfaction, then texted her client, Janos Pach, asking for a meeting ASAP.

It was August and steam-bath humid along the waterfront. She had grabbed the first flight that morning to New York to confirm her suspicions about Hudson Ventures. Now, night had fallen, and she was coming home with even more questions. Her townhouse, a blessedly cool oasis of calm where she did her best thinking, was within easy walking distance.

She tucked an errant curl of frizzy hair behind her ear. Her grey-green eyes narrowed. Should she call Carole? She really didn't want to. Damn. But she'd feel worse if she didn't.

Rachel keyed in the number.

"Hey, it's me. Yeah, it's been a while. Anyway, there's something you need to know. It's important. Obviously. I wouldn't have called if it wasn't. Get back to me as soon as you can."

She shrugged her shoulder until her laptop bag rode more comfortably and set off with a mile-eating, graceful gait, heading home along a familiar route, her brain running numbers. A sickening weight grew in her chest. Despite everything else, she didn't want to accept what the data revealed.

The sidewalks were crowded with locals, mostly young professionals enjoying the summer Friday night. On the narrow streets, runners and rollerbladers slipped around parked cars and turning cabs. A guy in a tight T-shirt and shorts checked her out as he ran by. She spotted a cyclist, a fit-looking woman wearing yellow spandex racing gear, resting on a bench. For a fleeting moment, Rachel considered getting out her bike and going for a ride. Fresh air and exercise would probably help clear her head, but a few more hours of online research would be more productive. And a cold beer would be a lifesaver.

Rachel reached her quiet cul-de-sac and approached her townhouse. She waved to a neighbour across the street who was trimming his rose bushes. She envied his devotion to the tiny front garden. He was a nice enough old guy, but tonight she had no patience for gossip. She twisted the key in her front door lock and stepped inside. Wonderful cool air washed—

He pounced.

She was yanked off her feet and slammed into the wall.

Shock and pain engulfed her. She panicked. A huge hand roughly grabbed her hair. Fingers like claws shoved her face to the wall, holding her there. Her right arm was wrenched up behind her back. Hot, fetid breath scorched her neck.

She heard the front door lock click shut. The foyer was instantly pitched into a murky half-light.

Her rage erupted. Chest tight. Acid bile in her throat. With a fierce burst of anger, she wrenched herself away from the wall. He slammed her back into it. She twisted. A mirror crashed to the floor and shattered. She blindly stomped back with her heel, but he was quick as a hunting cat.

She opened her mouth to scream. He jacked up her arm. Pain burned through her body. White light exploded across her vision.

"Not a word," he growled, his voice steady, his control unrelenting.

Rachel dragged in ragged gulps of air. She stood on her tiptoes, off balance, shivering in the darkness. Adrenalin raced through her body. A nightmare trapped her.

Silence except for the hoarse rasp of her breathing. He shifted his weight. Broken glass crunched under his feet.

"Your name is Rachel Elizabeth Lisgar. You are a professor of advanced mathematics. You hold the Canada Research Chair in Social Analytics. You also provide consulting services to the Emergent Investment Fund."

Still gasping for air, now totally confused, her mind spun. How did he know all this? Who was he? "What—"

"Shh," he whispered, bumping her forehead against the

wall. "Your parents are dead. You have a sister, Carole. She lives in Ottawa. I can give you her address."

"But—"

"Quiet," he snapped, smashing her face into the wall. She groaned in pain and confusion. Her eyes watered.

"We know everything," he hissed. "Where you work. Where Carole lives. Don't say a word, but nod if you understand."

Trapped, Rachel nodded.

"Okay," he said more calmly. "You and I are going to walk slowly over to your front window. You need to see something. Don't try to escape. Don't try to see my face. You'll only get hurt. Do you understand?"

She bowed her head. She clamped down on her anger. *How dare he do this? Stop it,* she told herself. *Now's not the time. Breathe. Keep it together. Live to fight another day.*

He pulled her away from the wall. He pushed her towards the front room. Together, they shuffled to the window.

Across the quiet street, her friendly old neighbour had interrupted his rose trimming to chat with a cyclist, the woman in yellow spandex racing gear she had seen earlier. A helmet and wraparound sunglasses hid her features.

"Pay attention," said the voice in her ear. From his pocket he pulled a laser pointer. He flashed it once out the window.

The cyclist, without interrupting the conversation, reached into her bike pannier and pulled out a silencer-equipped pistol.

Rachel gasped. Her neighbour froze in shock.

The cyclist, in one smooth motion, raised the weapon and shot the gardener in the face. His body crumpled to the sidewalk.

The cyclist threw one leg over the bike's crossbar, leaned

down and shot two more rounds into the body. She slid the gun back into the pannier, then rode away at a slow, steady pace.

The street was deserted.

Rachel, moaning, collapsed to the floor, numbed by the brutal murder.

He knelt beside her, grabbed her hair with one hand and her face with the other, holding her steady so she could not see him.

"I'm going to ask you a question. You need to tell the truth. If you lie, I will hurt you. Do you believe me?"

Rachel, her heart racing, gasped, "Yes."

He leaned closer, whispering. "Earlier today, you were given a flash drive—"

Her eyes widened in shock. *How could they know? How did they find out?* Without thinking, she started to turn her head.

"Don't." His grip on her tightened. He dug his bony knee into her back. He yanked on her hair and brought his mouth down close to her ear. "The flash drive. Where is it?"

"In my bag!" She squeezed her eyes shut. Hot tears of frustration and pain leaked out.

He increased the pressure. "Did you copy the files?"

"Only onto my laptop." Her voice broke in despair.

"Where else?" he demanded, his mouth so close his dank breath brushed her cheek. "The truth. Or Carole dies."

"No copies," she sobbed. She thought she might choke. *The bastards. Why do they always fucking win?*

He stroked her hair. "I believe you," he murmured.

Her panic began to ebb. Her ragged breathing eased. A glimmer of relief sparked hope. *Maybe that's all he wants. Maybe this will soon be over.*

Then he tightened his two-handed grip on her head.

He twisted it violently. Right. Left. Her neck snapped. Fragments of C_1 vertebrae were driven into her brain stem. He dropped her head and watched her eyes as Rachel's life faded to nothing.

In one fluid motion, he rose. He checked his watch. He had one more stop to make.

2

Collier Street runs for three quiet blocks near the high-rent shopping district in midtown Toronto. Rows of Victorian workers' cottages line the final stretch. At the end lies a small park with a shaded bench that offers a view across the wooded ravine to the old-money mansions of Rosedale. It was Monday morning. A light breeze lifted the growing humidity.

Neil Walker approached the park on foot. Out of habit, he used the tinted windows of parked cars to check the sidewalk behind him for a tail. He was clear. As he passed a dark blue luxury sedan, he checked his reflection in the side window.

Unconsciously, he straightened his shoulders in preparation for what could be a complicated meeting. He was in his mid-thirties, maybe a little heavy through the shoulders and arms. He wore jeans and a loose white shirt, the tails hanging out to cover the gun tucked in the small of his back. The deep-set eyes in his square face could keep secrets.

He spotted Janos Pach slumped on the park bench, head canted to one side, one finger picking absently at a semi-healed mosquito bite on his arm. Even while seated, Janos, with his broad forehead topped by white hair combed straight back to curl over his collar, displayed the urbane presence of an Eastern European aristocrat. He'd driven down from his cottage at Pointe au Baril on Georgian Bay, a three-hour drive, just for this meeting. The scruffy summer beard said Janos was still on vacation. The dark heaviness around his eyes told Neil something bad had happened.

Neil slipped onto the bench.

"Thank you for coming," Janos said. His Czech accent still lingered after four decades in Canada. Every syllable was precise, slightly exaggerated. "I was not sure you would."

"Just because we haven't talked in—what?—two years? Of course I'd come."

"You had dealings with the Lisgar family in the past." Janos gave him a sideways glance. "It did not work out so well."

"Says who?" Neil's grin flashed in the sunshine, breaking the tension. "Here I am, running my own business, just like you always wanted."

"But not like this."

Neil shrugged. "Kismet? Karma? Whatever. You called, I'm here. What's going on?"

Janos picked up the thread of their earlier phone conversation, his voice riddled with frustration.

"Rachel's neighbour? The gardener? It turns out he was a Serb. Ex-army colonel."

Neil stretched out his legs. "War crimes?"

Janos shrugged. "That is the police theory. They are interviewing people in the Serbian community."

Neil smiled. "And how's that working out?"

"Does not matter. The police believe Rachel died because

she witnessed a murder. They are wrong." He lapsed into brooding silence.

Neil looked out across the valley, enjoying the breeze as it drifted across his face, giving Janos time to collect his thoughts.

The Czech's disdain for the police came from bitter experience. Janos had been one of the student architects of the Prague Spring. When Soviet tanks rumbled through the streets, he slipped across the border one step ahead of the KGB. Today, he was a contrarian investor whose private equity fund, Emergent Investments, controlled more than a billion dollars in assets.

After a few moments, Janos touched Neil's arm gently. "I am sorry. This whole situation has me spinning. I do not like it."

Neil patted his hand, which fell away. "I take it Rachel Lisgar was more than just another consultant?"

Janos looked away for a moment. When his gaze swung back, his eyes were wet and haunted. "I have known Rachel since she was a child. She was a brilliant mathematician. Sure, with social causes, perhaps she could be a wing nut. But in the field of data analytics, she was a genius."

"And in the real world that means...?"

"She looked at information in new ways. And she could spot the bullshit in a balance sheet faster than anyone I have ever met. She got that from her father." Janos paused, lost for a moment in memories. "Thomas Lisgar, single-handedly, built Lisgar Investments into the biggest brokerage in the country."

"Always nice to see the rich get richer." The Lisgar family fortune stretched back to the era of sailing ships, the fur trade and the backroom political deals that produced Canada's first parliament.

"Tom Lisgar gave me my first job in this business. Everything I have I owe to him."

In the deep lines around Janos's mouth, Neil could see the pain and simmering anger. "Sorry for your loss."

"I do not need condolences. I need your help."

"So tell me what's happened. Start at the beginning."

Janos took a deep breath and let it out slowly. "One of my clients asked us to increase his exposure in social investment vehicles. You have heard of them? *Doing well by doing good?*"

"Sure."

"He specifically mentioned something called the Launchpad Fund. It is run out of New York by a company called Hudson Ventures. It helps countries and regions rebuild after natural disasters or wars. The Haitian earthquake. Pacific tsunamis. Like that."

"Got it," Neil said.

"I asked Rachel to perform a due diligence check. She mentors young activists in social entrepreneurship. This was right in her wheelhouse."

"Isn't she a high flyer? Why would she—"

"I give talks to her groups, from time to time. She helps out when we get swamped."

"Okay. I take it she looked into this Launchpad Fund. And?"

"Something about it bothered her. She said she needed to interview the CEO of Hudson Ventures, Stephen Howland."

Howland. The name rang a vague bell. What was it? Neil filed it away and pushed on. "Was there a problem?"

"She said Hudson Ventures was a Ponzi scheme."

"She could tell that fast?" Usually, Ponzi investigations took months, even years. "Based on what?"

"She compared the performance of the underlying investments against industry benchmarks." Janos shrugged. "She said the ROI was ridiculously high."

"And that was it?"

Janos paused. "There was something else. She said the corporate structure did not make sense."

Neil prompted him. "You mentioned she flew down to New York for the day to check it out."

"Yes, and when she got back, the first thing she did was leave a message for me. She wanted a meeting. Insisted on it being face-to-face."

"She knew you were up north?"

"She left the text on my work phone. I had turned it off. I did not pick it up until the next morning." Janos fell silent, then resumed the story. "Right after she left the message for me, she went home and was murdered. When the police discovered the body, her phone and laptop were missing."

"What's their theory?"

"That the Serb's killer had an accomplice watching from Rachel's townhouse. When she came home, she surprised him. After killing her, he stole her wallet and passport along with her phone and laptop. The police say the ID and electronics were probably fenced within hours."

Neil glanced at him. "It's possible, right?"

Janos shook his head. "There is more. Later that night, her office at the university was broken into."

"And what do the cops say about that?"

"The university did not report it. Apparently, nothing was missing. They did not want to make a fuss."

"Or do the paperwork."

"Detectives, inspectors, even the deputy chief—I have spent two days trying to get someone to listen."

"And?"

"They have settled on their theory. I could not budge them."

"And you are sure Rachel was the intended victim?"

"Not one hundred per cent," Janos admitted, "but if Rachel was killed because of research she did for me, I need to know."

"Now you want me to look into it?" Neil was pretty sure of the answer, but he had to ask.

"Find out what happened," Janos said, the skin around his eyes drawn tight and white.

Warily, Neil considered the obstacles. "The Toronto cops wouldn't be happy with me poking around."

"Not their jurisdiction." Janos sat up straighter. "This thing started in New York. That is where you will find answers. Do you have contacts there?"

"When I was on the force, I worked a couple of money laundering stings with investigators in the FBI's New York field office. A few of them should still be around." Neil glanced at Janos. "You know the Lisgar family lawyers will do everything they can to shut me out."

"Will that be a problem?"

"These are your friends, not mine."

They were quiet. A siren wailed in the distance, then faded.

Neil broke the silence. "Why me? Don't you own a piece of Securitec? They must have dozens of investigators on the payroll. Say the word, and they'll put a whole team on this."

"I do not need a team, Neil. I need one guy, the right guy and—you mentioned karma?—it turns out that guy is you." Janos pointed at Neil. "You were with the RCMP Financial Crimes Unit for—what?—ten years? You know the players.

The scams. You know how the financial world works. You can do this."

He had a point. Neil had a knack for financial investigations, something he discovered by accident while on the force. Money laundering, art fraud, stock swindles and more, he worked cases that crossed the spectrum. Nevertheless, this one promised to be complicated, not the least of which by the presence of Janos.

Janos grunted sourly. "You do not think I see the irony? When first you joined the RCMP, I asked myself why in God's name you would want to be a policeman."

"I remember. You weren't very happy."

"Even your mother agreed, which was shocking." He shook his head. "Yet today, here I am, asking for your help."

Neil laughed. Janos was really good about some things. His child support cheques arrived every month, starting the day Neil was born. He showed up once a year on Neil's birthday. But Janos admitting he was wrong? Rarely happened.

"Saying that must have cost you."

"You have no idea," Janos growled.

"Okay, I'll need to clear a few things off my desk."

"Thank you." The unexpected heartfelt gratitude in Janos's voice threatened to embarrass both of them. "Good." Janos pulled out his phone, relief showing on his face. "There are a few people you will want to talk to. I will make the calls."

Neil rested a cautionary hand on his arm. "If you're right about what happened to Rachel, be careful. They might come after you."

The look that flashed across Janos's face was one Neil had never seen but revealed a glimpse of something he had always suspected lay behind the friendly facade. It was cold, implacable, capable of anything.

His answer came as a guttural grunt. "Let them come."

Neil nodded. That tough determination was a good thing. Probably.

"I'll call you later." Neil stood and, with a small wave to Janos, walked back towards Yonge Street. He felt the beginning tingle of the hunt. Ponzi schemes. Huh. Bernie Madoff's Ponzi scheme had been worth sixty-four billion dollars. People have been killed for even a tiny piece of that.

Rachel had jumped into dangerous waters.

3

Neil stepped onto his front porch to find the door leading to the apartment upstairs open and the stairway blocked by a battered 200-pound Hammond B3 organ. That explained the van parked illegally by the fire hydrant out front.

"It's a fucking omen," rumbled Don Cale, the stocky white-haired musician who lived upstairs. He wore a heavy-duty black nylon vest with an attached lifting strap that disappeared under the dark brown wooden instrument.

Neil surveyed the scene. The organ, which was slightly larger than an apartment-sized piano, had become jammed at the landing where the stairs turned. "You need a hand?"

"I think we should forget the whole damn—"

"Yes, please," called out Moni Zetland, Don's long-standing and long-suffering girlfriend, who poked her head around the staircase corner and waved down to Neil. "Switch places with him. I'll go around front to make sure the van doesn't get a ticket."

Her head disappeared, followed a minute later by the sight of her nylon mover's vest being tossed on top of the B3.

Don rubbed the sweat off his face on the shoulder of his old Rush tour T-shirt. He looked at Neil and shrugged. "You sure you want to do this?"

"Be worth it just to see if you can squeeze up the stairs," Neil said with a grin. "Give me your vest, and get up to the top before I change my mind."

Neil had bought the century-old duplex near High Park while he was still on the force. The fact that he'd managed to keep up with the mortgage payments left him unexpectedly pleased.

He'd inherited Don as his tenant. By happy coincidence, Don had been with the Ontario Provincial Police as one of their top digital forensic techs. With retirement, he'd turned to music full time. Both of them were divorced. Don's ex lived in Scarborough. Neil's was in Prince Rupert, which established a reasonable buffer zone of two mountain ranges and a couple of thousand miles of prairie between them. More crucially, Neil and Don shared a love of Chicago blues, classic soul and east-coast singer-songwriters.

Neil tightened the strap attached to his vest and flexed his knees. He looked up at Don, checked he was ready. On his signal, they both lifted, shifting and twisting the massive wooden organ from where it had become jammed in the landing. Once freed, they eased it down the stairs, carefully keeping it from scraping the walls.

"You told me you retired this beast," Neil grunted. The Hammond B3, built circa 1963 and repaired with more parts than Frankenstein, had toured around the world a dozen times with various bands before Don meticulously restored it.

"I oughta have my head examined," Don said, avoiding a direct answer. "How'd it go with your dad?"

They made it to the front door and paused to catch their

breath. Neil could see Moni had the van's motor running and the back doors open.

"I have to go out of town for a couple of days," Neil said. "I'll try to be back by Thursday night." Don's band was booked into the Ace Hotel for a benefit. A traffic cop had been killed on duty, leaving four kids and a sick wife. This gig would be the first time they would play together in public. The crowd promised to be rowdy.

Don had bitched for days about not enough rehearsal time. Now he shook his head. "This thing could be a major fucking embarrassment. Might be better if nobody shows."

Together, they lifted the beast and gently carried it through the doorway, down the front steps and over to the van.

"If nobody turns up," Neil said cheerfully, "it won't matter how shitty you play."

"'Don't listen to the old man," Moni advised Neil in a loud stage whisper as she watched them maneuver the organ into the empty van and tie it down with straps. "He's just scared."

"Am not!" Don stumbled back out of the van into Moni's arms.

"Of course not," she laughed, pushing him gently around towards the passenger door. She reached over, hugged Neil and said *sotto voce*, "See you Thursday night? It would mean a lot to him."

"I'll do my best."

As the van pulled away, Neil stepped back onto the sidewalk. He checked his watch. *Pack a bag. Get changed. Send a couple of emails.* He had just enough time, even if he wasn't really sure what he was getting into.

4

The University of Toronto's Department of Mathematics occupies most of the sixth floor of the Goodman Centre for Information Technology, a modern glass-and-steel structure married to an old limestone and yellow-brick beaux arts–style administrative centre. A three-storey atrium connects the two buildings.

At the main floor reception desk, Neil watched the centre's executive director, Annie Da Silva, stride across the lobby to greet him. She was tall, well over six feet in her high heels, and dark, with exotic cat's eye makeup that somehow suited her. Janos Pach was a major donor to the centre. Annie was happy to make time for Neil's questions.

"The news was such a shock," she said, leading him across the atrium at a rapid clip. They were headed for the elevator, then Rachel's office.

"What can you tell me about Rachel?" Neil had to work hard to match her stride. "Last time you saw her, did you notice anything unusual? Was she nervous? Upset?"

"No, nothing. She was just...Rachel."

"What about her personal life—close friends, a jealous boyfriend, anything like that?"

"From what I saw, she wasn't seeing anyone. But how could she? She worked impossibly long hours, travelled constantly. Most of them do."

"Most of who?"

"You didn't know? In the world of mathematics, Rachel was a celebrity."

They stopped in front of a bank of elevators. Annie stabbed the Up button and turned to Neil. "What happened was a real tragedy. It's an overused word, but in this case it's true. She was someone people will write books about."

"Really? I heard she was smart but—"

"Try *genius*. Shortlisted for the Fields Medal. Twice. She was the real deal."

The elevator arrived, the doors opened. They waited for a handful of students to exit before they entered.

"Rachel had a gift for designing scalable pattern-recognition algorithms," Annie continued.

"Let's pretend I don't know what that means. Why is it important? In the real world?"

"She applies...applied...big data analytics to solve social problems," Annie explained as the door closed with a soft thud. "One of her algorithms, for example, drives smart transportation systems around the world. Another helps teachers improve educational outcomes for at-risk youth by seventy-eight to eighty-two per cent."

"I'm confused. How does Rachel's work here connect with what she was doing for Janos?"

"Sorry. No clue."

"Any idea what would make her jump on a plane to New York City?"

Annie shrugged. "Rachel kept the two worlds at arm's length." She fell silent. A text arrived on her phone. She glanced at it. Neil circled back to something she mentioned earlier.

"You said she was a rock star. What do you mean?"

The elevator doors opened, and they stepped out into a long hallway. Annie motioned to the left, and they started walking.

"In the academic world, competition for research talent is global, and it's fierce. Our mathematics department is ranked among the best in the world."

"Okay."

"Rachel's monographs were among the most cited publications to ever come out of this department. Ever. In the last hundred and fifty years."

"Wow."

"And that level of prestige attracts top scholars from around the world, more government funding and bigger corporate research partnerships. Because of that, the university ignored all the flack she caught for her off-campus campaigns."

"Her what?"

Annie glanced at him, clearly surprised at his ignorance. "Nobody told you? Rachel was an activist. Very vocal. Very involved in social justice issues. Reining in global corporations and their control of national economies was at the top of her list."

Neil stopped dead in his tracks. "Let me get this straight. She was an anti-globalism activist and a top-level financial consultant?"

"God love 'em, but mathematicians can be strange people," Annie said. "Lewis Carroll? The author of *Alice in Wonderland*? He was a mathematician."

"And was Rachel...?"

They stopped at Rachel's office. Neil examined the door. There were no obvious signs of a break-in.

"Rachel was...special." Annie swallowed and paled slightly, as if facing Rachel's office made her death more real. She cleared her throat. She swiped an electronic key card to open the door.

To Neil's eye, the office was small for a rock star academic. It measured about ten by fifteen feet with a window overlooking St. George Street. Framed degrees and certificates lined the walls. A bookcase sat stuffed with heavy texts and academic journals, some of them quite old. A cluttered desk and matching visitors' chairs, the blond-wood finish worn down by heavy use. On the desktop, there was a blank spot where Rachel would have positioned her computer.

"Anything missing?"

"Just the laptop. She carried it everywhere. It's not at her home?"

Neil shook his head.

"Other than that, it's hard to say for sure. There used to be piles of backup data disks and external storage drives everywhere. These days, the university insists that all backups be held on our secure network so..." Annie shrugged. "Could be just about anything. Who knows?"

"You knew her better than most—"

"Not really. We weren't all that close."

"I'm trying to understand who she was. You worked with her. What else can you tell me? Something other people might not realize?"

"Rachel was driven by her passions, both in the higher realms of advanced mathematics and at the grassroots community level. But underneath her public persona as a fearless social activist, Rachel was a shy introvert. She could be intellectually ruthless, but in her heart she cared deeply about people. She was complex, perhaps more than most people, but she gave more than most to the world."

Neil was beginning to believe he would have liked Rachel. "And her family? She has—had—a sister. Were they close?"

Annie's expression was carefully neutral. "Have you met her? Carole?"

Neil shrugged noncommittally.

"Then I won't say anything."

"Why—"

"It's best if you make up your own mind." Annie's phone beeped again. "I'm sorry. I have a meeting, and I'm already running a little late."

"Sure," said Neil, taking one final look around. He saw something lying on the floor behind Rachel's desk. "What's that?"

Annie bent down and picked up a framed black-and-white photo. It had probably been knocked down during the robbery. She brushed it off, a sad smile playing across her face.

It showed an elderly man with a shock of white hair; he was wearing a tweed suit and smoking a pipe. From his mouth emerged a cartoon bubble–quote: *One of the symptoms of an approaching nervous breakdown is the belief that one's work is terribly important.* The base of the frame held a small plaque inscribed, simply, *Bertrand Russell—mathematician, philosopher, peace activist.*

"This was one of her favourite quotes," Annie said. "Now you might understand why I liked her. A lot."

It was the type of self-deprecating humour that always made Neil smile, and it added another piece to the picture of Rachel that was forming in his mind.

Then his smile faded. Someone had callously killed this immensely talented, dazzlingly bright spirit.

They had made the world a little darker. They didn't care.

That was a mistake.

5

The broiling Haitian sun made the road shimmer in the high-noon heat. A government-issue SUV was parked at the edge of an abandoned neighbourhood in the Léogâne Arrondissement. Zhang Jie turned to address his two passengers. He pushed up his steel-framed glasses, then pointed accusingly through the windshield.

"The new homes that we paid for? The new school? Where are they?"

The pavement lay cracked and broken. During the years after the earthquake, tough, sturdy weeds had reclaimed whole sections of the abandoned roadway. Rows of devastated single-family homes baked alongside the road, their roofs collapsed, walls split, windows smashed. Piles of debris rose everywhere. A parched landscape stretched before them, devoid of life except for a pack of hungry feral dogs that rested in the shade of a derelict Toyota Corolla and watched to see whether these humans would offer food.

Zhang Jie, a civil engineer with the Red Cross Society of China, was on loan to the international disaster relief team. Two days ago, he had arrived in Haiti only to discover that his first job was to clean up the mess his predecessor left behind. That pissed him off, something he made crystal clear.

He glared at the passenger beside him, a slender, balding man in his early forties wearing an anonymous, grey business suit. Louis Brisbane, Grupo Muxia's VP for the Caribbean, had flown in just for this meeting. Brisbane's young female assistant, who had not been introduced, perched attentively in the back seat. She had a deep scar that ran down from the corner of her left eye and disappeared under her ear. He studiously avoided looking at it.

Zhang Jie continued. "According to Haitian ministry records, Grupo Muxia submitted construction status reports that detailed steady progress towards project milestones. Each report triggered multi-million-dollar payments." Zhang Jie pushed up his glasses and sniffed. "Obviously, your project managers falsified those documents."

Two days earlier, when Zhang Jie reported his suspicions to the ministry, he had felt flattered by the swift response from highly placed officials. Now, he cleared his throat and sat straighter in the SUV's driver's seat. "Minister Prevost personally asked that I meet with you privately before launching an official investigation."

"We came as soon as the minister conveyed his concerns," Brisbane replied, his tone clipped and precise. "We need to correct this situation immediately."

"And how could you possibly do that?"

"Our firm handles post-disaster reconstruction projects all over the world. In our experience, anything is possible. The key lies in having the right advisors on the ground. Someone like yourself, for example."

Silence filled the SUV.

"What are you suggesting?"

Brisbane leaned closer and lowered his voice, as if taking

Zhang Jie into his confidence. "I can see you are a man of the world. You understand what is needed. I'm sure your advice could be invaluable. That's why I'm prepared to offer you a substantial retainer to help us manage this project smoothly. I'm sure it could become a big success for all of us."

And there it was, hanging in the air between them, as transparent and electric and ugly as these things always are, the offer Zhang Jie had half expected.

The only sound in the SUV was a low-level white noise coming from the air conditioner.

Zhang Jie could ignore a little corruption as simply the cost of doing business. Several members of his extended family, he would admit privately, grew fat on loosely worded government contracts. But this level of greed left a bad taste in the back of his throat.

"What happened here is...criminal," Zhang Jie spat out. "Look around. Middle-class families lived on this street—doctors, teachers, shop owners and their children. We promised we would rebuild their homes. Months passed. Years. Nothing got done. Eventually, they emigrated to America or Canada. Do you understand what that means?"

"We understand your concerns—"

He raised his voice to override Brisbane. "Because of botched projects like this, Haiti lost a whole generation of educated professionals. The long-term economic impact—the social cost—cannot be measured."

Brisbane nodded and let out a sigh.

"Perhaps you should take photographs," he instructed his assistant, Karin Reichelt, who began rummaging in her tote bag. He turned back to Zhang Jie. "The minister told me of your determination, your passionate commitment to the project. I can see that he was right." Almost imperceptibly, Brisbane nodded to his assistant. "Did you happen to notice," he continued in a conversational tone, "that all those reports were signed off by the minister's cousin?"

Zhang Jie's eyes widened, instantly realizing his mistake—and what it meant.

From the back seat, a thin arm with the strength of steel slipped around the driver's headrest and pinned Zhang Jie to the seat. Shocked, he froze. He felt a searing pain as Reichelt's knife blade sliced expertly through the car seat, stabbing deep into his back and piercing his heart. He gasped, then thrashed momentarily before slumping, his head lolling, his lifeless body restrained by the seatbelt.

She withdrew her arm. Brisbane leaned over and placed two fingers against Zhang Jie's neck just below the jawline. She pulled out her phone and keyed in a text. Brisbane, satisfied there was no pulse, straightened Zhang Jie's glasses that had gone askew during his brief struggle.

A battered old Renault appeared from over the hill, negotiated the broken pavement and stopped beside the SUV. Brisbane and Reichelt climbed out and switched cars with the Renault's driver, a fat black man with dark glasses and a straw porkpie.

Without a word, the two of them drove off towards Aéroport International Toussaint Louverture just outside Port-au-Prince. The man in the hat dragged Zhang Jie's body from behind the wheel and dumped it in the ditch before starting the SUV and carefully driving back up and over the hill.

The dust settled. The silence resumed. One of the feral dogs sniffed the air, got to his feet and trotted over to Zhang Jie's body. The humans had brought food after all.

6

The former Toronto Stock Exchange building had been converted into an event space that tonight hosted *Global from the Get-Go*, a business networking dinner that billed itself as an opportunity for new tech entrepreneurs to connect with potential investors. For the occasion, Neil wore a dark summer-weight suit, which had been tailored to conceal his shoulder holster.

An attractive young hostess, one of the army of unpaid interns working the event in the desperate hope of landing a half-decent job, stopped him at the door.

"I'm meeting a friend," he said, giving his name.

"Oh, yes." She turned to the room and pointed. "Is that her?"

Neil scanned the crowd as he followed her gesture. Joanne Reynolds sat alone at a small table off to one side. As he approached, she removed her elegant red-framed glasses and smiled up at him. There were a few more lines around her mouth and at the corners of her eyes. *We all get a little older,* he thought, *but those seventy-hour corporate workweeks carry an extra cost.*

"It's great to see you." He leaned over and kissed her cheek before settling in his chair. During the five years they worked together in the RCMP's Financial Crimes Unit, they had developed a comfortable, no-bullshit rapport. Both resigned from the force within a few months of each other. Now she handled security for the Northern Bank. A daughter with special needs and an ex-husband with occasional bouts of alimony amnesia made her corporate paycheque one of life's little essentials.

After he left the Royal Canadian Mounted Police, Neil had just hung out for a few months. He worked on his house. The kitchen finally got painted, and he had new counters installed. At night, there was jazz and blues and singer-songwriters in the clubs along Roncy. He met a few friendly women. Had some fun. But after a while it seemed...pointless. So far, the private investigator thing was working out a lot better than he'd expected.

"Running your own business suits you," Joanne said, reaching out to smooth the lapel of his suit and pausing to finger the cloth. "Very nice."

He shifted his chair to let a server bearing a tray of drinks slip by. He had called Joanne earlier and asked if she would check around for any insider gossip that might be useful. "Were you able to find out anything?"

"We don't see each other for ages and it's straight to business? What's a girl going to think?" Joanne asked with a polished theatrical flair, a persona that masked the tough tomboy who had grown up in the east end of Toronto.

"She should realize the guy's in a hurry," he answered with a grin that showed he was genuinely glad to see her.

The hostess approached. "Sir, can I get you anything to start?"

"I won't be staying."

"A drink? Water?"

"Nothing, thanks." He turned back to Joanne.

The hostess persisted. "Some bread?"

"We're fine," Joanne assured her.

Neil glanced after the departing hostess. "She seems a little overeager."

"She's grateful," Joanne said. "Earlier today, I paid off the balance on her Mastercard."

"That was generous. Any chance you'll do the same for me?"

"It's the bank's money—an operational expense," she said. "I was particular about the seating arrangements." Her smartphone lay on the table. She adjusted the angle and glanced at the flickering signal-strength indicator monitoring one of the apps.

Who was she recording?

"Let me guess." He kept his eyes fastened on Joanne while he replayed his initial scan of the room. "Two guys—one European, about forty with that tanned, surfer dude look favoured by self-made rich guys. The other? Younger, late twenties, curly hair. Closely trimmed beard. Medium-grey suit. He looks like he runs his own business. Electronics? Software? Something like that."

"Good to see you haven't lost it." She took a sip of her wine. "I had the hostess slip a bug onto their table."

"All very illegal. I'm shocked. What's your interest in them?"

"The young guy, Carl Allwein. He's a bank client. When he was at the University of Waterloo, he developed a next-generation cybersecurity suite called ICE—Iron Clad Encryption. It's now used by a long list of blue-chip companies and a lot of the security services—CSE, NSA, GCHQ. The company's grown to a few hundred employees."

"You have a problem with that?"

"Me? Not at all. Now Carl wants to expand into China."

"Good for him."

"He came to us for backing. According to our guys, he's already overextended. We turned him down, so Carl started shopping around. I heard a whisper he was meeting with his new friend over there."

"So? You're afraid of a little competition?"

"The surfer dude, as you so aptly described him, calls himself Pol Luuckser, a VP for EuroDaag plc, supposedly a merchant bank based in Amsterdam."

"Who is he really?"

"I'm not sure...yet," she said. "But EuroDaag gets my yellow lights flashing. Now, there's a nasty organization. Corporate predators."

"Aren't they all?"

"He'll eat poor Carl alive." She shook her head. "Within a year, eighteen months, Luuckser will own the IP, Allwein will be out on his ass and a few hundred workers in Waterloo will lose their jobs when the operation moves offshore. My bank will then be the unhappy owner of an empty office building."

Neil gestured to the smartphone. "You're going to use this to show Carl the error of his ways?"

"Are you kidding? It's strictly internal use. Data for my report back up the chain. What happens next is someone else's decision."

"And Carl's company? And those hundreds of employees?"

"My job is to protect the bank," she said a little too sharply. "But enough about me. How are you? How's business?"

"It's good. I like being my own boss."

"Mr. Lone Wolf," she said with a mocking tone.

"More variety, fewer assholes."

"Who are you trying to fool? I know you. You've got more dog than lone wolf in your DNA."

"Meaning what?"

"I think you'd rather guard the sheep than gobble them up."

He laughed. "I don't know about that. A nice leg of lamb on the barbecue—"

"Yeah, yeah," she said with a wave of her hand. "Enough of the bullshit. What's your interest in Stephen Howland?"

"I'm looking into the murder of a woman, Rachel Lisgar."

"Any relation to—"

"Sister."

"You're kidding...wait. The other night? Down by the waterfront?"

"That's the one. The police think she was collateral damage—a witness to another killing. A friend of hers isn't so sure. Janos—"

"Janos Pach? My God. He's your client? How's that going?"

"We'll see." Neil leaned in closer and lowered his voice. "The reason I called you was that the victim met with Stephen Howland the day she died. Apparently, she thought his company, Hudson Ventures, was a massive fraud."

"No surprise there. Stevie's been a bad boy from way back."

"You almost got him once, didn't you? Before we worked together."

She held her thumb and forefinger a quarter inch apart. "I came this close. While I was pounding on his condo door, warrant in hand, he was boarding a private jet."

"Ouch. What can you tell me?"

"Howland made his first fortune orchestrating penny

stock pump-and-dumps. Over the years, he grew bolder. The Bre-X swindle? The Nortel implosion? Howland was involved in both. Then it was sub-prime mortgages during the US housing boom. He got out just ahead of the collapse of Bear Stearns and the Lehman Brothers."

"So...smart and lucky."

"Two other things you need to think about," she said soberly. "First, he's connected—"

"Mafia?"

"No, but he hangs around with a lot of rich people with solid political connections. You know what that means, better than most."

Neil shrugged. Policing, politics and power. He had learned a few tricks since the last time he slogged through that particular swamp. "Your second point?"

"Howland doesn't make many mistakes. At one time or another, everybody's had a crack at him. RCMP, FBI, SEC, Interpol, it's a long list. Every time, he slipped away."

"Maybe this time will be different."

She raised her glass in salute. "Gotta love an optimist."

He stood up. "And on that vote of confidence—"

She held him in place with the suddenly serious look in her eye. "Chances are he's got his bag packed and waiting by the door. You'd better hurry."

"My flight's already booked, last one out tonight." He checked his watch. "Right now, there's somewhere I need to be."

7

Parked limousines gleamed under the street lights along Alexander Boulevard. Drivers in dark suits with telltale security earpieces stood guard. Down the block, their masters and mistresses could be seen milling near the entrance to the ivy-covered Jackson Varley Funeral Home.

The ease with which the well-dressed crowd had commandeered the entire street reminded everyone that blue blood had coursed through the veins of the murdered mathematician.

Dozens of bicycles, some so battered and weather-stained that no thief would touch them, testified to the presence of academics and activists who had also come to mourn the loss of one of their own.

In death, as in life, Rachel's world was complicated.

"Are you staying for the service?" Neil asked Janos as they approached the front door. "I need to check out Rachel's townhouse before my flight."

"I am, but you do not have to. A quick word, that is all. I want to make sure they are aware you are working on this."

Inside, the air conditioning semi-successfully battled the

heat trapped in the heavy drapes, stuffed furniture and thick rugs. It was crowded. Power brokers in bespoke suits and politicians from all three levels of government stood next to academics in rumpled chinos. Janos smoothly worked his way through them with a sympathetic handshake here, a brief nod there. Neil ghosted along behind him.

"Do they know we're coming?" Neil asked.

"I left several messages," Janos replied.

Up ahead, people gathered in one of the visitation rooms. Commanding the epicentre was a woman in her mid-sixties with silver-blonde hair that fell to her shoulders in carefully controlled waves.

Neil recognized Isabelle Lisgar from news photos, television interviews and the covers of business magazines. She had turned a fading family fortune into a global network of regional banks, financial services and God knows what else. Widely celebrated as Canada's pre-eminent female entrepreneur, insiders knew her as a fierce backroom power broker in the Conservative Party.

Head high, back straight, Isabelle Lisgar was a striking woman who carried herself with regal bearing. For public appearances, she favoured minimal makeup and tailored suits with stiff mandarin collars. Tonight, her ensemble was cut from charcoal silk that whispered as she deftly managed the line of mourners, her attention focused subtly on a younger woman standing beside her wearing a black suit, her back to the room's entrance, her dark hair styled in an elegant French twist.

Sensing something, the younger woman turned.

Carole Lisgar's face was drawn and white, her eyes more weary than Neil remembered but still riveting. He'd heard she was now a special advisor for strategic relations to the former

Bay Street lobbyist who was Canada's minister of finance and deputy prime minister.

Janos reached out. "I am so sorry for your loss," he began. "This may not be the best time—"

Neil watched her expression shift rapidly from polite mask to cold fury.

She glared at Neil. Her voice was hoarse. "How dare you show up here."

"My condolences," Neil said. "I never met Rachel—"

"Fuck you," she hissed. "What do you want?"

Janos slid between them. "I have asked Neil to look into what happened to Rachel—"

"You what? You can't do that!" Her gaze flicked back to Neil. "And you're no longer with the RCMP."

"You're right, but—"

"In fact," she broke in, her voice laced with vindictive triumph, "after you bungled that so-called investigation, I heard you were fired."

"Not true," he snapped, "but no thanks to you."

Janos intervened, his voice quiet, forcing them both to lean in closer. "I think the police are making a big mistake—"

"Based on what?" she demanded, looking him straight in the eye.

"Well, what if—"

"That's the best you got? *What if?*" She stepped around Janos and faced Neil. Her eyes glinted like the edge of a razor blade. "I will not let you use Rachel's death to smear me or my family."

She raised her fist, her fingers clenched so tightly her knuckles turned white. Her forefinger shot out and jabbed like a knife at his chest. "You—"

"That's enough," interrupted Isabelle, who gently pulled down Carole's arm.

"I will stop you," Carole vowed, her voice as hard as carbon steel. "Count on it." Suddenly aware that the confrontation had drawn attention, she looked around defiantly. Her eyes daring anyone to say a word, she walked from the room.

"Janos, are you crazy?" Isabelle whispered in her restrained, moneyed voice, looking past him and nodding to the mourners nearby.

"Let me explain," Janos said. "But first, have you two met? Isabelle Lisgar, this is Neil Walker."

"Please accept my condolences," Neil said.

"I know who you are," she responded with cool grace. "You should leave. Both of you."

"Will you talk to Carole?" Janos pleaded. "Ask her to call me?"

"You saw how she felt," Isabelle answered. "She's not going to change her mind."

"But she might be able to help us discover what really happened that night," Janos said, pushing back. "She might have information about Rachel, her friends, anything at all."

"This is a family matter. Leave it alone." Without another word, she turned and walked away.

Janos stared after her, trying to understand the fierceness of the two women's reactions.

"I'm out of here." Neil began edging through the crowd. After a moment, Janos fell in behind.

Outside, they made their way through the smokers grabbing last cigarettes before heading into the chapel for the service.

"What is the story with you two?"

Neil glanced around. There was no one within earshot. He kept his voice low, and they walked a little more slowly.

"Remember that thing with Senator Christian Bouchard? A few years back?"

"Vaguely. At the time, my wife was in and out of the hospital with cancer. I didn't pay much attention to anything else."

"Sorry. I forgot."

"Something about kickbacks for contracts awarded through Public Works Canada?"

"I was still on the force. The lead investigator."

"And?"

"Carole Lisgar was the senator's policy advisor."

"Uh-oh. So, what happened?"

"We recovered a series of emails from her computer that proved she ran the whole thing through a Quebec bagman."

"She left emails? I find it hard to believe she would be that stupid." Janos sounded skeptical.

"She was arrested. Obstruction of justice. She faced ten years. The crown attorney planned to flip her."

"And?"

"While in the evidence lock-up, the computer hard drives containing the incriminating emails were completely destroyed. Accidentally, of course."

"And the charges?"

"Dropped. I was ordered to apologize. It didn't happen."

"Ahh—that was it? You never told me why you left the force."

"More like the straw that broke the camel's back," said Neil. They had reached his car. He pulled out his keys. "Can I drop you somewhere?"

Janos glanced back as the last smokers disappeared through the funeral home doors. "I will try to talk with Carole after the service."

"You still want me to go ahead?"

Janos stared at the ground for a minute, jingling the change in his pocket.

"I cannot let this rest." He looked at Neil. "What happened to Rachel? Maybe the police are right. Maybe not. I have to know for certain."

"Understood."

"Can you work around the family?" Janos asked quietly.

"Try to keep them off my back," Neil replied, opening his car door. "But, I tell you, Carole Lisgar's reaction? It will make it a lot harder to find the truth behind Rachel's murder."

8

Magdalene Court lay quiet. A cool evening breeze off the lake blew away the lingering humidity and muted the rumble of traffic on Lakeshore Boulevard. Rachel's townhouse sat on the north side of the street about halfway down the short block.

Neil slowly, methodically, catalogued the scene. Twelve red-brick Victorian-style row houses overlooked a circular flower bed at the centre of the narrow cul-de-sac. Each had a token front yard surrounded by a low brick wall. The only signs of life were the blue light of a television flickering from a neighbour's second-storey window and a guy parked at the corner who was checking his phone.

Neil gave one more sweeping look, then climbed the front steps of Rachel's townhouse, skirting a pot of red geraniums on the small porch. Yellow police tape crossed the black-painted front door. Through a frosted glass panel with a border of clear glass shone a dim light in the hallway.

He leaned forward, cupping his hand over his eyes to make out whatever details he could of Rachel's life. Because he no longer had a badge and with Rachel's family against him, he knew he wouldn't get inside to see the actual crime scene. But he had to take a look. Seeing how and where the victim had lived often helped him understand the crime in ways that files and reports could not.

Given Rachel's wealth, she could have lived anywhere. An upscale condo in the Entertainment District. A sprawling suburban estate. Something modern in midtown. But Rachel had picked this house in this neighbourhood because it had appealed to her. Why?

The foyer still showed the scars of her desperate struggle. Broken glass lay on the tiled floor. Farther along the front hallway, Neil saw a bike hanging on wall pegs. It was an old beater, the kind that long-time city cyclists gravitate to after their first few bikes are stolen. The ride from here to the university campus would take about twenty minutes max, he calculated. He pictured her route, most of it through Queen West and Chinatown. Quick, cheap and easier than public transit. *So, she had a practical streak*, Neil thought.

"Can I help you?"

Neil froze. The voice came from behind him, male, maybe in his thirties, probably standing on the sidewalk.

"Sir? Please turn around."

Aw, shit. It was a cop. Under the circumstances, no one else would project that calm, assured and polite tone of command. The guy from the car parked at the corner?

"I'm turning." Neil held his hands away from his body and slowly twisted around.

The cop stood easy on the sidewalk, a few feet back from the steps, enough to give him room to move in case Neil tried something. He was a big guy, a few inches over six feet and outweighing Neil by thirty pounds. He wore faded jeans, a polo shirt and a light windbreaker to cover the weapon—a

Glock—holstered on his belt and displayed as casually as his gold shield.

"I'm going to reach into my pocket for my wallet," Neil said calmly.

"Okay," said the cop, watching both Neil's hands. "What are you doing here?"

"I'm a private investigator," Neil responded, holding open his wallet to show his licence and stepping down to the sidewalk so he would not be looming over the cop. "You're metro police. Homicide?"

"Good guess," the cop said, moving back to maintain some distance. "Take your licence out of the wallet and hand it to me."

"When I was with the RCMP, I worked with a lot of Toronto cops," Neil said, passing it over.

"RCMP, huh?" The cop examined the licence. A small grin twitched at his lips. "I suppose you were getting ready to break in."

It was a tired, old joke. In the bad old days, the RCMP had been caught in a couple of headline-making embarrassments involving picked locks on the back doors of suspected political dissidents. The rivalry between the Toronto cops and the RCMP, one with local jurisdiction and the other national, was inevitable.

"And you are?" Neil asked.

"Detective Danny Relf, Homicide Squad." He handed the licence back to Neil. "You've worked with us before? Anyone I might know?"

"I was a sergeant, Commercial Crimes. Mainly I worked with your Financial Crimes Unit. Stanley Kwan?"

"Yeah, I know Stan," Relf said. "Have you seen him lately? You wouldn't recognize him. Must have lost a hundred and fifty pounds."

"Sorry to hear that," Neil replied. "Stanley never weighed more than a hundred and seventy-five pounds in his life."

Relf nodded. "Okay. So, what's up?"

"You knew Rachel Lisgar was a financial consultant, right? An investment fund she was researching appeared to be questionable. I'm seeing if there's any connection."

Relf bristled. "This is an ongoing investigation. You know better—"

"This all happened in New York City. Nothing to do with your investigation," Neil assured him, starting to back away.

"Hey! Wait."

"Nice talking with you, but I've got a plane to catch. I just stopped by the townhouse for a quick look-see."

"Stop!" Relf grabbed Neil's arm. "What investment fund?"

Neil shook off Relf's grip. "Check your case file. It should be there. Janos Pach reported all this yesterday."

"It's the first I've heard of it," Relf said, a skeptical expression narrowing his eyes.

Neil sensed an opportunity to make an ally. "You're working a theory that this was a professional hit and she was just an innocent bystander, right? That the neighbour—some retired Serbian warlord—was the target?"

"No comment."

"Let me suggest three facts you could consider." Neil squared himself. "First, a respected financial analyst investigating a multi-million-dollar fraud has been murdered by a professional. Second, despite your deputy chief being informed of this alternate interpretation of the facts, you were not briefed on it. And third, a few years ago, an investigation into financial corruption involving the murder victim's sister was derailed when all the evidence was mysteriously destroyed while in RCMP custody."

"Shit." Relf sighed. His double murder case had just got a lot more complicated.

"Carole Lisgar. That's the victim's sister. I'd keep an eye open for her name in this."

"You think she was involved?"

Neil checked his watch. "I'm getting on a plane to New York to see if there's anything to this. Do you want to know what I find out?"

"Yeah, sure. Of course."

"And in return?"

"We can work something out."

"Give me your card," Neil offered. "I'll keep you in the loop."

"I expect I'll regret this," Relf said, digging out one his business cards.

"I keep my promises. Ask around."

"I will," Relf said. "Call me, one way or another. Okay?"

"You got it. Now, I really gotta go."

9

As the lights of Toronto disappeared beneath the tilting night horizon, passengers settled in for the ninety-minute flight to New York.

Neil opened his laptop and started clicking through the background files he'd received from Don Cale. He needed to get his head around this thing.

How was he going to get Stephen Howland to open up? He'd only get one chance. Howland wouldn't have lasted this long if he didn't have the survival instincts of a skittish coyote. Neil needed leverage, and that meant information.

When he turned private, Neil had lost access to law enforcement databases. Don Cale filled that gap and then some. From what Neil could piece together, Don had gotten into computers back in the days when there were mail-order kits for hobbyists. By the time he'd put in his twenty-five and taken early retirement, he'd chased pedophiles, dope dealers and terrorists from community chat rooms to the darkest realms of cyberspace.

Now, Don supplemented his pension with occasional gigs as a white-hat hacker. If there was digital data connected to an

IP address anywhere in the world, Don could access it. He had yet to meet a firewall he couldn't slip through. The tougher the security, the higher his fees.

Tax records, real estate transactions, birth and death records, court transcripts, business licences, SEC and OSC filings, regulatory compliance reports, vital statistics, election polling lists, DMV records, police reports, security profiles, social media sites—Don roamed freely through all of them. He was worth every penny of his often exorbitant fee, something he'd once again demonstrated with the data he had assembled.

Neil gave in to temptation. He opened the files on Carole Lisgar first. What had she been up to? He scrolled through the summary. Huh. A couple of surprises. She'd co-authored a paper in *New Policy Directions* that discussed the bottom-line business benefits of better public health care. Her master's thesis in political management at Carlton University was cited in several academic articles on crowdsourcing political decision-making. Those were dangerous ideas among the hard-core conservatives she worked with in the current administration.

"Sir? A snack? Something to drink?"

Neil looked up. A flight attendant stood poised over the cumbersome stainless steel drinks trolley that filled the narrow aisle.

"Nothing, thanks."

She flashed a smile before moving on.

He returned to the laptop. Not surprisingly, the files on Isabelle Lisgar were more voluminous. As a glittering star in Canada's blue-chip firmament and winner of several CEO of the Year or Woman of the Year awards, she'd been the subject of glowing profiles in the business press. They detailed how, following the death of her brother Thomas, she had rebuilt the Lisgar family holding company, Bala Bay Financial, from near bankruptcy to being Canada's largest privately held financial services conglomerate.

Neil had first run into Bala Bay during his time with the Commercial Crimes Unit. One of Bala Bay's subsidiaries provided anti–money laundering compliance systems and training for financial institutions, banks, government agencies and non-governmental organizations around the world.

Isabelle had also won kudos as a vocal champion of technology start-ups, receiving plaudits as Angel of the Year from *Tech Investor Quarterly* and *TechBiz Today*, a top-rated television show on one of the international business television channels.

During the 2008 global banking crises, Bala Bay had expanded internationally by acquiring control of a small but highly respected US merchant bank that was teetering on the verge of collapse. Thompson Trust was a 150-year-old, family-held regional merchant bank in the northeast US that had roots in the days of whaling fleets and transatlantic steamships. Isabelle Lisgar skilfully leveraged its gilt-edged reputation for traditional merchant bank services—trade financing, letters of credit and foreign corporate investing—and optimized those services for web-based companies needing to hedge currencies and transfer funds seamlessly worldwide.

Neil leaned back and gazed out the window into the dark night sky. Despite the volume of information, stuff was missing. Where was the dirt? Where were the rumours that she was a greedy, corrupt, backstabbing, ruthless bitch who should be in jail? The online reports were suspiciously clean.

Reputation management ruled the corporate world. There were online services that constantly scanned web news and used whatever tactics necessary to delete or discourage negative coverage from pit-bull lawyers with libel suits to midnight hackers with search-and-replace programs. Still, he reasoned, there must be traces. Few digital files ever totally disappear. As soon as he got off the plane, he would ask Don to dig deeper.

He opened the package on Rachel. There were a few new details. She had an eight-figure trust fund and a big chunk of shares in the family holding company. There were numerous links to esoteric academic papers and an online video, dated the previous December, of a TED talk lecture taped at the Court Theatre in Chicago.

The video opened with Rachel striding onstage in a packed theatre. Jeans, leather jacket, hair tied back, a big smile and a wave.

"How are you? Feeling good? Great! I just got back from a math colloquium in London. Man, what an expensive city! But fun? Absolutely amazing!"

She glided easily around the stage, energetic, engaging, comfortably at home.

"And math can be fun, right? That's what I try to teach the kids at this community drop-in centre back home. Some of the kids don't do so well in math. In fact, this particular community centre is in a crappy part of town, so the people, including the kids, aren't doing so well. Period. Not a lot of money. Or hope. Sometimes not enough food. You probably have those neighbourhoods in your city, right?"

The camera panned the audience, mainly middle-aged and older, casually well-dressed, relaxed and paying attention.

"Anyway, I teach these kids that math is useful. Do well in math, do well in school, and they've got a better shot at getting out of the housing projects. But I show them that math can be fun, too.

"You want an example? When I teach them basic

geometric formulas—like how to find the area of a circle—I make it fun. You all remember the formula, right? Pi r-squared, where r stands for *radius*?

"Imagine a pizza, I tell them, 'cos they all know what pizzas are, even the kids that are three weeks off the refugee plane from Somalia. Pizza is one of those cheap, sort of tasty but pretty unhealthy foods that people survive on when they don't have much money."

Rachel strode to the whiteboard and picked up a marker and looked at the audience with mock surprise. "Hey, this is math! You didn't think we could avoid the whiteboard, did you?"

Easy laughter rolled through the theatre, and she paused to let it die down before continuing.

"Anyway, if you use Z to stand for the radius instead of the letter r, when you write out the formula, what you get is $Pi \times Z \times Z = A$." She wrote the final letter with a flourish and stepped back to face the audience.

Scattered applause arose, which Rachel acknowledged with a short pause before continuing.

"What I love is the way they laugh and their eyes light up when I show them that one. And I tell them that math can help them figure out things that are really complicated. Best of all, they don't have to have a lot of fancy equipment or super computers."

Rachel's tone became more serious. "I tell them about Eratosthenes, a mathematician who lived in Egypt more than two thousand years ago. This guy, using just his brain and his math skills, calculated that the Earth's circumference was 25,000 miles. How close did he come? Today's super computers tell us that the circumference is actually 24,901 miles. In other words, his calculation was off by less than one hundred miles.

"When the kids hear that, they're amazed. And rightly so. It's an incredible feat. Partly because one hundred is a number these kids can get their heads around. That might be how much money their mom gets for food from welfare every month. Or the sticker price on a crappy, second-hand laptop.

"There are a lot of numbers around these days that these kids just can't fathom. A ten-million-dollar lottery win? What's that? What's it look like? Or a billion dollars?

"I show them a way to understand those huge numbers. I tell them to think of them in terms of minutes and seconds and days. Here's how the math works out.

"One million seconds equals eleven-and-a-half days.

"One billion seconds equals thirty-one-and-three-quarters years.

"Let me say that again. Slowly, in case some of you are math-phobic."

Laughter, some of it a little uncomfortable, rippled through the house.

"One billion seconds equals thirty-one-and-three-quarters years."

She paused to let that magnitude sink in.

"One way of looking at it is that thirty-one years is roughly the life expectancy of people living in some of these projects."

Silence filled the theatre.

"Here's another way of looking at it. For a kid who lives in a world where a hundred dollars can make a big difference, how do you imagine they will react when they discover that their community after-school programs are cancelled so our government can give tax cuts to billionaires?

"How would you react if you were in their shoes?

"It's something we all should think about. And maybe do something about it. Because we don't need more poor, pissed-off teenagers who believe our government is stealing their future."

The audience broke into thunderous applause. Rachel, wearing an ear-to-ear grin, basked in it for a minute, then brought her palms together under her chin and bowed to the audience. As the applause continued, she backed gracefully off the stage.

Neil was left shaking his head as the laptop screen froze on Rachel's delight-filled smile.

Smart, committed...what a loss.

There was a lot to process. He pulled up his music, picked a playlist of Eric Clapton, Colin James and the Tedeschi Trucks Band, closed his eyes and let his brain wander.

10

Carole slid through the morning commuters crowding the Ottawa airport with practised ease, a wheeled carry-on trailing behind her. It wasn't until the limousine pulled away from the curb and headed downtown towards her Slater Street condo that she finally let out a long, deep breath.

Rachel had pissed her off more and more over the years. Carole had bailed out her little sister after demonstrations and burned up political capital to save her research grants. At best, all she ever got was a grudging thanks.

To some people, Rachel was a genius. Maybe she was. But for a smart person, she sure made a long line of stupid decisions. It would be laughable if it weren't so...awful.

Carole's throat tightened. A heavy weight pressed down on her chest. It hurt a lot more than she expected.

Pull yourself together, she told herself. She looked out the window. There was a nice bright blue sky. The green parklands along the Rideau Canal were more lush than she remembered, even though she had driven this same route just a few days earlier. She lowered the window a few inches. Humid summer air flowed in, redolent with the smell of freshly cut grass. *Suck it in. Clear your head. Focus.* Stuff needed to get done.

———

Carole unlocked the door to her condo, pushed in her suitcase to prop it open, stepped back across the hall and knocked three times.

"Hey, Rae. I'm back," she called out before turning back, grabbing her suitcase and heading in towards the living room. The spectacular view of the Ottawa skyline, with the river snaking off into the distance, never failed to sooth her soul.

Rae Kornisglass crossed the hall from the condo where she lived with her husband Paul Collacchi and their newborn son. She was a delightfully vicious Party lawyer and Carole's best friend since university. As she entered, Carole's two cats, Gabe and Rafael, scooted across the hall from her condo to Carole's. Rae followed them in carrying baby Charlie in her arms.

Carole had flopped on the couch. She needed to catch her breath before going in the office. She bent down as both cats came by to rub against her leg. "Hey, guys. Miss me?"

"How did it go?" Rae asked.

"I'm just glad it's over," Carole said, scratching Rafael's back. "Thanks for looking after these guys. How's Charlie?"

Rae beamed. "He slept from one to almost six this morning. A new all-time record!"

"Way to go, champ!"

Rae plunked down beside Carole. "So, was Jason there? Any chance of you two getting back together?"

"Like I need that now." She rolled her eyes in exasperation. Her relationship with Jason McKendry, an oil-patch lawyer and lobbyist, had tanked right after her arrest. She wasn't ready for that kind of complication. "You know who did show up? Neil Walker. You remember him?"

Rae nodded. "Back when you were arrested, I checked him out. What did he want?"

"I suspect he's using Rachel's death to take another run at me."

Rae rocked Charlie and studied her. "That sounds a little paranoid."

"I've finally put all that crap behind me. I can't get dragged into a murder investigation—"

"What investigation?"

"Something to do with Rachel's death."

"And why would he target you?"

"I don't know," Carole shot back in frustration. "My guess? He's still pissed at how the Bouchard case fell apart."

Senator Christian Bouchard, leader of the Quebec caucus within the Canadian Senate, was the go-to guy who connected Quebec's business elite with federal-government procurement contracts, agricultural subsidies and international development projects. Carole had been an up-and-coming player. She earned a reputation for pushing through win–win deals that balanced pragmatic politics with good public policy. She prided herself on working her ass off to keep the bleeding-heart lefties from screwing up the country.

When the forged emails turned up on her computer, the scandal had nearly killed her. All the charges were dropped, but the memories still triggered hot acid in her gut. The anger and frustration she'd felt when no one believed her innocence. The shame when she'd been arrested in the Senate foyer under the glare of the television cameras.

"Carole, let it go. It's ancient history," Rae counselled.

"Not for me."

"There was a silver lining." Self-satisfied amusement crept into Rae's voice. "The RCMP was badly embarrassed. It gave us the perfect excuse to appoint a new commissioner and clean house over there. I'd say they learned who signed their paycheques."

"But what about me? Walker shows up two years later at my goddamn sister's funeral, and I lose it." She stood up. "Jesus, Rae. My reputation—"

"Are you kidding? The way you handled yourself? You kept your head straight and your mouth shut. People noticed. I hear they've got something else lined up for you."

"Yeah? Maybe I'm not interested," she sighed and looked down at Gabe who was rubbing his forehead against her leg. She picked him up and scratched under his chin. "I could use some downtime."

"This is different." Rae's tone caused Carole to look up. "Paul's signed on. He said it looked interesting."

Carole eyed her warily. "What's the deal?"

Charlie stirred. Rae kissed him gently on the forehead. "Thanks to this little guy, my brain's a mush. Something about new OECD regulations governing cross-border capital transfers. A vote is on the agenda for the upcoming G7 ministers' conference in Paris. They want you to lead the Canadian team."

"Jobs like that can be a real meat grinder," Carole shook her head. "All-night sessions where you spend more time negotiating prepositions in the press communiqué than you do discussing policy. No thanks. Give it to somebody else."

"The banks are going ballistic."

"No surprise there. I'm sure compliance will be a pain in the ass. They'll get over it."

"Apparently, the costs will be huge. Not only that, they say they'll have to eat them to stay competitive. They are so pissed. If you'd picked the family business instead of politics, you'd be yelling about it yourself."

"Trust me, they can afford it." Despite her better judgement, Carole felt her interest piqued. Over the past few months, she'd noticed a growing restlessness. Paris for the G7? How bad could it be? "What else?"

"Quite a few major Party donors are upset. They claim it would be a massive intrusion into the privacy of their clients."

Carole burst out laughing. "I can see why they might be concerned."

WikiLeaks had just published yet another cache of hacked files detailing secret offshore accounts being used to hide assets from tax collectors, bankruptcy courts and divorce lawyers. Greater scrutiny of cross-border financial transactions could make life more complicated for many friends of the Party.

"Whatever," Rae said. "These people support us when we need it, and now they want the Canadian government to stop this thing. Your guy, as Canada's minister of finance, is carrying the can for this. Which means you have the lead."

"Whose bright idea was this?" Her laugh turned sour.

"Isabelle made the call."

"Are you sure?" Isabelle was her mentor in the Party. What was going on?

Rae shrugged and leaned over to kiss the head of the still-sleeping Charlie. "At least think about it," she suggested.

Carole stood for a moment, weighing her options. "If I do this—and I'm not saying I will—I need something in return. Find me a way to stop Walker."

"For God's sake, Carole—"

"You have contacts in the RCMP. The provincial government. Call in a favour. Lean on someone. Get his licence pulled."

"Have you seen Walker's record? More commendations than any RCMP officer in the last twenty years. High-profile joint operations with Interpol and the FBI. Successful undercover stings against the Hell's Angels and the Mafia. Hell, he put Nick Pasatti away for life."

"I don't care," Carole said, her voice hard. "If Walker comes after me, I want to bury him."

"You're serious?"

"That's the deal."

"Okay," Rae conceded. "Leave it with me."

11

The reception area outside the minister's office was quiet when Carole strode through to drop the suitcase in her corner office. The sign on the door read *Special Advisor for Strategic Relations*. The title was deliberately vague. In reality, she was the Party's fixer on temporary assignment to the minister of finance.

She looked up when she heard the door to the minister's office open. Isabelle was wrapping up a conversation with Finance Minister Peter Lattimer.

He was a couple of inches over six feet, fiftyish, with a comb-over and a pot belly protruding from underneath an impeccably cut Savile Row suit. He favoured crisp white shirts, flamboyant Hermès ties and Tory-blue suspenders.

"Find us something interesting, okay?" he said to Isabelle. "Line up a few options."

"I'll make some calls," she promised.

Lattimer glanced at Carole. "How are you holding up? Doing okay?"

"Fine," Carole said. "There's a lot of work on my desk."

"Then, I won't keep you." He ducked back into his office.

Carole turned to Isabelle. "What's going on? I—"

"Not here," Isabelle said, flashing a brief smile at the receptionist.

Once inside her office, Carole shut the door and turned on her aunt. "What's this OECD thing really about? What are you not telling me?"

"There's something you need to know." Isabelle sat down in one of the guest chairs and crossed her legs. "Right after the election, if we win—and every poll says we will—the prime minister plans to resign."

"What?" Carole's eyes widened. "Why?"

"He's not well. I've watched him for a while now and wondered."

Carole leaned against her desk and ran her hands through her hair, considering the implications. "You're sure?"

"My source is...impeccable."

"How sick is he?"

Isabelle shrugged. "Mostly, he's tired. He's pushing himself through one last campaign just so the history books will show he was prime minister longer than any of his predecessors."

"That sounds like him," Carole muttered. Absurd, but typical. History shaped by the small needs of big egos.

"Once the prime minister resigns, his successor will want to bring in his own staff," Isabelle pointed out.

"Of course." Carole visualized the dominoes falling. Until the Party could elect a new leader, the deputy prime minister would step in. And that was her current boss, the finance minister. And he was an idiot. A Bay Street party boy and a powerhouse fundraiser, as interim PM he would be a disaster. No way she wanted to ride his coattails into the PMO.

"It'll be a mess," Isabelle continued. "None of the leadership contenders has the smarts to manage our east–west coalition. Within a year, the whole Party will fall apart."

"And you're willing to let that happen?"

"It's time to retreat from the political trenches, at least for a few years. We had a great run while our guy was PM. We put some sane policies into place. We made some money. But the world is changing. It's time to move on."

"Maybe," Carole said. Politics had consumed her life, but in the past few years, the games had gotten dirtier. She admitted to herself it wasn't as much fun as it used to be.

"Think about it," Isabelle suggested. "This OECD issue creates a right-time, right-place opportunity. Leading the Canadian government team will raise your profile with people that count, both here and internationally. Those contacts will be useful when you take over from me at Bala Bay."

"I can't see you retiring," Carole scoffed. "Summers in Muskoka? Winters in Boca Raton? Really?"

Isabelle leaned back. "I'm not getting any younger."

Carole studied her aunt. In the nearly two decades since her parents' deaths, Isabelle had been more than her aunt. She had guided Carole's career and stood by her when there was trouble. "And the OECD issue would be a good stepping stone?"

Isabelle simply nodded.

Carole waved a hand in acceptance. "You've never steered me wrong in the past."

Isabelle tipped her head in the direction of the minister's office. "He'll need someone to feed him his lines and keep him on track."

"Doesn't he always?"

"Managing the media will be essential. Paul Collacchi's on board. He can help."

"No problem. But what about you? What are you going to say about this OECD directive?"

Isabelle folded her hands and showed a small smile. "Nothing."

"But you head the regulatory committee of the Canadian Bankers' Institute. The media will be all over you for a quote."

"I can't be seen taking a stand. Next week the prime minister will announce my appointment as Canada's representative to IFIA."

Enormous power and inner-circle prestige accompanied a seat on the International Financial Intelligence Alliance. It was a closed-door forum for global bankers and national security services. IFIA initiatives had quietly and successfully shut down the financial networks of cartels and terrorist groups by sharing highly classified data and executing joint strategies. Now it was Canada's turn to chair the alliance. Isabelle would set the group's agenda, shape its priorities. Billions, even trillions of dollars were at stake. The job was a pressure cooker.

"Are you sure you should take that on?" Carole reached out, concern written across her face. "It's been less than a year since your last heart attack."

"Really, I'm fine."

"All right, if you say so." Carole blew out a slow breath. "This OECD thing, it all starts when?"

"The G7 conference is next week in Paris, but we've worked out a joint Canada–US strategy. We'll start with Lattimer's speech at the Global Financial Institute conference in New York."

Carole sat up straight. "You mean the conference that starts tomorrow?"

"I just spoke with the minister, and he's totally on board," Isabelle said with satisfaction in her voice. "With some luck and by pushing the right buttons, we should be able to torpedo this disaster before the G7 conference even starts."

Carole pictured her still-unpacked carry-on standing in her condo hallway. "I had hoped to stay in town for a few days, catch up with a few friends."

"I'll tell you what," Isabelle said brightly, deliberately changing the subject. "I have to be in New York on business. You keep the minister on message and out of trouble. I'll do some face time with a few big clients. We'll do a little shopping. Get tickets to a Broadway show. Have some fun."

With part of her brain, she had to admire how Isabelle had sold her on taking this project. A little flattery, some whispered super-secret insider information and assurances it would be a no-brainer. *Was she that easy to con?* she chided herself.

"Let me get my head around this. Can I call you later?"

"Of course," Isabelle stood up. She clasped Carole's hands in her own. "I've got a feeling that this is going to work out well for you. Something new is about to begin."

12

Carole, juggling her phone, notebook and a heavy briefing binder, had just left her office when a bell chimed and the elevator doors opened.

Paul Collacchi, slightly dishevelled and sleep-deprived, spilled into the reception area. He was pushing fifty and overweight, a former journalist who had crossed over to the dark side and become a political speech writer.

"You definitely need more coffee." Carole signalled for an assistant to bring a pot into the meeting.

"What I need is a cigarette," he grumbled. He'd quit smoking right after the baby was born. Since then, he'd been restless and twitchy, some days better than others.

"Hang in there, buddy," Carole consoled him as she gently steered him towards the conference room.

Waiting for them was Rob Goodyear, the assistant deputy minister for finance policy. He was the scholarly, button-down collar and knit-tie type.

"Hey, Rob," Carole said, sliding into her chair at the head of the table, as Paul dropped down next to her and opened the briefing binder. "Bring me up to speed. Where do we stand?"

"The day after tomorrow, Minister Lattimer will deliver opening remarks at the Global Financial Institute's annual conference in New York. At dinner, he will give the keynote address at the Canada–US Chamber of Commerce Innovation Awards."

Rob pushed a revised conference itinerary across the table. "The OECD's proposed directive on financial reporting would make it easier for police to investigate suspected cross-border money laundering."

"Before we get into the weeds, I need context," she said. "Why should I care? Joe Public doesn't give a damn about international money laundering."

"They should," Rob said sharply. "A money launderer is like the getaway driver after a bank robbery. They make it easier for corrupt officials to hide their bribes, for human traffickers to turn women and children into sex slaves and for terrorists to buy bomb-making material."

"And this new directive would stop that?" Carole's skepticism was clear.

"Follow the money, catch the bad guys. It works. Ask Al Capone." Rob flipped through the briefing binder. "Look at page seventeen. Financial institutions would be required to report all potentially suspicious cross-border banking transactions to the OECD's Financial Action Task Force. These reports would be mandatory, not voluntary."

"No wonder the banks are up in arms."

"In essence, it would establish international public-sector monitoring of the global financial system. Until now, this has been the responsibility of private-sector bank officers on a voluntary basis."

"I was told they were pissed off by the costs of compliance," Carole said. "But this? There's no way they will sit still for it."

"Critics would say they brought it on themselves," Rob countered. "Many of the world's largest banks—JP Morgan, Deutsche Bank, HSBC—have paid billions in fines for money laundering."

Carole tapped her pen on the table. "Automatically sharing sensitive financial information is hugely problematic. Especially when the data would be held by an international non-governmental organization. What are the controls?"

"The OECD's proposal is thin on implementation details," Rob acknowledged, flipping a page. "The official Canadian response is that we would support additional research and pilot-project initiatives to fine-tune the directive."

"In other words, stall," Carole said, half to herself, visualizing how it would play out. Carole looked at Paul to see if he had any questions. He shook his head.

"Okay. Is that it? Are we done?"

Rob flipped through his notepad. "Unless you have something else, that should do it."

"Good. And thanks."

Rob nodded, gathered his binder and slipped out, closing the door softly behind him.

She checked her watch. It had been a long day already. She was feeling a little…not quite light-headed but…hollow. It was something she'd noticed after the funeral and hadn't been able to shake.

Paul leaned back. "What about Lattimer? Do you think he'll have any ideas? Suggestions? Objections?"

"Maybe, if he gave it a minute of his time," she said dryly. "The problem is, when it comes to public policy, he just doesn't care enough."

"The minister of finance doesn't care about public policy?"

"What can I say?" Carole responded, as she picked up her binder and stood. "He says it's not sexy."

13

Hudson Ventures occupied half of the thirty-sixth floor of a nice but not too flashy office building in midtown Manhattan. Neil pushed through the glass entry doors into a beige reception area commanded by a smiling older woman behind the reception desk. She wore a blue silk blouse and had the open friendly face and salt-and-pepper hair often seen in ads for seniors' fitness clubs and cruises to Alaska.

"May I help you?" Her voice was gracious and upbeat.

"My name is Walker. I have an appointment."

"Mr. Howland will be with you in a few minutes. Can I get you anything while you wait—coffee, water, soda?"

"No thanks."

Neil took a seat on the sectional sofa. It wrapped around a squat, sturdy table that held a Frederic Remington–style bronze sculpture, about eighteen inches high, of a cowboy astride a wildly bucking long-horned bull. Seriously? Is that how Howland saw himself? A heroic Wall Street cowboy riding a volatile bull market?

Two doors led off the reception area, a clear glass one leading towards internal offices and, behind and to the right of the receptionist, a solid wooden one. Just as Neil settled in to wait, it was opened by Stephen Howland, who was talking with someone back in the office.

Neil recognized Howland from online photos. He was tanned and fit, wearing a striped silk tie and a white shirt with the sleeves rolled casually to below the elbow. A successful guy, the image conveyed, and a pragmatic hard worker. It projected a persona that played well on the television business shows where Howland sat in regularly as a financial commentator.

Howland flashed Neil a charismatic smile that came straight out of Dale Carnegie's *How to Win Friends and Influence People*. He ushered a retirement-aged couple out of his office. The three of them stopped to chat for a minute, wrapping up their meeting with a brief social visit.

The couple looked like they'd dressed up for the event. She was taller than her husband. He was a little overweight. They appeared comfortably well-off, not rich but not too worried about money. Maybe he had been a suburban professional—an engineer—and they had saved steadily and raised a couple of kids. Decent. Educated. People who followed the rules and built a good life for themselves and their children. But if they were investing with Hudson Ventures, Neil was pretty sure, sooner or later, they would get badly screwed over.

She reached out to shake Howland's hand. "Thanks for looking after us so well."

"Think about the Launchpad Fund," he replied, enveloping her hand with both of his.

"Don't work too hard," she said with a smile.

"What can I do?" Howland shrugged elaborately. "It's my curse."

"Better you than me," the husband muttered. All three of them chuckled.

"You two take care, and I'll see you in a few months." Howland let the glass door close behind them and turned towards Neil, who stood up.

"Mr. Walker? Stephen Howland." His handshake was firm and dry.

"Thanks for seeing me."

"Come in," he said, waving Neil into his office. The decor was surprisingly modest. A sleek wooden desk abutted the wall where a presentation-sized display monitor showed the stock market ticker.

"You're the second person Mr. Pach has sent to see me," Howland said while indicating Neil should take one of the visitors' chairs as he settled into his own executive-style chair. "I'm flattered, especially since I've never met the man. Recognize his name, of course. He's brilliant. A visionary. And we know many of the same people."

"It's about your meeting with Rachel Lisgar." Neil leaned forward with a friendly but serious expression on his face. "Could you tell me what you two discussed?"

"Why don't you ask her?" Howland had a wary look.

"Because she's dead." Neil's tone was clipped.

Howland's head jerked back. "I'm so sorry to hear that," he said, the shock clear in his voice. "What happened?"

"She was killed in Toronto. Murdered."

"My God! That's terrible."

But there it was.

The eye twitch.

Just a slight shift to the right.

Neil had been watching for it. Such a little thing, it spoke volumes. Howland knew something. Adrenalin quickened Neil's pulse. He kept his expression neutral.

"Rachel's last meeting that day was with you," Neil said, letting a hint of accusation slip into his tone. "She had questions about the Launchpad Fund. Is that right, Stephen?"

Howland straightened up in his chair. "Before I say anything more, who are you? Exactly?"

"I work with Janos Pach. We need—"

"So, you're not with the police?" Howland's voice sounded tighter.

Good. It was the sound of fear. Some people turn quiet when scared. A con man believes he can always bullshit his way out of any trouble. Neil needed Howland nervous so he would keep talking. The tougher question was what made an experienced con artist like Howland grow so skittish so fast?

"We will keep this unofficial. At least, for now." Neil sweetened the pot. "I will, of course, let Mr. Pach know how much you helped. He can be very appreciative."

For anyone running an investment fund, a recommendation from Janos meant money in the bank. It could cause stock prices to skyrocket. Neil watched greed versus fear wrestle behind Howland's eyes.

"Yes, certainly," Howland said with a renewed sparkle in his smile. He pulled over his keyboard. A series of file folders popped up on the display monitor.

"Actually, the Launchpad Fund did not come up," he continued. "Ms. Lisgar and I discussed a recent FINRA report—you're familiar with the Financial Industry Regulatory Authority? She shared her insights into the impact of artificial intelligence programs on flash trading in the futures market. I'll make a copy of the report for you."

Howland stood up and headed for the door. "Let me get it from the print room. A glass of water? I'm getting one for myself...No? I'll be right back."

Neil quickly studied the file folder names displayed on

the monitor. As far as he could see, the labels were just numbers and letters. They offered no clues to the contents. He'd dearly love to take a peek inside them.

Neil fingered the thumb drive he always kept on his key chain. Would he have time? He glanced over his shoulder at the open door.

No sign of Howland.

He looked at the screen. Awfully tempting.

He listened for any sound from the reception area.

As silent as death.

He got to his feet and made a show of stretching. He had ten seconds, tops.

He slipped over to Howland's side of the desk. The desktop's CPU was on the floor. He searched for a USB slot.

Couldn't find one.

He checked the side of the monitor.

Yes! He slipped his thumb drive into one of the slots.

Five seconds to go.

He called up the directory. Looked for any promising folders.

Four seconds. *There! Clients.* He clicked to open it. The icon spun. It must be a big sucker.

Enter password.

Fuck! He'd expected it but was still frustrated.

Three seconds.

Where do people write down their passwords? He checked the back of the monitor. Nothing.

Two seconds.

He yanked open the desk drawer.

The cursor blinked, demanding a response.

One second.

He pawed through the loose papers, discarded pens and rubber bands. Nothing.

Frustrated, he yanked out the thumb drive.

One, two, three long strides.

He sat back in his chair. He took in a deep breath and let it out slowly. It had been a long shot, but worth trying. He checked over his shoulder.

The reception area remained silent. Not a sound. Not a phone ringing. Not a door closing. Nothing.

That was weird.

Neil stepped over to the doorway. There was no sign of the receptionist. There were no waiting clients. The reception area was empty.

And Howland? Gone.

Neil saw movement behind the door leading to the inner offices.

Cautiously, he crossed over and pulled open the heavy glass door.

He heard people chatting on phones. The rapid clicks of keyboards being worked. The slam of file drawers being kicked shut. All the usual office sounds.

As if everything was normal.

He eased down the short hallway, his steps muffled by the carpet. He paused just before reaching an open office door. The nameplate said *Tonya Clarke*. He heard a woman speaking on the phone.

"Listen, I gotta go...No, no. There's no way I can make it before seven, seven thirty."

Neil peered around the doorway. An African-American woman sat behind a desk talking into a headset. She was in her mid-forties, wearing rimless glasses and an emerald green T-shirt, her hair tied back in long braids. Her desk overflowed with file folders, notepads, a giant coffee cup and three computer screens. She glanced up when she saw Neil.

"Somebody's here...Yeah, yeah. Okay. Later." She pulled off the headset. "Can I help you?"

"I'm looking for Stephen Howland?"

"He should be in his office. Ask Marta. The receptionist." She turned back to her monitor.

"She's not at her desk."

"Say what?"

"There's no one in reception," Neil explained. "And Howland's not in his office."

Annoyed, she looked up. "I'm sure they will be back in a moment. If you could wait in reception..."

"But there's no one around. It's like everyone just left."

"Really?" She got to her feet. She brushed past Neil and paused when she reached the empty reception area. She walked over to Howland's office, checked inside, shrugged to herself and closed the door, twisting the handle to make sure it was locked. She scanned the reception desk. There was no note, nothing to explain why Marta had left or when she might return.

"You should come back later."

"Has this ever happened before? Everyone just disappearing?"

"Sorry, I can't help you." An impatient edge had crept into her voice. "I've got my own work to take care of." And with that, she turned on her heel and headed back to her office, her headset and the blinking screens.

"But—"

She stopped and spun around. "Do I need to call security?"

"No," Neil said, backing towards the exit. "I'll catch up with Mr. Howland later."

She crossed her arms. "If I see him, I'll be sure to let him know."

He grinned. She was tough. He liked her spirit. With a nod, he left. As Neil waited for the elevator, a wisp of an idea, a fleeting connection to something he had seen or read in the past twenty-four hours, stirred in the back of his mind.

What was it? He could sense it floating just over the horizon.

Patience, he told himself. *Let it come.*

A bell chimed, the elevator doors opened and the slim thread of memory snapped.

14

Two black Chevy Suburbans eased to a stop on East Fifty-Seventh near Park Avenue just outside the Four Seasons Hotel. From beneath the marquee, a doorman and a pair of porters stepped out smartly.

The rear doors of both limousines opened simultaneously. Out stepped the plain-clothes RCMP security detail for the finance minister. They checked the street and rooftops before opening the doors wider and allowing the passengers to disembark. Minister Lattimer climbed from the first vehicle followed by Carole Lisgar and Jack O'Connell, the minister's personal gofer. From the second vehicle, Cindy Altara, the finance minister's assistant, and Paul Collacchi stepped onto the sidewalk. Paul looked wistfully at two guys lighting cigarettes under the marquee. He sidled over and sucked in a lungful of second-hand smoke.

Carole led the minister, O'Connell and the security team leader, Cal Sturman, through the revolving front doors into the hotel's soaring three-storey lobby. It was sleek and austere, with soft lighting, polished limestone columns and high-gloss marble floors. Broad steps led up to the long reception counter. Four clerks, dressed in simple dark blazers and pale shirts, waited for them.

"Welcome to the Four Seasons," greeted the most senior of the clerks, an Asian woman in her late thirties.

"The Canadian Department of Finance made reservations—a suite plus an adjacent block of four rooms." Carole slid a corporate credit card onto the counter.

"Yes." She confirmed the booking on the computer. "And how many key cards?"

Carole's phone buzzed. She glanced at the caller ID, then turned to Cindy. "Take care of this, will you?"

Carole stepped away before answering the phone. "Are you on your way?"

"We're leaving the townhouse now," Isabelle Lisgar responded. "How was your flight?"

"We took one of the Challengers. It was okay."

"You sound a little tired."

"I'm fine," Carole assured her. She watched porters load the luggage onto trolleys. Cindy had collected the key cards. Carole signalled Cal Sturman to lead the group towards the elevator bank.

She trailed behind, phone to her ear. "We're in the Oak Suite. Thirty-second floor. See you soon."

Thirty-six hours in Manhattan, she thought, babysitting a pair of overgrown frat boys. All Lattimer had to do was deliver two speeches and make a couple of corporate calls on company CEOs thinking about expanding into Canada. All routine stuff. What could go wrong? Just about anything, but probably nothing. She was paid to worry about it.

―――

In the back of a Bentley inching down Fifth Avenue

beside Central Park, Isabelle Lisgar slipped her phone into her purse, thinking about Carole and the fatigue in her voice. Maybe it had been a mistake to put Carole on this project. If it hadn't been for Rachel's...never mind.

With a deliberate effort, Isabelle shook off her concern. "All set," she said to the squat woman beside her, who had been checking text messages on her phone.

"Good," Christina Smarland grunted with a forced smile, a troll's passing nod to civility.

Tina was well-known to senators, congressmen and high rollers in both Washington and New York as a tireless Republican lobbyist and backroom deal broker. She had a round face, thick lips and massive shoulders that stretched the seams of her black suit jacket in ways that would make a tailor weep. Through her company, Washington-based Sentinel Strategies, Tina commanded a guerrilla army of secret soldiers in the ongoing war against corporate taxes, gun control and any kind of regulatory oversight of industry. They specialized in scorched-earth victories for Republican candidates in districts across the US.

"Carole will make sure Lattimer stays on message," Isabelle said, handing Tina a short list of names. "Your job is to generate the media pressure we need."

"You got it," Tina responded, turning to face Isabelle. "Tell me about Minister Lattimer."

"What about him?"

"I've watched him on video. I'd guess he likes to cut loose from time to time?"

"Why do you ask?"

"My people in Washington need him to be seen as the straight laced, sober, thoughtful Canadian who is outraged by these invasive new OECD regulations."

"Don't worry. Carole and I have him under control."

"Are you sure?"

"Focus on supporting Carole," Isabelle ordered. "Your role is to facilitate, not direct. We have this under control."

"Isabelle, we've known each other for a long time. Don't get me wrong. I have complete confidence in you." Tina shrugged. "But Carole? Her I don't know. Is she up to it?"

As the limo continued down Fifth Avenue, passing the entrance to the zoo, Isabelle studied Tina critically.

"You know in Canada we're about to start a federal election, right?"

"Of course."

"If I hadn't called in a lot of favours, Carole would be running the national re-election campaign."

"Really?"

"Don't underestimate her," Isabelle warned. "You won't like the result."

Tina flashed another quick, appeasing smile. "I'm sure everything will be fine."

"Certainly," Isabelle said, patting Tina's arm. The car turned off Fifth Avenue. The Four Seasons was just three blocks away. "One other thing."

"Yes?"

"Carole's sister Rachel—"

"The mathematician?"

"She died three days ago. The funeral was last night."

"Good lord. And you're sure Carole can keep her head on straight?"

"She's a pro. She does whatever needs to be done."

As the limo pulled up in front of the hotel, Isabelle cemented Tina's commitment by dangling a carrot.

"The Party needs to shore up a handful of candidates in BC. I can put Sentinel Strategies at the top of a short list. This is an opportunity to showcase what you do best." She paused with one hand on the door handle. "Don't fuck it up."

Without another word, Isabelle stepped out.

"We're good?" Carole asked Cal Sturman as he finished sweeping the thirty-second-floor suite for electronic bugs.

With two bedrooms and a media room, a large sitting room and wraparound terrace with a spectacular view of the city, the Oak Suite had the sprawling elegance of a luxury Manhattan apartment. Everyone milled near the entrance, waiting for clearance from the security team.

"We're good," Sturman said, logging the results on his phone.

Immediately everyone spread out. Carole claimed the round conference-cum-dining room table and opened her briefcase. The minister headed straight for the larger bedroom and used the ensuite. Jack O'Connell wandered out onto the terrace for a smoke. Paul Collacchi sat down across from Carole, opened his laptop and added notes for the minister's speech. She noticed Paul had deliberately chosen a spot where he didn't face O'Connell with his cigarette. She hoped he would beat the habit.

The porter unloaded the luggage trolley. He would be expecting a tip from someone.

"Cindy, would you take care of that?" Carole asked, then raised her voice so the minister was able to hear her. "OP Analytics is thinking about opening a twenty-seven-million-dollar software development lab in Markham next month. At five o'clock, you're meeting with the co-founders, Jeremy Ogden and Tom Platz—"

"Which riding?" he called through the half-closed bedroom door. "Markham east or west?"

"West," Carole answered without looking up from the minister's schedule. "One of ours. Janet Chen."

"Oh, her." Lattimer appeared in the bedroom doorway and saw the porter pushing the luggage trolley out. "Thanks for your help," he called out, then waited for the sound of the door closing before continuing. "Who are we up against?"

"North Carolina. The Research Triangle. They're offering twenty-year tax abatements and a five-million-dollar matching grant for leasehold improvements."

"And our pitch?"

"Markham's offering turnkey space down the road from IBM's big R and D centre, so the local IT infrastructure is superb. To sweeten that, we'll guarantee OP gets priority access to employment programs and R and D tax credits that will cut their talent costs by forty to fifty per cent."

"Is that enough?"

"OP's focus is software development. It's all about talent, and we've got an edge on the talent pool. Property taxes are not a big budget item, so North Carolina's tax abatement doesn't count for much. As for leasehold improvements, all these guys need are fibre-optic connections with zero downtime, enough power to run their servers and cappuccino machines, and a lot of local restaurants that deliver."

"Anything else?" Lattimer brushed a bit of lint off his jacket sleeve. Carole knew what he was really asking. Business schools and the media push a myth that corporate decisions are always driven by hard data and cold facts. The truth is that most multi-million-dollar deals are shaped by the personal quirks of the people sitting around the table.

Carole flipped through the file. "Two things. Jeremy Ogden is a University of Waterloo grad—computers and risk management—so this would be a successful homecoming for him."

"And the other?"

"Tom Platz is gay. Married."

Lattimer scowled. "Like we need more of those."

Carole held her annoyance in check. "His husband's a top-ranked medical researcher. Cancer genetics. Currently, he's doing some work with Memorial Sloan Kettering. We could get Health Canada to fund some kind of research project. Maybe in connection with the Ontario Genomics Institute."

"Good," Lattimer said, nodding his head as he worked through the pitch. "Get me a backgrounder on gay rights in North Carolina and a few research highlights from Princess Margaret. High level. Two, three paragraphs on each."

"Paul?"

"No problem. Give me twenty minutes."

"We could make the announcement next week in Markham," Lattimer continued with a big grin. "Twenty-seven million? That should get us front-page headlines."

Carole caught his eye. "You should leave yourself wiggle room on any research funding."

"Why? If we lose the election, too bad, so sad. We won't have to deliver on anyone's research grant."

The house phone rang. Cindy answered, then announced, "Isabelle Lisgar and Tina Smarland are on their way up."

15

"**Shit." Paul spun his laptop around** to show Carole and Lattimer. "CBC just broke the navy retrofit story. A three point seven billion-dollar cost overrun on the destroyer program."

"Goddamn," Lattimer winced. "Jim Matusak swore he buried that under—"

Before he got into a full-tilt rant, Carole interrupted him. "You weren't anywhere near that, right?"

"What? No, no." But his eyes slid away.

"You're sure? Because I can do stuff now that—"

"Forget it. It's okay," he insisted, and then there was no stopping him. "But how the hell did they get that story? Somebody leaked something. Fucking Grits turned somebody. Shit. Shit. Shit." He was practically frothing. "Cindy! Get me Matusak! We need to—"

"Hello, everyone!" Isabelle swept into the room with her thousand-watt smile and went straight to Peter Lattimer, opening her arms wide. "We need to what?"

"CBC's got the goddamn destroyer retrofit," he

responded, giving her a hug and allowing her to kiss him on both cheeks.

She waved away his concerns. "We knew there was a good chance it would come out."

"Yes, but—"

"Don't worry. I talked with the prime minister's office. They're on it." She patted him on the chest and lowered her voice. "While we're here, let's have some fun." She stepped back and gestured for Tina to come forward.

"Minister Lattimer, this is Christina Smarland."

"It's an honour to meet you, sir." Tina extended her hand, which he enveloped in both of his.

"I understand you're going to help us derail this OECD proposal," he said. "Good. Like I always say, we need more global trade, not more global regulation."

"Absolutely," Tina said.

"And this is my niece, Carole Lisgar, the minister's special advisor for strategic relations and acting chief of staff."

"Welcome to the team," Carole said as they shook hands.

"Call me Tina, please."

"Okay, Tina." She pointed with her chin across the table. "This is Paul Collacchi, the minister's speech writer, researcher extraordinaire and, in his spare time, an award-winning travel writer."

"Hi, Paul. I'm suitably impressed."

"Fortunately, I'm also modest." He grinned and waved. "Looking forward to working with you."

"Fabulous draft, Paul," Isabelle said, pulling a copy of the minister's speech out of her handbag and passing it over to him. "I made a few suggestions, but I'll leave it up to you."

"Thanks," Carole said, intercepting the marked-up speech and putting it on the conference table. "We'll look after it."

"Excellent," Isabelle said with an easy smile, then turned to Minister Lattimer. "May I make a suggestion? We could all do with a break. A little downtime. Why not bump the OP meeting 'til tomorrow?" Her voice adopted a mock-confidential whisper. "I'm told the bar downstairs has a new single-malt whisky that will change your life. What do you think? My treat."

"Paul and I need to go over the details of tomorrow's speech with Tina," Carole said. "We need to work out our approaches—"

"Absolutely," Isabelle said. "We'll get out of your hair so you can work in peace."

Carole looked across the room. "Minister, what do you think?"

"The OP thing is just a meet-and-greet with a little side deal," he said. "It will be fine."

Carole was torn. Her professional instincts whispered she should not let Lattimer out of her sight, but when she considered Isabelle's offer to take over at least some of her responsibilities, she felt her shoulders loosen in relief.

"Okay," Carole agreed. "And thanks. I'll catch up with you later."

Isabelle pulled her aside. "You're exhausted. Why don't you take the night off?"

"I'm fine." Carole gritted her teeth. Isabelle's concern, while touching, was getting on her nerves.

"Take your ego out of this," Isabelle urged. "The last three days have been an absolute hell. Nobody's saying you're not up to the job. You are. No question about that."

"But—"

"The next forty-eight hours will be critical." Isabelle held up her hand and with her fingers ticked off the itinerary. "The minister's speeches in the morning and the dinner tomorrow night. Back to his riding for a fundraiser the next night. Then the G7 conference in Paris next week. To make this all work, you're going to need to bring your A game."

"I don't know…"

Carole glanced over at the minister and O'Connell who were deep in quiet conversation. She caught his eye. He had the playful look of a guilty little boy.

"Come on, ladies. It's need-to-know time," Lattimer called out. "What's this event you've lined up for tonight?"

"I'll keep him busy. You look after yourself," Isabelle whispered, giving Carole a comforting pat on the arm before turning to address the minister.

"You asked me to find something interesting? Well, after dinner I've made reservations at the downtown helipad for a flight to one of the most beautiful estates you will ever see in your life."

"Are you kidding?" O'Connell's face split with a grin.

"I've got you on the guest list for a party that promises to be very special. Very private. Very exclusive."

A glint of excitement in his eyes, Lattimer asked, "What kind of party?"

"It's a fundraiser for one of those international do-gooders," Isabelle shrugged. "Disaster relief? Who knows? Frankly, who cares? What's important is the people who will be there. CEOs from offshore multinationals. Senior people from the UN, the World Bank, the IOC. A few celebrities."

"Let's do it." Lattimer exchanged fist bumps with Jack O'Connell.

Isabelle laughed. "A glorious summer evening. A lovely estate. Interesting people. It should be fun."

"Cal?" Carole asked the security team leader. "You're okay with this?"

He nodded. "Isabelle gave us a heads-up. We've checked it out."

"Cal will keep a close eye on them," Isabelle said. "I wish I could join you—"

Carole broke in, concern in her voice. "What? I thought—"

"Unfortunately, I have a business dinner I can't reschedule," Isabelle explained. "A banker from Beijing and his wife. Apparently, she's a big fan of Billy Joel so I've got us tickets for tonight's concert at Madison Square Garden. You wouldn't believe what the scalpers charged. I think I'm in the wrong business."

Still unconvinced, Carole turned to the minister. "And you're sure you don't need me for this?"

"We'll be fine," he assured her.

"Okay. We'll stay here and polish your speech for the morning."

He laughed. "Are you trying to make me feel guilty? I warn you. It won't work."

"Go," she responded with a playful push. "Have fun, but not too much. You've got an early morning."

"Yes, boss." Lattimer made an elaborate bow.

"Go on, get out of here," Carole ordered with mock severity.

He saluted and slipped on his suit jacket. Cal called ahead to have the limo brought around.

Carole pulled Cindy aside and whispered in her ear. "You know how he gets—"

"Don't worry," Cindy whispered back. "I'll have my eye on him all night long."

Within minutes, they were all ready, and Cal led them out. No sooner had the suite's door closed than Carole's lower back muscles loosened just a notch. She slid into a chair at the conference table, leaned back and kicked off her shoes.

"Before we get started, I've got a few calls to make," Tina said, waving her phone and heading for the terrace.

"Take your time," Carole called out. She looked over at Paul, who watched Tina and waited until she was outside.

"I checked her out," Paul said. "Her reputation is pretty sleazy."

Carole shrugged. "The Canadian Bankers' Institute is paying her fees."

"Still..."

"We're clean. There's no paper trail." Carole rubbed her eyes in bone-crushing fatigue. "Isabelle has known her for years. That's good enough for me."

16

Through the floor-to-ceiling windows of Chris Rader's twenty-third-floor office in the FBI's Manhattan field office, One World Trade Center rose phoenix-like, partially blocking the setting sun.

"Doesn't this make you a little nervous?" Neil turned to Rader. "Anyone with a grudge and a sniper rifle could really mess up your day."

"If you want the corner office, you take a few risks," Chris replied, brushing lint from his trouser leg. He was sitting at his desk, a phone to his ear, waiting patiently on hold.

A slim, elegant and soft-spoken man with silver-grey hair and a gracious ease that belied the ravages of high stress and overwork, Chris Rader was the FBI's point man on the US government's Financial Fraud Enforcement Task Force. It was a massive inter-agency behemoth that involved twenty federal agencies, ninety-four US attorneys' offices, state regulators and local law enforcement. While the intention had been to focus on strategy, the reality involved a lot of firefighting.

"Yes?" Chris said into the phone, jotting notes while he

talked. "Anybody else need a briefing note for this thing?" He paused, tapped his pen repeatedly. "That's it?" He hung up and grimaced at Neil.

"I'll have to ask for a rain check on dinner." He waved Neil into the visitor's chair opposite his desk.

"It's not my day," Neil replied. "At least you didn't walk out for a glass of water and disappear."

Chris laughed. "You don't know how many times I wish I could."

"Seriously, that's what happened earlier today," Neil said, segueing neatly into the main reason he had contacted Rader. He was betting the FBI had a file on Howland, and he wanted a peek at it.

"The guy's got a successful Ponzi scheme going here in town," Neil continued. "As soon as I mention the murder of this mathematician—"

"Okay, you have my attention." Chris leaned back. "I can give you, like, thirty seconds. What's up?"

"Not sure," Neil admitted. "It started with a murder in Toronto. A mathematician, Rachel Lisgar. A thin thread linked her to this Ponzi scheme here in New York—possibly—but when I interviewed the CEO, this guy Howland, he did a runner."

"You're kidding."

"We were talking in his office. He left to get some information. Never came back. Boom. Elvis has left the building."

"What scared him off?"

Neil shook his head. "No idea. Usually these guys go for the bullshit, not the exit."

"What was his name again?" Chris tapped his fingers on the desk.

"Stephen Howland. CEO, Hudson Ventures. Offices in midtown."

"Hudson Ventures? That rings a bell." He picked up his phone and punched a four-digit extension. "Good, you haven't left. There's a guy here you should talk to." He hung up the phone. "What have you got into?"

"I'm not sure. The murder victim's sister works for the Canadian minister of finance."

"You have my sympathy."

A sharp knock on the door frame got their attention.

"Hey, boss. What's up?"

A woman stood in the doorway, slightly out of breath. She was in her forties, tall and thin like a hydro pole, with a long, narrow face and dark eyes set close together. She wore a loose cotton shirt and chinos, her credentials hanging on a blue lanyard around her neck.

Rader waved her in. "Special Agent Alexandra Gorka, this is Neil Walker. He and I worked together on a few things when he was with the RCMP. Now he's a PI looking into a murder up in Toronto."

"Call me Ali," she said to Neil, looking him in the eye as they shook hands.

Chris asked her, "Does the name Hudson Ventures mean anything to you?"

"Sure." She stepped back, her eyes flicking between Chris and Neil. "We looked at them, there was something definitely not kosher, but we got pulled into the tail end of the Madoff file. Talk to Ted. He knows it better than me." She checked her watch. "Listen, I'm running late on this surveillance thing—you know the one?—and traffic's a bitch."

"Yeah, yeah. Ted's part of your team, isn't he?"

"He's out there now. I'm relieving him on post." She fidgeted with her car keys.

"Okay," Chris said. "Take Neil with you—"

"What? That's not—"

"You and Ted need to compare notes with him."

"But—"

"There's a political angle as well." Chris's voice held cynical delight. "A Canadian finance minister."

She measured Neil anew. "This should be an interesting drive."

"What are your plans for tomorrow?" Chris asked Neil.

"Wide open. At this point, I'm making it up as I go along."

"Good," Chris said, ushering them out the door. "You heard about the OECD's new AML directive?"

"Sure." It had been a hot topic on the anti–money laundering blogs Neil followed.

"There's a conference starting tomorrow morning. You should come. I can introduce you to a couple of people. They might be useful."

"Sounds good," Neil said. "Thanks."

"I'll send you the details," Chris said with a distracted wave as his phone rang again.

"Where are we going?" Neil asked Ali as he stretched to match her fast walk to the elevator.

"It's a lovely summer day," she answered brightly. "We're going to the beach."

17

"There you are," Carole said, welcoming Tina back into the suite with what she hoped was a collegial smile. "We need tomorrow's event to generate lots of good media back home. Who have you lined up for sound bites?"

"What's the headline?" Tina picked up the draft speech and skimmed rapidly through the pages.

"What the f—" Paul reached across the table.

Carole silently raised her hand just above the table, palm up, stopping him, her attention focused on Tina. "We've hand-picked the journalists who'll be there—"

"Yeah, yeah. The Canadians, fine." Tina sniffed. "CNN, *Wall Street Journal*, Breitbart—we need to spoon-feed them something provocative, a real barnburner that'll light up their comment boards." She tossed the draft speech back. "This won't cut it."

"What we need," Carole said slowly and clearly, "is sound bites from two or three credible names from US financial circles who will say good things—"

"But—"

Carole overrode her. "—say good things about the Canadian position on this issue. Your task was to line up those people. Where do we stand?"

"It's done, we're good," Tina assured her. "But we need to talk about this speech. First, though, my condolences on your sister's passing."

"Thanks."

"I saw online a TED talk she gave. Kind of a flake, wasn't she?"

Carole bristled slightly, surprising herself, but quickly suppressed it. "You were saying about the speech?"

Tina switched her attention to Paul. "You need to hammer the privacy angle a lot harder."

He sat back in his chair, his arms crossed, not budging.

"Really fire up the online trolls," Tina pushed. "Get them screaming that this is the stuff of nightmares." She shook her head and raised her voice. "What happened to our right to privacy? The presumption of innocence? In America, these are basic human rights. That's what we're fighting for here. We ask our men and women to risk their lives in God-forsaken parts of the world to protect something we turn around and give away because some Frenchies want to snoop in our bank accounts? No friggin' way!"

Tina was breathing hard by the time she finished, her chest heaving, her face red, her gaze shifting between Paul and Carole.

Paul rolled his eyes.

"I hear you, but my guy is not the best person to sell that message," Carole said calmly. "You have people who can do that much more effectively. Minister Lattimer has a different role. We position him as a cool, strategic voice who supports you. We need him to appear to be more centrist, more thoughtful. A statesman. It strengthens your hand in Washington, and it plays well for us back home."

"We need to hit 'em hard," Tina insisted.

"And we will," Carole says. "Two voices, working together. Between us, we can get this thing sidelined. Raise enough doubts to bury it in some subcommittee."

"The EU hates our guts," Tina muttered, closing her eyes and rubbing her temples. "They hate our business smarts, but they'll steal our technology every chance they get. And what about all those crazy Muslims? Don't get me started!"

"Let's not go there," Carole said. "Let's get back to—"

"I like that about you—one hundred per cent focused," Tina said with a grin, her mood flipping a hundred and eighty degrees. "Just how Isabelle described you."

"Isabelle told you about me?" Carole said, sliding her chair back a few inches, her expression watchful. "I'm flattered. Isabelle doesn't usually talk much about family. She must like you."

"And I'm a huge fan of hers."

"You two must know each other pretty well," Carole said, masking her surprise with an attentive look, her unspoken question probing for more details about the apparent closeness of Isabelle's relationship with Tina.

Tina nodded. "One time, she invited me to a meeting at the Hay-Adams in Washington. Your prime minister was there—I really like him—anyway, we were talking about this pipeline thing I was working on. Some idiots from Ducks Unlimited in Saskatchewan were bitching—I should say they were *quacking*—about some environmental bullshit."

"They have a lot of support out west," Carole acknowledged evenly.

"They were holding up the whole goddamn parade! So, Isabelle had a quiet word with your PM. Five minutes later he tells us not to worry, he'd fix it through—whatchamacallit—not *executive order*, but what do you call it up there? *Order-*

in-Council? Right. Three weeks later, by God, the man delivered."

"That's Isabelle for you," Carole said, her tone encouraging Tina to continue. "She can get seemingly impossible things done."

"You heard about a certain congressman from Delaware?" Tina raised her eyebrows and lowered her voice.

"Wasn't that amazing?" Carole responded with a gossipy tone.

"The only reason that guy's not in jail is thanks to Isabelle and the digital voodoo pulled off by her Waterloo computer geeks. By the time the SEC got their subpoena, the financial files were spotless." Tina grinned with delight. "Now she owns that guy's ass. And guess who sits on the senate subcommittee reviewing this new OECD directive? Bingo! That's one vote in the bag!"

Tina checked her watch. "Whoa! The time! Gotta run." She grabbed her briefcase and practically raced for the door.

"Hey—we're not finished," Carole called out. "The sound bites? Who have you got lined up?"

"Call me," Tina shouted back, just before the door slammed shut.

The sudden silence in the room grew uncomfortable.

"Honest to God, I try to keep my cynicism at bay," Paul said. "But, holy fuck, this makes it hard."

Carole picked up her phone. She found in Paul's doubts an echo of her own. She tapped in Isabelle's number. It rang and rang, then went to voice mail.

18

The FBI sedan headed east through Queens along the Long Island Expressway. Low-rise factories and distribution warehouses, bleached grey-beige by the late-afternoon August heat, gradually gave way to sunburnt suburban bungalows, then dusty farmland.

Construction crews had torn up long stretches of the highway. There was so much road noise that Neil had trouble prying information out of the two FBI agents sitting up front. The driver, introduced by Ali Gorka as her new partner Special Agent Ken Merkel, muttered a steady stream of curses aimed at the drivers cutting in and out of lanes.

"You'll have to forgive our young special agent," Ali mocked, glancing over her shoulder at Neil. "This is his first week here after a posting in Alaska, where he grew up—"

"Hey! I spent the last six months in Vegas—"

"Right, but none of it prepared him for driving in New York City."

"I can sympathize," Neil near shouted. "I was posted for eighteen months in the Yukon. Spectacular country." They hit a bump that rocked Neil up from his seat, then the road smoothed out. "So, where are we going?"

"Ted Boyce, the guy you need to talk with about Hudson Ventures, is on a surveillance job out in the Hamptons," Ali replied. "It's part of a joint US–UK task force, a money laundering thing. This Spanish dude is throwing a big party tonight at his ginormous beachfront estate."

"What's his name? The Spanish guy?"

"Santiago. He's the CEO of Grupo Muxia."

"Doesn't ring any bells," Neil said. "So, tell me about Hudson Ventures. You mentioned you looked into it a few years ago. What happened?"

"It looked good at the start but then just sort of petered out," Ali said. "It went cold. Other files got hot. You know how it goes."

"I hear you."

"Talk to Boyce. He'll fill you in," Ali promised. "Is that what brought you here on this lovely summer day? Hudson Ventures?"

"Indirectly. The victim—Rachel Lisgar—met with the CEO, Stephen Howland. She flew back to Toronto and within an hour she's dead. Howland was the last—"

"How'd she die?" Ali glanced at Merkel before locking eyes with Neil.

"Murdered. Why?"

"Our investigation into Hudson Ventures lost steam because the guy who filed the original SEC complaint—this accountant in Staten Island?—he died, too.

"Really?"

"Yeah," said Ali, watching Neil in the rear-view mirror. "An accident while renovating his house. The story was he used an off-the-books electrician. Somehow, wires got crossed.

A power surge electrocuted him in his home office. Fried his computer at the same time."

There was a moment of silence as they thought about the coincidence. Merkel, recently arrived from the Las Vegas office, spoke up. "What are the odds?"

19

Merkel parked on a gravel road just behind an oversized FBI surveillance truck. Ali rapped twice on the truck's back door, then stuck her head inside.

Neil paused to stretch the kinks out of his back and suck in a deep lungful of the sultry Atlantic breeze. Gulls wheeled overhead. Whitecaps topped the waves rolling across the broad bay. A handful of teenagers in bikinis and board shorts were hanging out on the beach, catching the last rays of the setting sun. All in all, a pretty nice summer evening.

Ali waved Neil over. The mobile command centre was big enough to hold ten people, multiple workstations and a ton of rack-mounted digital equipment. Ali made the introductions. Special Agent Ted Boyce was built solid, with big, scarred hands and eyes that had seen everything. He looked like the guy you'd pick to play on your side in any contact sport. Brian Haffey, from the UK's National Crime Agency, was thin, ginger-haired, intense and wrapped a little too tightly.

Wall-mounted monitors showed a half-dozen video feeds streaming from the party across the bay. The main house was a sprawling two-storey, glass-and-stone showcase with tennis courts and two swimming pools, spread across acres of prime real estate. A hundred or so wealthy guests milled about on the perfect lawn that rolled down to a groomed, private beachfront. Catering staff circulated with trays of drinks and food. The dress code was silks, linens, deep tans and chunky, glittery jewellery.

"What's the party for?" Neil asked.

"Supposedly a fundraiser for—" Boyce looked down at his notes "—African humanitarian aid."

"Fat cats for famine relief," Ali deadpanned.

Hiding his irritation, Boyce continued. "Guests are A-listers from business, the UN, various global aid groups. It's a who's who of CEOs, wealthy donors, NGO executives, politicians, diplomats and backroom fixers."

Ali blew a rude sound. "It's like a pickup bar. A place to start conversations that can be continued later behind closed doors."

One of the techies called out, "Go to a lot of pickup bars, do you?"

Boyce shook his head with a gesture that said *Look what I have to put up with.*

Suppressing a grin, Neil asked, "Who's the host?"

"Paolo Santiago, CEO of Grupo Muxia," Boyce said, glancing across the bay to the party underway. "He's Spanish royalty of some kind, an engineer by training. He made a fortune from Spain's infrastructure and green energy boom."

"Infrastructure projects," Neil grunted. "No-bid contracts. Kickbacks. Usually, a lot of cash ends up in briefcases."

"The business press says he's a shrewd guy. But that's PR bullshit. He's shrewd like John Gotti was shrewd. From time to time, his competitors turn up dead."

"But, so far, nothing has stuck?"

"Not for lack of trying. Interpol has a thick file on him. Grupo Muxia specializes in international development projects. There's evidence of massive fraud, bribing government officials, money laundering—he's a real piece of work." Boyce jerked his chin at the video feeds. "We're tagging the guests we have files on and running the others through facial recognition software."

"Security is pretty heavy," Neil noted. Uniformed guards stood watch at the front gate, and two-man teams circled the perimeter.

"Echelon Security Systems. They're private contractors," Ali said. "I was an MP in Iraq, two tours. I recognize the type."

"They probably know you're here," Neil said.

"Sure," Boyce said. "But they haven't found the cameras and bugs the catering staff planted earlier."

Skeptically, Neil asked, "And security isn't sweeping—"

"Frequency-hopping microburst transmissions," Boyce replied with a quick grin. "Too fast for signal tracking."

"You guys get all the good toys," Neil said, brown-nosing just a little.

"Yeah, yeah," Boyce replied. "So—Hudson Ventures. What's up?"

"A financial analyst was murdered in Toronto. Her last appointment was here in New York at Hudson Ventures. I was there this afternoon. It raised some flags."

Boyce glanced at the screens, then looked back at Neil. "So, what do you want from us?"

"Could I take a look at your files on Hudson Ventures?"

"I don't—"

Ali spoke up. "Remember Ed Kosnik?"

"Remind me."

"Three years ago. The Staten Island accountant who blew the whistle on Hudson Ventures? Then died suddenly? As I recall, the timing was pretty convenient. What if that wasn't an accident?"

Boyce paused. "Tell me about this murder."

Neil sketched what had happened on Magdalene Court. "If we're right, Rachel Lisgar did something or saw something during her meeting with Howland here in New York that led her to death a few hours later in Toronto." He held up his hand and used his fingers to list his points. "First: the killers. It was a team of two, possibly more. Highly skilled, well equipped and very professional. Second: the fast, cross-border response. That means an organization with international reach, deep pockets and direct access to contract killers. Mafia? Terrorists? The options are all bad."

Boyce nodded, then looked over at Ali. "Get him the files on Hudson Ventures."

Ali asked Boyce, "How about we take another look ourselves?"

"Based on what? A potential connection to a possible murder case in Canada?"

"That, and Howland's connection to Santiago."

Neil spoke up. "Say again?"

"When we looked at Hudson Ventures, there were ongoing transactions with Grupo Muxia," Ali told Neil, but she was watching for Boyce's reaction. "We'd just scratched the surface when the case fell apart."

"Boss," Merkel broke in. "You're going to want to see this."

Onscreen, they watched as a blue-and-white helicopter, sparkling in the setting sun, swept in for a spectacular entrance to the party. The FBI cameras zoomed in on the passengers as they disembarked, walking hunched over until they were beyond the whirling blades.

Neil froze.

Not many things could astonish him, but this one came out of the blue.

He recognized one of the passengers. Leading the way was Peter Lattimer, Canada's minister of finance.

20

A beautiful Filipina hostess, whose gossamer sarong swirled in the helicopter's updraft, greeted them at the edge of the helipad. She led Minister Lattimer, his driver, Cindy and the security team across the south lawn to where the party was in full swing. Within moments, servers were on hand offering drinks and trays of food.

Neil finally found his voice. "There's something you don't see every day."

"Lattimer was a last-minute addition to the guest list." Boyce gave Neil a sidelong glance, then refocused on the monitors. They saw Santiago shake Lattimer's hand with obvious respect.

Paolo Santiago, the man under the intense microscope of an international police investigation, appeared to be relaxed and enjoying himself. He was about five foot eight and wearing a simple top and pants cut loosely from monochrome grey linen. Round tinted glasses gave him a quiet, old-fashioned, intellectual air.

"Who's the little guy?" Boyce asked.

"Jack something...O'Connell," Neil said. "Officially, he's

the minister's driver. Truth is, he's Lattimer's wingman, his party buddy. Has been since they were at university together."

Jack got into the party mood, dancing a little as he reached out and grabbed a drink off a passing tray.

"Any chance we could hear what they're saying?" Neil asked.

"Lisa?" Boyce asked the audio technician.

"One minute..." she muttered, her fingers flying over the keyboard. "Got it!"

Santiago's voice was soft and husky, with only a trace of Spanish accent. "...so glad you could join us," he said to Lattimer. "With your upcoming election campaign, I imagine your schedule is hectic. I hope you will take this time to relax and refresh yourself."

"At a party like this, on a night like tonight, it would be hard not to," the minister said, his eyes glued to a pair of voluptuous young hostesses in matching red gowns.

"*Bueno.*" Santiago beckoned the two women with a wave of his hand. "Let Michelle and Angelique show you around."

"What do you think, Jack?" Lattimer's eyes glittered.

"We'd be rude not to accept such fine hospitality," Jack answered as he slipped his arm around Michelle's waist.

The RCMP security team leader shot a questioning look at Lattimer. "Give us a little space," Lattimer ordered, looking first at Cindy, then Cal.

Jack leaned over and whispered something to the two hostesses. They giggled.

"May I impose on you for advice about doing business in Canada?" Santiago asked Lattimer. "It will take only a minute or two. Perhaps your friends could go ahead."

"Of course," Lattimer said graciously, albeit reluctantly. With hungry eyes, he followed the seductive young women in red as they linked arms with Jack. Together, they strolled across the lawn towards the dance floor, trailed by a stone-faced Cindy and the security team. Lattimer, only half paying attention to Santiago, asked, "How can I help?"

In the surveillance truck, Boyce ordered the audio techs to stay with the signal. He glanced at the guy controlling the camera feed. "In case we lose the audio, zoom in close enough so lip-readers can figure it out later."

Everyone focused on the monitors.

"I plan to open a new engineering and project-management operations centre," Santiago explained. "Locating it in Canada would enable us to reach disaster zones in the western hemisphere more quickly and efficiently."

"If there's anything I can do to streamline your start-up process, let me know." Lattimer's gaze swept the lavish grounds.

"I have a question about taxes." Santiago nodded thoughtfully. "Our work is in disaster relief projects. Many of our clients are charities. Every penny we can save them provides more food and medical supplies for the victims."

Lattimer accepted a glass of champagne from a passing server. "Tight budgets are a fact of life these days."

"Since our work impacts the social welfare of millions worldwide, I wondered if a Canadian engineering centre could be structured under Canadian tax laws as a non-profit social enterprise."

"As such, it would be tax-exempt." Lattimer's eyes narrowed as he studied Santiago. "It would require pushing the boundaries of current definitions."

Across the bay, inside the truck, the FBI tech called out. "Five seconds."

"Keep it live," Boyce ordered.

"But—"

"Wait 'til I tell you!"

It was risky. The longer they listened, the greater the chance Santiago's security would detect and jam the signal. The tech turned up the volume.

They watched Santiago respond to Lattimer with a shrug.

"True innovation often calls for rules and regulations to be stretched, no?"

Lattimer tilted his head in silent agreement.

"In my experience," Santiago continued, "success requires two things: first, the support of influential people with vision and, second, a willingness to invest in local expertise."

Lattimer took a sip of champagne and spoke over the rim of the glass. "Such expertise can be expensive. Lawyers, accountants, various consultants."

"Whatever initial costs of securing tax-exempt status would be more than paid back over the long term."

"In terms of benefits for your clients, the charitable organizations," Lattimer said, a smile tugging at the corners of his lips.

"Exactly," Santiago said, with a brief bow of his head. "Now, enough of business! This is a party. Shall we finish our conversation at a later date?"

"Of course," Lattimer replied, then leaned closer and continued more softly.

"And cut it!" Boyce shouted.

Silence reigned in the surveillance truck. Neil looked at Boyce. They both recognized what appeared to be the opening moves in a dirty dance. If Grupo Muxia splashed around a lot of money to the right people, Lattimer would help them avoid millions in taxes.

Neil took a deep breath while he thought through his options. He had witnessed a senior Canadian cabinet minister engaged in an oblique discussion about taking bribes for special tax status. He had no definitive proof. He had no authority to act. Who should he tell?

He stepped out of the truck, grabbing a pair of binoculars off a hook, and walked away a few paces in the soft summer night.

The exchange raised a raft of questions. Why had Peter Lattimer shown up at a party thrown by an international thug like Paolo Santiago? What had happened to his political sense? The remote location might have lulled Lattimer into thinking no one would find out, but a hundred or more people watched him make a splashy entrance. Could he be that brazen?

None of those questions had anything to do with Rachel's death.

Neil held up the binoculars and studied the party across the bay. *Lattimer may believe he's smart enough to handle Santiago,* Neil thought, *but he's way out of his league. He'll get eaten alive.*

Not that Neil gave a shit.

But it gave him an idea.

He hung the binoculars around his neck. He pulled out his phone and made a call.

"Janos? Pull up your contacts list. I need a number."

21

Carole swiped her hotel key card, *snick-click*, followed by a solid *clunk* as she pushed open the room's heavy door.

"Have you even had time to unpack since the funeral?" Paul Collacchi's room was almost directly across the hall. She saw concern in his eyes.

"Not a problem," she replied as lightly as possible, pulling her carry-on. "This is New York City. Everybody always wears black."

As the door closed behind her, she heard him laugh. Good. He always wrote better when he was relaxed, and tomorrow was a big day. Isabelle needed a solid win. It was up to her to deliver.

She heaved her suitcase up onto the luggage stand, kicked off her shoes and surveyed the room. King-sized bed, soft grey walls, artful lighting, floor-to-ceiling windows with a slice of the sparkling New York skyline showing between heavy dark drapes. It would do. She opened one of the lower cabinets and was rewarded with the mini-bar. She poured herself a scotch, made it a double and collapsed on the couch. Feet up on the coffee table, she leaned back and closed her eyes.

The last three days had been a marathon, and she was still standing. She took a measure of pride in being able to roll with whatever happened, think on her feet, find ways to move forward. That's what separated the winners from the rest of the pack.

Organizing Rachel's funeral had been a logistical nightmare that blew everything else off her priority list. The arrangements, reaching out to people she needed to connect with, being nice to the horde of Rachel's students and fellow travellers who felt compelled to show up and say something. Basically, a three-ring circus with her as reluctant ringmaster.

Isabelle had been a lifesaver. She must find a gift for her, a token, something sparkly.

Carole took a long, slow sip, feeling the icy-fiery liquid slip down her throat, coating and soothing raw nerve ends, muscles melting in relief.

Rachel. She'd left a mess. Typical. She could have at least let Carole know she was named executor—executrix?—of her estate. Was that too much to ask?

They hadn't spoken in almost two years. In the decade before that, the contacts had decreased in frequency as they increased in bitterness. Polite exchanges had degenerated into snarls and stinging insults. Eventually, even those had stopped. Mercifully.

Rachel. When they were kids, she'd been the brilliant one. Eighteen months younger and quick with a cutting remark. Both parents, when they were around, were obviously delighted and amused by the precocious Rachel, expecting Carole to fend for herself.

And she became good at it. She'd learned how to put the pain into little boxes, close the lid and put them on a shelf. As she grew older, Carole discovered that compartmentalizing things was a useful life skill.

She lifted her drink and tried making a short toast to Rachel, but the right words eluded her. Too many conflicting emotions. Residual anger. Sudden hollowness. Regret. Impossible to sort out.

Most of all, what she felt was tired.

She sat for a moment, head back, eyes closed, letting the air fill her lungs, then slowly releasing it. She started drifting off, caught herself, stood up and got ready for bed.

Soon, she was under the covers, lights out. Thirty seconds later, she was gone.

———

An insistent cellphone ring broke into Carole's sleep.

She opened her eyes. It was still dark. Where was she? Hotel room. New York.

Another ring. She groped for the phone.

"Yeah?"

"Carole Lisgar?"

"Who is this?"

"Neil Walker. I know it's late but—"

"Who?" She sat up.

"Neil Walker. I—"

Without a word, she hung up and tossed the phone back on the nightstand. She rolled over and slid back down under the covers.

It started ringing again. She squeezed her eyes and pulled the pillow close around her ears. She waited. It went to voice mail. She waited, knowing...

Again, it started ringing. She snatched up the phone.

"Go away," she snapped.

"You're a dealmaker, right?" he said in a rush. "So, let's make a deal."

"Not interested." She started to put the phone down.

"Don't hang up! I have information you need to know. All I want is a few minutes of your time."

"Bullshit." Carole rubbed her eyes but couldn't stop herself from listening.

"A few questions about Rachel," he said, his tone softening. "Let me buy you breakfast."

Carole sat up in bed. "Where are you calling from?"

"I'm here in New York."

"What are you doing here? Never mind." Almost against her better instincts, she leaned back against the headboard. She cursed her weakness for secrets. "What's this information I need to know?"

"No, no. In the morning. A trade—"

Carole broke in, her voice harsh. "Give me something now or I'm hanging up."

"Tomorrow. I promise."

"Like I'm going to trust you. Don't call again." She held the phone away from her ear as if she were going to disconnect.

"Okay, okay!" Neil shouted.

"I'm listening."

"Do you know where your boss is right now?"

Carole sat up straight, her political radar flashing yellow and heading for red. "Minister Lattimer?"

"Yeah. This very minute."

"Do tell," she said with forced calm. Juggling her cell, she reached for the bedside phone.

"So, he slipped the leash," Neil said, his tone sympathetic. "Lattimer's partying with an A-list of corporate thugs, corrupt politicians and international money launderers."

"That's ridiculous." Carole quickly punched Isabelle's number into the hotel phone. She loaded her voice with all the skepticism her still-foggy brain could muster. "And you know this how?"

"Because I saw him arrive. Nice helicopter, by the way."

"You just happened to be in the neighbourhood?"

"No, I was sitting in an FBI surveillance van. There he was on the monitors. Captured on video for posterity."

"I don't believe you," Carole snapped, silently urging her call on the other line to go through.

"So, call him."

Carole, frustrated, heard Lattimer's phone go to voice mail.

Neil, studying the party guests through binoculars, saw Lattimer glance at his phone.

"Uh-oh, he's not taking your call."

"Say again?" Carole stalled, hitting redial and willing Isabelle to pick up.

"I'm watching Lattimer put his phone back into his pocket. He's having a wonderful time. Oh, and that's a nice babe he's with. A little young, maybe, but I'm sure her ID says she's eighteen."

"Okay, okay," Carole said. She hung up the hotel phone and rubbed the sleep from her eyes. *What a disaster! How could this be happening? What was Lattimer doing?*

Neil's voice cut through her thoughts. "Tomorrow? Breakfast?"

"Okay, but I've got something first thing." Carole shook her head to clear the remaining dregs of sleep. "Later. Around nine?"

"Where?"

"Financial District. I'll text you the address.

22

It was morning before Carole could talk to the minister alone, or almost alone. Outside the Four Seasons, as they climbed into the Suburbans, she signalled Cindy to ride in the other car with Paul. That left her, the minister and Cal Sturman, the RCMP security team lead. She closed the driver's partition.

"Interesting guests at the party last night?" She kept her tone carefully neutral. She needed to manage this guy, not antagonize him, even if he was an idiot.

"The usual," Lattimer responded absently, his head down, scanning his speech notes, deliberately not looking at her.

"How about you, Cal?" Carole again kept her tone even. "Anything come up?"

"Nah." He glanced at her, then quickly shifted his attention back to the passing traffic. "Same old, same old."

"I'm surprised the FBI didn't give you a heads-up."

"The FBI?"

Lattimer looked up. "What—"

She overrode him, her focus on Cal. "Did you check with them?"

"Sure," Sturman answered, perplexed. "What are you talking about?"

"Last night's party was under FBI surveillance." She glanced at the minister. "They have it all on video."

"What's going on?" Lattimer seemed annoyed by the interruption.

"Money laundering, apparently," Carole responded. "It's somewhat ironic, given the speech you're delivering in about fifteen minutes." She shifted her attention back to Cal. "Two things you might want to consider. Did the FBI not tell you because they don't trust you? And what else are they keeping from you?" Her voice hardened. "And when I say *you*, I mean *us*."

"I'll look into it," Sturman promised, red-faced.

"Do that." Her voice held a sharp edge. "I'm counting on you, Cal."

"From the time we left the hotel to the time we returned, security was tight," Sturman protested. "My job is to protect the principal, not offer political advice."

"Cut him some slack," Lattimer said. "It was my call, not his. For God's sake, it was a charity fundraiser. Besides, I met serious players last night, people with the kind of international connections that can make big trade and investment deals happen."

"The FBI claims—"

"Who knows what the FBI is really up to?" he said, then threw in a dig. "Not too long ago, you were facing charges yourself."

She felt her face flush but held her anger in check. "This is not about me. You're the one running for re-election."

"I checked. None of my constituents were at the party." He smiled and patted her leg. "Relax. You worry too much."

She gritted her teeth. *Condescending jerk.* "I'm paid to worry about this stuff."

"Everything is fine. Talk to Isabelle. She arranged everything."

"That's a whole different conversation," Carole said coolly.

She looked up when the limo stopped at a traffic light. She realized they were only two or three minutes to their destination.

Shit! Her priority was to keep Lattimer focused. The federal election campaign was starting soon. Opposing the OECD proposal sent a message to Wall Street and the folks back home that Canada's business-friendly tax and regulatory environment was in good hands. There was nothing to worry about. Nearly two billion dollars' worth of trade and investment flowed across the Canada–US border every day. A lot of jobs were at stake.

She pulled out the day's schedule. "How about a quick run-through of today's itinerary?"

Lattimer grunted a response.

"After the presentation, you have a series of corporate calls. Rick Skelton from the consulate—you met him yesterday at the airport—he knows the companies. He'll introduce you."

She realized Lattimer was only half paying attention, but that was okay. She was barely paying attention herself.

Mostly, she was trying to figure out Neil Walker's agenda.

23

The Hotel Astley's mezzanine-level coffee shop had floor-to-ceiling windows that overlooked the hotel entrance and the few loitering protestors who had no better place to go.

Carole slid into the banquette across from Neil. "It must piss you off that you need my help."

His expression neutral, Neil said, "Actually, I am trying to figure out what I did to deserve such weird karma."

"Let's start with you having me arrested on national television, even though I was innocent," she said, her face pale and sharp with anger.

Burned into her memory was the humiliation of being handcuffed and led down the broad steps of Parliament's Centre Block. Television cameras and reporters had tracked her every move. She could still feel being pushed into the back of an RCMP squad car.

"Arresting you was not my choice," Neil responded, looking her straight in the eye.

"Really?" She snorted. "That's not what they told me."

"The decision came down from the assistant superintendent's office."

"And you were just following orders? Where have I heard that before?"

"Actually, I refused to sign the warrant." Neil shrugged. "The brass assigned another guy as co-lead investigator, who was happy to go along."

Carole leaned back. His cool, matter-of-fact tone made her pause. She watched his eyes, the set of his mouth, his posture. Having been raised on backroom politics, she'd run into a lot of liars.

"Those emails on your computer?" He waved his hand in dismissal. "I was pretty sure they were fake—"

Carole wasn't sure she'd heard correctly. "You knew I didn't write them?"

"You're obviously not stupid, and only an idiot would have used her own computer to send those emails." He tipped his head. "The other thing was timing. They appeared at just the right time, supplying exactly the evidence we needed. According to the digital forensics, the metadata was consistent with all your other emails. But I was not convinced. I thought they were too good to be true."

She shook her head. "RCMP techies planted them on my computer."

"And why would they do that?"

"It was all politics. Dirty tricks. The senator cut the RCMP budget. Your bosses wanted him gone."

"We didn't need them," he said simply. "We had the senator's offshore accounts. We had a guy ready to sign a plea deal. We were within days of tracking the money trail through a string of anonymous shell companies. When the emails turned up, they immediately became the centre of the case. Someone leaked that we had them. The brass felt they had no option but to arrest you. Once the emails were publicly discredited, any chance of successfully prosecuting Senator Bouchard disappeared."

Carole was stunned. All she could do was stare. This was a completely different scenario than she had been living with for three long years. The problem was, it carried the ring of truth.

When she spoke, her voice was rough and raw. "Is that really why you were fired? Because you refused to arrest me?"

"I told you, I resigned," Neil said, letting out an exasperated sigh. "I quit, not because I was pissed off. Well, I was, but it was more than that." He spun the salt and pepper shakers. "I found myself in a lot of meetings with RCMP brass and political staff from the minister's office where there were odd comments and looks I didn't understand."

Carole sat silent, frozen in place, staring blankly. It was like she was hearing a weird alternate-reality version of the disaster that had nearly destroyed her life.

Neil swept aside some salt that had been spilled on the table. "Do you play poker?"

Surprised, she refocused on him, her eyes narrowing. "What's that got to do with anything?"

"There's an old saying. *If you look around the table and can't spot the patsy, chances are it's you.*"

A grin flickered across Carole's face. She couldn't help it.

"Now I get to choose the cases I want," Neil said. "Finding out what happened to Rachel is one of them."

Carole glanced out the window, buying time. As much as she didn't want to admit it, even to herself, his story sounded true.

And that changed everything.

Because those emails did exist.

Someone had created them. Somehow, they got onto her computer. If it wasn't the RCMP, who was it?

She didn't know what to think. Or what to say.

He leaned forward. "How about you and I agree to throw pixie dust all over the past? Further, let's agree to put it on the back burner. Okay?"

Carole nodded, now on firmer ground.

"Good. Let's talk about Rachel." Neil pulled out a notebook and pen. "When was the last time you saw her?"

"Maybe two years ago? Something like that."

"Okay. What about friends she might talk to. Boyfriend? Girlfriend? Best friend?"

"I don't know anything about her personal life. We hadn't even talked in a long time. Except..."

"Yes?"

"She left a message the night she died. She wanted me to call. Said it was important."

"And did you?"

"No." She knew it sounded bad. She felt compelled to explain. "Every time we talked, we ended up fighting. I didn't want to get into it."

"Did Rachel say why she wanted you to call? Just that it was important?"

Stung, defensive, she pushed back. "Important to who? Rachel? It could be some anti-poverty regulation she wanted to vent about. I thought, if it was urgent, she would call again."

Neil closed his notebook and placed his pen on the table.

"Sorry." Carole let out a long breath and shifted topics. "Why are you asking all this? The police say Rachel was killed because she was a witness. Are they wrong?"

"Maybe," Neil said. "The problem is that theory ignores certain other facts."

"Like what?"

"On the day she died, Rachel made a round-trip flight from Toronto to New York to meet with the CEO of Hudson Ventures. Have you heard of it?"

"Hudson Ventures?" She searched her memory. "No."

"How about its CEO, Stephen Howland?"

"Not that I recall. Who is he?"

"He's a con man. He started with penny stocks on the Vancouver Stock Exchange. He skipped out of Canada just as the RCMP was closing in."

"And he's operating here in New York City?"

"Has been for a few years now. Successfully, by all accounts. The thing is, Rachel's research strongly suggested that Hudson Ventures is probably a Ponzi scheme. She could have simply written a report to that effect. Why the face-to-face meeting?"

"Wait a minute," Carole said. "If it's a Ponzi scheme, why hasn't the district attorney shut it down?"

"They tried a few years ago. The FBI investigation fell apart when the financial analyst who filed the original SEC complaint died in a freak accident."

"Really? Is that true?"

"According to the FBI."

"Okay. It could be a coincidence."

"Possibly," Neil said, clearly not convinced. "You've never heard of Stephen Howland or Hudson Ventures. How about Grupo Muxia?"

"No," Carole replied, shaking her head slowly as she again searched her memory. "What is it?"

"I did some online digging last night. It's a privately controlled corporation based in Switzerland. Supposedly, it's a design-build engineering company. It specializes in infrastructure projects, mainly in the Third World, usually after some natural disaster—an earthquake, tsunami, volcanic eruption. Like that. What connects all the projects is the litany of accusations against Grupo Muxia that inevitably follows: bribery, corruption, sub-standard construction and often sheer theft. AidWatch International ranks it as the worst among the so-called rogue corporations."

"What does a Ponzi scheme have to do with infrastructure projects?"

"Don't know," Neil admitted. "One thing I noticed was that Grupo Muxia maintains a highly trained security force. I saw them in the Hamptons. Some of them looked like they have special forces background."

"So? The world can be a dangerous place."

"Spec Ops are an interesting breed. Most are quiet, solid guys. Others are no different than bikers with better guns. My point is that, by definition, Grupo Muxia security contractors would have the training and skills to murder Rachel."

"That's a leap," Carole scoffed.

"Somewhat," Neil agreed. "But according to the FBI, Hudson Ventures did business with Grupo Muxia and, from what I could piece together about Rachel, Grupo Muxia is exactly the type of corrupt global corporation that she hated."

"That's true," Carole conceded. There was something in his voice. "You sound like you admired her."

"From what I've learned, a lot of people liked Rachel," Neil said. "Have you seen any of the stuff online? Like the TED talks? She was pretty interesting."

"I can tell you, she wasn't perfect."

"Few of us are," Neil said. "But getting back to the topic at hand, what can you tell me about Peter Lattimer's connection to Grupo Muxia?"

"The minister? As far as I'm aware, there's absolutely none," Carole replied. "What makes you think there is?"

"You don't know?"

"Know what?"

"Last night's party in the Hamptons?"

"What about it?"

"The host was Paolo Santiago, CEO of Grupo Muxia."

"Oh, no," Carole said with a sinking feeling. This was not good. Her mind whirled.

Neil's voice brought her back. "My understanding is that a cabinet minister's schedule is tightly controlled. Events are always vetted. If Lattimer didn't know Santiago, who arranged for the invitation?"

Carole cleared her throat. "Isabelle."

He stared at her. "Isabelle Lisgar knows Paolo Santiago?"

"Not necessarily," she said, confused. "I don't know."

Why would Isabelle risk the political reputation of the minister by having him photographed shaking hands with someone like Paolo Santiago? Especially when she knew Carole was responsible for keeping Lattimer out of trouble? It was insane. How could she do this? Carole trusted her. They were family.

Neil broke into her thoughts. "Look, do you think you could help me out here?"

Carole stared at him while her brain raced. The barrage of information, first about the email, then about last night's party, had cracked the foundation of her world. What was going on?

"I'm going to keep looking into Rachel's death," Neil said. "If something comes up, would it be okay to call you?"

She made a decision. "Can you keep me in the loop on what you find out?"

He paused. She watched him weigh his answer.

"On one condition," he said. "You don't tell anyone

without checking with me."

Carole realized he meant Lattimer and Isabelle. "I can do that," she promised.

They sat at the table, a little awkwardly. Carole realized she would have to trust a person who, until fifteen minutes ago, had been her sworn enemy.

Best to take it one step at a time. Look at things with fresh eyes. She knew where to start. "You mentioned one of Rachel's TED talks. Could you send me the link?"

"My pleasure," Neil said.

24

Police barricades outside the Hotel Astley held back the two hundred or so demonstrators jostling for space and waving placards that urged *Break the Chains of Corporate Corruption* and warned *Global Banking—a Conspiracy of the Corrupt*. Neil's personal favourite said simply *Fuck the Greedy—Feed the Needy*.

Inside, the Global Financial Institute's annual conference on trends in foreign direct investment had already started. Neil arrived with Chris Rader, who flashed his FBI creds and got them into the Vanderbilt Room.

The cavernous, low-ceilinged hall buzzed with testosterone. The event had drawn C-suite executives, politicians and high-priced consultants. Serious young guys in expensive suits, eyes sparkling, hustled to make insider connections. Older guys held court, posing as potential mentors, their smiles bland, their instincts predatory.

The Canadian Department of Foreign Affairs and International Trade was a gold sponsor of the conference, and that bought Finance Minister Peter Lattimer top spot at the podium. His speech was already underway. A few hundred executives, both men and women, sat in rows of chairs listening politely.

Neil spotted Carole at the front near the stage. Beside her, a big guy in a black suit hung on the minister's every word. Neil studied Carole, barely paying attention as Lattimer droned on about how, after the election, more taxes would be cut and red tape slashed. Meanwhile, Canada and the United States had to work together as like-minded neighbours to deal with a number of serious challenges.

"The International Monetary Fund said in their most recent report that the next financial crisis is coming. It's just a matter of time," said Lattimer. "I believe them.

"I also believe time is racing ahead faster than many of us realize—or want to recognize. The problem is that we haven't finished fixing the systemic flaws exposed by the last global financial crisis.

"Remember? We promised to fix the system. To restore confidence. To make pensions safe. And those reforms are now underway. Legislation is in development. Regulations are drafted, waiting to be implemented.

"Yet, before we are able to fulfill our promises with real, concrete actions, the OECD's Financial Action Task Force has proposed new and different regulations. The proposed anti–money laundering directives may be well-intended, but is this the time to rethink regulations—again?

"I believe piling new regulations willy-nilly on top of old ones is a recipe for disaster. It will burn up scarce resources chasing an elusive target. If I was more cynical, I'd suspect the old bureaucrats' two-step—use a problem as an opportunity to grab more power."

Applause rippled through the audience.

"I am also troubled by the loss of personal privacy that comes with the sweeping new regulations proposed by the

OECD bureaucrats. Yes, of course we need to stop terrorists and drug traffickers, and, yes, we need to give our security services the tools they need.

"But are we not putting at risk something precious? With these new regulations, is the cost to our privacy, our personal freedom, too high? Freedom that is at the core of every human dream? I don't have answers. But I believe in my heart that we must ask the questions because we are putting at risk a piece of our soul."

The crowd broke into wild applause and stood up. Neil's attention shifted to Carole. She was grinning hugely and giving a high-five to the big guy next to her. *Good,* he thought. *Maybe that will make her easier to deal with.*

Neil and Rader drifted with the crowd back out to the reception area. People lined up at the buffet tables for coffee and pastries or broke into conversational groups.

Neil spotted Minister Lattimer smiling broadly and shaking hands with well-wishers. Isabelle Lisgar was whispering something in the minister's ear.

A short, pushy woman broke away from the group and snagged the arm of a burly guy with a neatly trimmed beard. They quickly huddled. Neil recognized him from the Hamptons party.

Rader noticed Neil's interest. "Now, there's a pair worth keeping an eye on. Tina Smarland's a particularly slippery lobbyist, the kind that preaches there's no such thing as a good regulation."

"Our prime minister is on record as saying the same thing about taxes," Neil said, nodding. "Who's she talking to?"

"Pyotr Arakelova. He's a VP for one of those Russian oligarchs, but who knows?"

Neil raised an eyebrow. "What do you mean?"

"Until a few years ago, he was head of the anti–money

laundering unit for the Russian security service, the FSB, Federalnaya Sluzhba Bezopasnosti. I worked with him once. He's a good guy. Now he's on the other side? I find the switch a little hard to believe."

Neil deadpanned. "Maybe he's a deep-cover penetration agent."

Rader laughed, then stuck out his hand. "Listen, I'm out of here. I've got a stack of reports that need to be signed off."

"Thanks for your help," Neil said. "I'll call you later about those files on Howland."

"You haven't got them yet? Talk to Ali Gorka. I'll have a word with her."

As Rader worked his way to the exit, Neil saw Carole stop Isabelle and lean in, asking a question. Isabelle shook her head and moved away. Carole followed for a step or two, clearly wanting to talk, but Isabelle, without looking back, pushed on, heading straight for Neil.

"You are making a nuisance of yourself," Isabelle said, slowing as she passed, measuring Neil with a flat expression.

"You seem to know a lot of people," he countered. "How about Stephen Howland? Used to be a player on the Vancouver Stock Exchange? Ring any bells?"

"I'll have a word with Janos," she said over her shoulder as she slid through a gap in the crowd. Neil tracked her progress, pondering the fact that she hadn't answered his question about knowing Stephen Howland. Did that mean anything?

A small group of journalists and videographers, media credentials on lanyards, were clustered at the back by the exit. He recognized one or two of them from his days on the force. Carole chatted easily with them. One of them, a brunette in jeans with her hair tied back, nodded and laughed.

"She's got them eating out of her hand," said an admiring

voice at his shoulder. Neil turned. It was the big guy in the black suit.

"She's good at schmoozing the press," the guy said. He held out his hand. "Paul Collacchi."

"Neil Walker." They measured each other openly.

"Thought so," Paul said. "I saw you watching her."

Neil jerked his chin at the journalists. "Didn't you used to be one of them?"

"Yeah," Collacchi said. "Now I've moved over to the dark side."

"Journalist to speech writer. Huh. You figure that's up or down the food chain?"

"Some days it's hard to tell." Collacchi laughed. "I know I breathe a little easier when it's time to write those alimony cheques."

"And that's important," Neil agreed as Carole came over to join them.

"Paul, you need to be more careful about the company you keep," Carole said, her eyes on Neil.

"A bad habit I picked up as a reporter," Paul responded. His eyes flicked between the two of them. "I can't help it. I'm always drawn to the most interesting story."

"Something we have in common," Neil replied, then asked Carole. "We're still on?"

"Give me five more minutes," she responded. "Paul? Two things. Would you ride along with the minister on his corporate calls? Try to keep him on message?"

"Sure."

"Second," she said, continuing to talk to Paul but looking straight at Neil, "just in case I can't get rid of this guy once and for all, dazzle me with your research skills and find me some ammunition I can use."

Paul looked at Neil coolly. "You got it."

25

The beeping alarm of a delivery truck backing up snapped Neil back to reality, the West Village and a mess of disturbing questions.

Ostensibly, he was waiting for Stephen Howland to emerge from his luxury condominium on West Twelfth Street. In reality, he was trying to figure out whether he could trust Carole.

He had expected the hostility. Her willingness to set that aside took him by surprise. It showed a cool self-control he didn't remember from their last run-in.

And what about Isabelle? Apparently, she knew Santiago well enough to arrange an invitation for Lattimer. Did it mean anything? Isabelle was famous for knowing everyone.

And was any of this connected to Rachel's murder?

Three Lisgar women. Each of them a high performer. Figuring out the family dynamics would take years. Fortunately, there was a shortcut. He pulled out his phone and called his father.

"That is a complicated question," said Janos. "What exactly do you want to know?"

"The three of them are so different. I'm looking for a common thread. Any ideas?"

After a moment of silence, Janos spoke. "The family business."

"Bala Bay? Doesn't Isabelle control it?"

"Yes, but she does not own all the shares. In his will, Thomas Lisgar split corporate ownership of Bala Bay Financial equally between Isabelle, Carole and Rachel. Isabelle runs it because both sisters were more interested in other things. For Carole, it is politics. For Rachel, it was higher math and social justice.

"The two sisters fought constantly over business decisions. Both girls trusted me, so they asked me to find a solution," Janos said. "We deposited Rachel's shares into a trust fund. With that money, she made investments she felt were ethical, ones that would spark social transformations. She wanted to make a difference."

"I can see how that might not go over well with Carole or Isabelle."

"For Isabelle, anyone who does not maximize profit is a fool."

"There's a lot of that going around. I think it's like the flu."

"She has a particularly bad case of it."

Neil grunted and switched topics. "Are you familiar with Grupo Muxia and Paolo Santiago?"

"They appeared on my radar several years ago. There was an investigation into the collapse of his green energy companies."

"What happened?"

"Spanish prosecutors closed the file after the death of a key government witness."

"Huh. The same thing happened to the FBI investigation into Hudson Ventures."

"I would not do business with any company linked to Grupo Muxia," Janos responded.

"Where did Santiago get the money to start Grupo Muxia?"

"That was a mystery. He went from being a minor Spanish aristocrat with a meagre trust fund to the head of Grupo Muxia and a green energy champion."

"Could you find out?"

"Possibly, but why?" Janos said. "That was quite a few years ago."

"At some point, I may want to talk to Santiago. When I do, I'll need leverage. Maybe there's a connection I can use."

"Good. Following the money has always been a smart strategy."

"While you do that, I'll take another run at Howland. He knows more than he's been willing to say."

"You think he will talk with you?"

"Howland uses his profile from television business shows to attract more suckers for his Ponzi scheme. I'm going to convince him that his links to Grupo Muxia and the FBI investigation will destroy his reputation. No television producer would touch him."

"That will be enough?"

"Like bad gamblers, a lot of con men are addicted to taking risks and trying to get away with things," Neil said. "It's their ego. They see themselves as smarter and luckier and ballsier than Joe Lunch Bucket. Nothing's more important than the heart-stopping thrills they get from playing the game. It's compulsive behaviour. They can't stop it. That's why most grifters end up losing everything. And that's Howland's weakness. I will use it to drive a wedge between Howland and Santiago."

"Call me if I can help."

"There is something. According to the Toronto cops, there were two killers, one of them female. Now, in all the time I spent with bikers and Mafia hoods, I never heard of anything like that. But in the military, two-man kill teams are standard. Another thing. The way Rachel was killed. The coroner's report says her neck was snapped by a violent, twisting movement from behind. It's a silent killing technique taught in the armed forces, particularly the special forces."

Janos was dubious. "It is also shown in every action movie. Anyone can learn how to do that."

"Bullshit. Those films have all these cool martial arts moves, like spin kicks. They look easy. You ever see an amateur try a spin kick? They end up flat on their ass every time."

"You are convinced these killers have had professional military training?"

"Yeah, and Santiago's security team includes ex-military contractors. I have absolutely no evidence to connect the two, but what are the odds?"

"Okay. Where does that get you?"

"Elite specialists are rare. How many male–female killer teams could there be?"

"And?"

"You're on the board of Securitec, which hires ex-military types. Could you ask them to check their sources for information on any teams that might fit the profile?"

"No problem."

"I'll see if I can sweet talk the FBI into running the same search query, including whatever other databases they can access through Homeland Security, NSA, the CIA or anyone else."

"No friggin' way." Ali Gorka's refusal to run the search was not a huge surprise to Neil, but he was taken aback by its vehemence.

"We keep all these lists," she said, her frustration clear. "You wanna know why all these suspects slip through the cracks? Fucking software is a piece of shit. You either get no results or fifty thousand hits. What good is that? Drives me nuts every time I use it."

"It's probably some version of CIRT from AccessData, right?" The Cyber Intelligence and Response Technology platform was adopted by the Five Eyes security alliance and used by most intelligence and national police services across Canada, the US, the UK, New Zealand and Australia.

"Are you some kind of expert?" Her tone held deep suspicion.

"God, no. I've had my own battles with it."

"But you know how to use it?"

"In a sort of half-assed way."

"Why didn't you say so?" Ali said. "Come on down. If Chris says it's okay, I'll get you access, and you can do all the keyword bullshit. That way, any time wasted will be yours, not mine and not the US taxpayers'."

"One thing," Neil said. "Given there are roughly five million Americans with security clearance, what are the chances that Santiago will have insiders that might tip him off?"

"I'm told the encryption is pretty good. Without my access code, your searches look like gobbledygook to anyone else. That being said, you know nothing is one hundred per cent secure."

"Still—"

"Life's full of risks," she said impatiently. "You want the search done, you take your chances."

"Are you getting a little testy with me?"
"Piss off. And bring me a Diet Coke. Make sure it's cold."
"Yes, boss."

———

Neil hoped Joanne Reynolds was in her office. He got lucky. "I'm taking another run at Stephen Howland. Do you have a minute?"

"Sure. Let me get the door." The background noise dropped, then she came back on the line.

"What's up?"

"When you chased Howland, did you come across any connections to Grupo Muxia?"

"Anyone with half a brain stays well away from them. Why?"

"Bear with me here. Howland is a con man, sure. But a murderer?"

"Not his style. I'm sure he'd say he was more a lover than a fighter." She made a farting noise, which Neil ignored.

"Would Howland have the connections to send a hit team from New York to Toronto?"

"Unlikely," Joanne said. "Ordering a hit, even if he had the contacts, would not be his first response. His ego is too big. He'd figure he could bullshit his way out of just about anything."

"Right."

"And his fallback would be lawyers. But Santiago and the Grupo Muxia crew? I suspect murder is just another business tool. And you think they're connected? How?"

"The FBI says they've done business. Exactly what and how often isn't clear. But it occurred to me that an organization like Grupo Muxia would need to move millions of dollars for bribes and payoffs. Hudson Ventures, as an investment firm with a brokerage licence, would be the perfect vehicle to launder as much money as they wanted."

"Interesting theory," Joanne said. "Wish I could help you, but connections between Howland and Santiago? It's news to me, and it's something I would remember."

"Okay. How about Isabelle Lisgar?"

"Tell me it's a coincidence you should mention her," Joanne said sharply. "Bala Bay Financial just announced it was acquiring ICE Technology, that Waterloo tech company with the encryption technology. The deal should go through next week. I had hoped it was one less thing I had to worry about."

"I wouldn't get too comfortable," Neil warned her. "Last night, I sat in an FBI surveillance truck and saw Peter Lattimer welcomed to a flashy party in the Hamptons. The host was Paolo Santiago."

"Our finance minister met with Santiago?"

"Apparently, the invitation was arranged by Isabelle Lisgar."

"Shit." Joanne sighed. "I better flag all this to Llewelyn—"

"Tom Llewelyn? Are you working with him?" Tom Llewelyn had been on the RCMP at the same time as Neil. They hadn't ever butted heads, but the chemistry wasn't good.

"Oh, my. Do I detect some anger issues?"

"Let's just say you have my sympathies," Neil retorted. "When I count up the good things about being an independent, not having to deal with people like him is right near the top."

"You forget. It's a small world around here. We're like family. We don't always get along, but we stay in touch."

"You do, but not me. Remember? I signed the divorce papers."

From the tone of her voice, Neil could picture her quirky grin when she said, "Remember that time we followed a load of BC bud to Northern Ireland?"

"Belfast." He shuddered. "It rained for three weeks straight. What of it?"

"I was told the IRA had an unwritten membership rule. Once in, never out."

"You're saying it's like that?"

All he heard was her laughter as she cut the connection.

26

OP Analytics made a ton of money for Wall Street clients but did the actual work in an anonymous industrial strip mall in Queens. It was a no-brainer. Cheap rents, easy parking and direct access to one hundred gigabit-per-second digital pipelines trumped rubbing shoulders with flashy suits. In fact, the only people wearing suits in OP's darkened conference room were in the finance minister's entourage.

As Jeremy Ogden and Tom Platz began their PowerPoint pitch for the proposed software development centre in Markham, Carole slipped out into the open-concept reception area. The minister caught her eye through the glass door and frowned. She held up her phone and mimed that she had calls she needed to return. He looked pissed off. Too bad. She had more important things on her mind.

The sprawling reception area included two full-sized snooker tables, an English pub-style bar running along one wall, a professional kitchen and communal dining tables. In honour of the minister's visit, a caterer had laid out trays heaped with food. At a gesture from Carole, a young server brought an espresso to where she settled at one of the communal tables.

What if Walker was right?

The question looped through her mind like a hamster on speed.

She needed facts, data points she could trust.

First, Grupo Muxia. Phone in hand, she pulled up a search engine and started hunting for reliable information.

And it was bad.

Bribery, corruption, links to warlords and mercenaries. A long list of charges from activists and public advocacy groups. Some of them seemed credible, she admitted, even if they were lefties.

The more she read, the more pissed off she got. Why the hell would Isabelle expose Peter Lattimer to anything this politically toxic?

Carole called her. Straight to voice mail. She cut the connection without leaving a message. She'd give it a minute, then call back. Meanwhile, she had other things to check.

She scrolled through her contact list. Danny Relf, the Toronto homicide cop, had interviewed her about Rachel. She punched his number into her phone.

"Relf."

She could hear road noise in the background and guessed he was driving. "Hi. It's Carole Lisgar. Do you have a minute?"

"Ms. Lisgar. Sure. What's up?"

"I wanted to find out if there were any developments. Anything new?"

"I'm on my way to interview someone right now."

"A witness?"

"More like a possible informant. That's how these cases often move forward. Information is traded that leads to evidence we can take to court. But, at this point, there's no real news to report."

"And this Serbian neighbour. You still consider him the—what?—main victim?"

"It seems most likely."

"What about alternative theories? Neil Walker suggested that Rachel's death might be connected to her trip to New York."

Relf sounded doubtful. "The Serb was a warlord guilty of crimes against humanity. It looks like his past caught up with him. But your sister? I'm not aware of anything in her life that would lead to murder. Are you suggesting there was?"

"No, but Rachel met with a guy in New York who—apparently—runs a Ponzi scheme worth hundreds of millions of dollars. Knowing Rachel, she probably confronted him."

"But wasn't she an analyst? An academic?"

"Rachel had a tendency to jump into action. Would you agree it's worth looking into?"

"Me? In New York? I have no jurisdiction."

"But, hypothetically, if it was in Toronto, you'd investigate it?"

"Of course. But—"

"Let me be direct. Is it possible that my sister, not this neighbour, was the primary victim?"

"Anything's possible."

"So, Walker might be right."

"Like I said, anything's possible."

Carole was silent for a moment. "Do you know Walker?"

"I met him the other night."

"And?"

"And what?"

"What's his reputation?"

At first, he didn't respond. As the silence lengthened, she found herself gripping her phone more tightly.

He cleared his throat. "I asked around. Some people I respect say he's a natural-born hunter. Give him a question, and he'll come back with answers. Whether you like them is another question."

"But wasn't he fired from the RCMP?"

"Yeah, well. I heard he quit."

She said nothing, hoping to draw him out. It worked.

"The RCMP doesn't like people who rock the boat."

Carole let out a long breath she didn't realize she'd been holding. "I see."

"For someone in your situation, maybe that's what you need."

"What do you mean?"

"Ms. Lisgar, I have to go now," Relf said, his tone more official. "If you find out anything that might help us with this investigation, call me or send me an email."

"And Walker?"

"What about him?"

"Since you're working two sides of the same investigation, wouldn't it make sense for you two to talk? I'll get him to call you, okay?"

"Yeah, sure. Now, I gotta go. Please keep me informed."

The phone went dead. Carole placed it carefully on the table. She took a slow sip of her espresso in the echoing silence.

Maybe she had to revise her thinking about Walker. Maybe he wasn't the vindictive RCMP detective who planted false evidence. Or a partisan political tool. Or her enemy.

Sudden laughter in the distance made her look towards the conference room. Someone had opened the door. Good, the boys were keeping themselves amused. She picked up her phone and tried Isabelle's number again, this time getting through.

She didn't let Isabelle get beyond saying hello before charging in. "Grupo Muxia? What were you thinking?"

"Calm down." Isabelle's tone was quiet, measured.

"How long before some FBI flunky peddles the surveillance video to the *Toronto Sun*?"

"There is nothing wrong with Grupo Muxia."

"That's not what I've been reading online."

"Grupo Muxia helps countries get back on their feet after natural disasters. Does it occasionally pay bribes to get things done? Probably. It's the way business works in those places. And what thanks does it receive? It gets pilloried by a bunch to hand-wringing, know-nothing activists, academics and limousine liberals."

"And the FBI surveillance in the Hamptons?"

"So what? These days, everybody's being watched by someone. FBI. RCMP. Pah. I have no patience for them. The paparazzi of the police state. What a waste of taxpayer money."

Carole couldn't help but smile. Typical Isabelle. Outrageous. "I still don't understand why you sent Lattimer to that party. Why take the political risk?"

"It's simple. Bala Bay is expanding into regions that overlap with Grupo Muxia strengths, mostly in the South Pacific and Africa. Depending on how the election pans out, I'm considering putting him on the board of directors for one of our subsidiaries. Peter executed several highly profitable takeovers during his time on Bay Street, and he's done well in Ottawa. I wanted to see how he handled himself in that crowd."

Carole, somewhat mollified but clearly not happy, asked, "So, how did he do?"

"Not too bad."

There was silence for a minute.

Finally, Isabelle said. "Spit it out. What's really going on?"

"I've been thinking about Rachel," Carole admitted. "Were you aware that she came here to New York? And met with Stephen Howland? Do you know him?"

"What's this all about?"

"It seems Rachel getting killed might not be as random as they told us."

"What? Who said that?"

"It doesn't matter. I just talked to the Toronto Police. They don't seem to be getting anywhere. Maybe I should make some calls, crank up the pressure. Sean Poulsen over at Public Safety could lean on them. He owes me."

"Leave it to me," Isabelle offered. "You have enough on your plate with this pain in the ass OECD directive."

"No, I'd feel better—"

"You need to stay focused."

"I can handle—"

"You cannot intervene," Isabelle insisted. "If it got out—and it would—the media would be all over you. Interfering with a police investigation. A lot of history would be dredged up and hung out again. You'd be crucified."

"There's no connection—"

"The Liberals would turn it into a scandal and smear it over everything."

"But I can't just let it go!"

"Yes, you can! If we can't persuade the Americans to kill this OECD directive, you may have to take the minister to Paris ahead of time—"

"Paris? When? Why?"

"Possibly as early as tomorrow. Why? He may need to meet directly with the OECD and get this thing derailed."

"No can do! Tomorrow he has a fundraiser in his riding. Big donors—"

"They can wait!"

Confused, Carole fell silent. Was Isabelle really saying Lattimer should cancel a long-planned fundraiser at the last minute? Now? On the eve of an election campaign? These were busy people with deep pockets and high expectations about what their contributions bought them. At the top of the list was access. They all wanted to whisper in the minister's ear about an issue or pet project. Any schedule changes at the eleventh hour might put a cramp in their cheque-writing hand.

"We can't afford to piss off these people."

"Sure we can," Isabelle continued, her voice returning to normal tones. "Do a photo op in Paris. Something military. Wounded soldiers. Foreign aid. Who cares? This is more important. I'd go myself, but I have meetings in Singapore and Beijing. I'm counting on you to derail this OECD directive."

Carole looked up to see Peter Lattimer and the OP guys coming down the hallway. The presentations were finished. Time to go.

"Okay," she said, getting to her feet. "But this isn't over. We need to talk."

"About?"

"About Grupo Muxia and this Stephen Howland that Rachel met with. He's a Canadian. Have you heard of him?"

Isabelle took a deep breath before answering smoothly. "Yes, let's clear the air. Where are you?"

"Queens. We're just heading back into Manhattan."

"Have you eaten? Perhaps we should talk over a late lunch/early dinner? Landry's on East Seventeenth? I'll call Jessica and have them open for us. We'll have the place to ourselves."

"Okay," Carole said, gathering her purse and fending off a glare from Peter Lattimer as he headed out the door. "One last thing. Did Rachel try to call you?"

"When?"

"The day she died."

"Who put that idea into your head? Rachel and I hadn't spoken in at least two years."

"That's what I thought."

Paul Collacchi waved to her from the front entrance. Outside, Lattimer's Suburban waited, the engine running. She shouldered her purse.

Three hours until she met Isabelle at Landry's. She'd wait that long for answers. She had no choice.

27

"So, my friend has this dog," Neil said casually.

"What?" Startled, Stephen Howland backed away from him. Mid-afternoon crowds swirled around them on the sidewalk outside Howland's condo in the West Village.

"Right," Neil continued, his tone friendly. "And whenever it does something bad, it hides behind the drapes, but its tail always sticks out. And when the drape's pulled back? The expression in its eyes? It's sort of like yours is now."

He got into Howland's face. "Did you think I wouldn't find you? We were talking in your office. You stepped out and —what?—forgot to return?"

"I'm so, so sorry." Howland glanced back into the building lobby. The doorman clung to his post in the air conditioning. "Food poisoning. Marta, the receptionist, she told you, didn't she?"

"No—"

"All of a sudden, I had to hit the can." Howland's face twisted in a mock grimace. "Bad shrimp for lunch off the food truck is my best guess." He scanned the traffic crawling by.

"I'm glad you're feeling better," Neil said with equal sincerity. "After your meeting with Rachel Lisgar—"

"Marta didn't mention it?"

"She disappeared, too. Maybe she had the same shrimp."

"I'm on my way back to the office now. I'll have a talk with her." A sleek black limousine rolled to a stop at the curb. Howland stepped towards it.

"Just a couple more questions." Neil kept pace with him. "Did you mention your meeting with Rachel to anyone after she left?"

"Why would I do that?" He tried to step around Neil.

Neil took a chance. "You're a friend of Paolo Santiago, right? Now, there's a guy who could have someone murdered." As Howland reached for the rear passenger door handle, Neil blocked his path. "What's the connection between your Launchpad Fund and Santiago's Grupo Muxia?"

Howland's face froze for a flicker before turning bland. It had lasted just a flash, but Neil knew he had scored.

He heard the driver's door open. He quickly checked over his shoulder. African-American guy, medium build, alert. Neil tracked him around the front bumper. Light on his feet. Moved like a cat.

Neil realized had a few seconds. He leaned towards Howland, his voice dropping. "The FBI is all over Grupo Muxia. They know about your Ponzi scheme. They're talking warrants, asset seizures, the whole nine yards."

Howland's eyes narrowed.

Neil's tone turned urgent. "How long before someone flips and links you to Rachel's murder?"

"I don't—"

"Work with me. Worst case, you'd serve your time in Canada. You wouldn't like US prisons. Nasty places."

"Mr. Howland? Is there a problem?" The voice was low-key, confident. The driver stopped slightly behind Neil, flanking him, forcing him to turn, and opening the space between Howland and the limo.

Howland slipped into the rear passenger seat.

"I can help you get on the right side of this thing," Neil called out. "They want Santiago more than you." Howland stared resolutely forward.

The driver withdrew but kept his eye on Neil until he was back in the limo behind the wheel. Neil recognized a professional when he saw one. This guy had all the right moves. Why would Howland need such expensive security? Why not some minimum-wage rent-a-cop, some working-class guy holding down two jobs just to pay the bills?

Huh.

The limo pulled away from the curb. As it did, Howland looked back, his expression thoughtful, as if he was measuring Neil and weighing his options. Neil kept his eyes on the limo until it turned onto Eighth Avenue, wishing again he had a badge. It made asking questions so much easier.

He paused. The doorman.

Neil crossed the marble-clad condo lobby to the sleek, dark wooden desk.

"May I help you, sir?" The doorman was in his late forties, heavy-set with close-cropped steel grey hair. His eyes rested steadily on Neil's face. Likely an ex-cop.

Neil waved over his shoulder towards the sidewalk. "My friend Steve? He's been raving about this place since he moved in. He said you could give me some information about available units?"

The doorman shook his head. "You would have to talk with the property management about that, sir."

"And who would that be?"

The doorman plucked a card from under his desk and handed it to Neil. "I'd start with them."

"Right. Thanks. I'll tell them you've been very helpful."

By the time Neil was back on the sidewalk, he'd done a quick inventory of the security systems spread throughout the lobby. He recognized the cameras and monitoring system. That was embassy-grade tech. Backed by guys with training in close personal protection. Bodyguards. Professionals.

One thing was clear. This whole thing was much bigger than a murder to cover up a Ponzi scheme.

28

The Grand Central Gun Club, tucked out of sight on the top floor high above the ornate domed ceiling of Grand Central Terminal in midtown Manhattan, was established in 1871 as a private shooting range for wealthy sporting types.

It billed itself as a comfortable place for members to pause before the commute to their country estates, somewhere to drink and socialize while workers hooked up their luxurious private railway cars on the dirty, dangerous tracks six stories below. Now, corporate names dominated the membership list, the accounts paid mostly through anonymous, offshore shell companies. The traditional fittings, from the intricate floor mosaics to the huge, churchlike chandeliers that cast soft light on the century-old wood panelling, offered many members the reassuring ambience of privilege.

Karin Reichelt fired off the last two rounds from her Glock, hit the retrieval button and looked around as the paper target raced sixty feet back to her. Absently, she scratched the scar that started under her left eye. If this wasn't the oddest shooting range she'd ever seen, it was near the top of the list. A former member of Norway's Jegertroppen—the world's first and only all-female special operations unit—she was still getting used to life in the private sector.

She glanced down when her cellphone lit up. It lay on the hip-high wooden counter that generations of gun oil had stained dark. She took off her shooter's ear muffs.

"How soon can you get to Forty-Ninth Street and Seventh Avenue?" It was Brisbane.

"Ten minutes, maybe fifteen. What's up?" The conversation was encrypted. Even so, they were careful. She unclipped the tattered target. The bullet holes drifted a little high and to the right, but none were more than a quarter inch off.

"You need to take a meeting, ASAP. I'm texting you the details now."

"What's the op plan?" She folded the target into quarters, then again.

"Remember Lausanne? Same plan." Six months earlier, she had killed a mid-level official with the International Olympic Committee in his office. What had he done? She didn't know. Didn't care.

"But planning for that took weeks." Her voice dropped to a whisper, but the intensity increased.

"This set up is almost identical."

"*Almost*? What does that mean?" She collected her spent brass in a cup for disposal.

"Don't worry. The plan worked then. It will work today."

"What about building security? My exit? My backup?" She slipped her pistol into a belly holster.

"You're covered. We've hacked into security. All recordings will be suspended until you're off-site. We'll feed real-time video to your phone."

She looked around and wiped any surface that might hold her fingerprints. "I don't like it. There is a high probability this could go sideways."

"Simple is best," Brisbane reassured her. "We'll create a distraction. You take care of business and slip out before anyone knows you were even there."

"To do it like Lausanne, I will need to pick up a few things."

"Make it fast. The clock is ticking."

"I say again: I don't like it."

"So what? In a perfect world, we would have fail-safes and backups. But the world ain't fucking perfect." She could hear frustration building in Brisbane's voice. "Just do your job."

"So I exaggerated a little," Neil said. He was in an FBI briefing room comparing notes with Chris Rader, Ali Gorka and Ken Merkel. Pinned to the wall were photos and bios of the more high-profile guests at the Hamptons fundraiser and a complicated organizational chart of Grupo Muxia's known subsidiaries, corporate holdings and shell companies.

"Why tell Howland anything at all, let alone that we were watching Grupo Muxia?" Ali asked, clearly a little pissed. "We trusted you to keep it confidential."

"Confidential? Who from? Santiago and his security guys knew you were there."

"Still—"

"I wanted Howland to see his links to Santiago as a threat. I needed to rattle him."

Rader nodded. "Did it work? How did he react?"

"He didn't deny them," Neil said. "If Howland thinks Santiago is about to be arrested, he might jump to our side. He knows the first person to talk gets the best deal."

"And that will be enough?" Ali sounded skeptical.

"Most con artists get bored easily. They need to dream up new moves and take bigger risks to make the game more interesting. If we can convince Howland that talking to us is risky but the smart move, his ego will tell him to go for it."

"I noticed you slipped a *we* in there," Rader said.

"I think Rachel's questions made Howland nervous," Neil said. "He called Santiago, and Santiago sent a hit team to Toronto to deal with the problem. If I'm right, we need Howland to admit he made that phone call."

"And how will you do that?" Rader looked skeptical.

"I'm still working on it," Neil confessed. "Meanwhile, I had hoped you could help me identify the hit team."

"You don't ask for much, do you?"

"Hey, if I'm right, they came from your backyard. I'm doing you a favour here."

"Spare me the bullshit."

Reichelt cocked her head, listening to the faint sound of music echoing down the office stairwell to the thirty-sixth floor. Satisfied it presented no danger, she refocused her attention on the cellphone in her gloved hand.

A video link from the building security feed showed the reception area of Hudson Ventures. Marta sat behind the reception desk, signing for a FedEx courier package. Other than that, it was quiet.

Reichelt wore a Yankees baseball cap, mirrored sunglasses

and a baggy blue hoodie she'd bought off a street vendor's cart. The rough-and-ready outfit disguised her blonde hair and body shape. She'd dump it as soon as the job was done. Under the hoodie, she had a throat mic and earpiece, her communications link to Brisbane, who was monitoring the hit.

A rustling sound from behind caught her attention. She spun around.

A discarded fast-food clamshell lay in the corner of the landing. A hungry rat, nosing for crumbs, had tipped it over. Reichelt hated rats. She was, she admitted to herself but no one else, becoming a germophobe. And it was getting worse. She stamped her foot, hoping to scare the rat. It stared at her for a moment, then stuck its nose back in the clamshell.

She shuddered and turned to the phone in her hand. As soon as the reception area was empty, she touched her throat mic.

"Going in now."

She slipped out of the stairwell and glided towards the closed door of Howland's office.

"What I've got is a partial description of the shooter and some reasonable assumptions—"

"Pretty thin," Ali scoffed.

"It's a start," Neil protested. "What do you want from me?"

"Okay. Gimme some keywords for the search. Let's see how far this piece of shit software will let us get before I shoot it."

Neil and Ali were alone in the briefing room. Laptop open, Ali logged in to a combined FBI, Homeland Security and NSA database. Neil sat across from her, pushing an empty coffee cup in circles while he worked through what might fit the search template.

"Toronto Police got a description of the woman," he said. "A witness saw her talking to the neighbour on the sidewalk. Our killer is definitely female, about thirty years old with a slim, athletic build. She's a little taller than the neighbour, which would make her at least five foot nine. Probably blonde. And, according to the witness, she's—quote—*hot*."

"Really?"

"Witness was a guy waiting for his girlfriend."

"Typical, and absolutely useless." Ali looked up from the screen. "Anything else?"

"Here's where it gets speculative. For a bunch of reasons, I think she might have a military background, likely in special forces."

"That narrows things down. A lot. For one thing, she's not one of ours."

"And you know that because...?"

"The US military throws up every barrier it can to keep women out of combat roles. Could you imagine it letting women into the SEALs or Rangers?"

"Okay. If not the US, then where? Israel? New Zealand? One of the Scandinavian countries? Do you have access to their data?"

"Not a chance. The good news is that if she ever applied for security clearance through any US military contractors like Blackwater or MVM, there's a good chance she'd be here."

"Good. Who knows? Maybe we'll get lucky."

Howland's body sprawled face down across his desk, blood from the knife wound in his chest pooling among the papers. His eyes had already dulled, his TV-handsome face slack and empty.

Reichelt, standing just inside Howland's office, breathed steadily, evenly, her attention laser-focused on the video streaming to her phone. Marta sat behind the reception desk, entering data from a file.

The hit had unfolded like the whisper of silk.

She had entered his office unannounced. At first he was startled but quickly rolled with the interruption.

Howland saw a smiling, attractive woman striding towards him, her hand stretched out to shake his. Responding automatically, he stood up from behind his desk and extended his own hand.

"I'm sorry. Did we have a meeting? I don't—"

Reichelt grabbed his right hand. She yanked him forward, off balance. From the sleeve of her hoodie, a black tactical stiletto dropped into her left hand. With the speed of a snake's tongue, she shoved the knife between his ribs. It pierced the left ventricle of his heart, throwing his whole system into shock. She gripped Howland's hand, pinning him in place, and twisted the blade, ripping his heart beyond repair.

His eyes widened with a spark of panic, and then he was gone.

She pulled out the stiletto. He collapsed. She tossed the knife on the desk.

By the doorway, she touched her throat mic. "I need that distraction."

Marta's phone lit up with multiple calls. "Good afternoon, Hudson Ventures. Could you hold for a minute?" *Click.* "Good afternoon, Hudson Ventures. Could you hold? Thanks so much!" *Click.* "Good afternoon..."

Reichelt moved fast. While Marta focused on answering the lines, her back to Howland's office, the assassin strode across the reception area to the stairway and silently disappeared through the fire door.

29

Midtown traffic was nearly gridlocked, which jacked up their frustration another couple of levels.

Ken Merkel braked the FBI sedan to a jarring stop outside Howland's building. Neil and Ali slid out. They threaded their way across the plaza crowded with tourists. In the elevator, they exchanged glances. They had little information, but Neil could bet that the same questions were rolling through Ali's mind.

What were the chances Howland's death had nothing to do with their investigation?

Possible but, realistically, just about zero.

He had hoped Howland would confirm that Santiago was behind Rachel's murder. That wasn't going to happen.

Identifying the hit team through a database search? It always worked better on television than in real life. He admitted to himself it was a long shot.

He clung to one central idea: somebody, likely Santiago, was desperate enough to have Howland killed. That meant Neil had uncovered something.

Unfortunately, he didn't have a clue what it was.

The elevator doors opened onto a hallway jammed with NYPD uniforms and curious office workers. Ali held up her FBI credentials and jerked her thumb to indicate that Neil was with her. One of the uniforms waved them through.

When Neil entered the reception area, Marta stared at him, then turned her back and whispered urgently to the plain-clothes detective interviewing her. The cop, a squat, balding bodybuilder-type in a wrinkled black suit, looked over, eye-checked Neil and jotted something in his notebook. Ali scanned the room, spotted the detective in charge and made her way over to sort out jurisdiction.

Neil skirted the knot of cops and stopped at the doorway to Howland's office. The pooled blood on the desktop had started to darken and dry. Howland's office chair lay on its side. He thought about the hit. Right in the middle of a private office, right in the middle of a busy workday. That took arrogance. How had they gotten away with it?

"A ten-minute blank in the security recording," the detective in charge said to Ali as Neil wandered over to stand beside her. "They're not willing to admit they were hacked, but that would be my guess."

"So, a sophisticated, well-coordinated, well-equipped team," Neil suggested.

"And you are?"

Ali made the introductions, sketching in Neil's link to Howland through the murder of Rachel Lisgar.

Homicide Detective Sergeant Jim Adler was a thin guy in a well-cut suit with the dark circles under his eyes that come from too many years of working long hours.

The detective who had been interviewing Marta joined the group. "You had an altercation with Howland earlier this afternoon? And confronted him yesterday?"

"I wouldn't call it an altercation," Neil said. "A conversation."

"And, for the record, where were you this afternoon at two forty-five?"

Neil tipped his head towards Ali. "I was at the FBI offices with Special Agent Ali Gorka and Special Agent in Charge Chris Rader. In fact, we were discussing Stephen Howland and trying to identify a hit team."

The detectives exchanged looks. "That's quite a coincidence."

"Rachel Lisgar was also murdered by a pair of pros," said Neil. "That was a few hours after she met with Howland."

"We'll need a statement from you."

"No problem."

Adler turned to Ali. "What about the vic? What can you give us?"

"What do you need?"

While Ali and the detectives conferred about how and what information to share, Neil half listened to the conversation and scanned the room. He spotted Tonya Clarke, the analyst he had spoken to on his previous visit. Her dreadlocks wrapped in a purple scarf, she hovered on the other side of the glass door that led to the back offices. He caught her eye and walked over.

"Tonya, right?"

"You're the detective? The one investigating Rachel Lisgar's murder?"

Neil nodded.

She crossed her arms and shivered. "First her, now Stephen? What's going on?"

"That's what we're trying to figure out. Did you see anything?"

Tonya shook her head. "What a waste."

"Howland?"

"Well, yeah. But I was thinking more of Rachel Lisgar. She was brilliant. I met her once, you know?"

"A few days ago? When she was here?"

"No. I mean, yes." She rubbed her chin and looked at Neil. "I met her the first time four years ago at a math colloquium in Glasgow. She gave a presentation on the application of chaos theory to social justice models. The place was jammed. Standing room only. Afterwards, I tracked her down and introduced myself. We hit it off." She looked a little embarrassed. "What can I say? I was a fan. Her death...what a fucking tragedy."

"And when she was here the other day, you said hello?"

Tonya nodded.

"What did you talk about?"

"Rachel asked how Hudson Ventures got started. Who were the initial investors? Who are the major shareholders? That sort of thing."

"She wanted to identify the beneficial owners?"

Tonya looked at him sharply. Evidently, she recognized the legal term that names the real people hiding behind the veil of secrecy surrounding shell corporations often used by drug dealers, stock swindlers and money launderers. She seemed disturbed when Neil applied it to Hudson Ventures.

"I suppose so."

"But the initial investors would be listed with the SEC, right? A Schedule 13D?"

"Stephen never filed a 13D," Tonya admitted.

"But—"

"So, yeah, I showed Rachel the list. There was one company she appeared to recognize, one of the original investors that is still a shareholder."

"Which one?"

Tonya shook her head. "She didn't say."

"I'd like to see the list."

"I can't do that. The information is confidential."

"You're afraid of getting into trouble? With who? Your boss is dead."

"The board of directors will appoint someone—"

"You said you admired Rachel. These two murders are connected. Help me find out why she was killed."

Neil could see Tonya weighing his argument.

"Show me the list," he said softly. "It might help. It certainly can't hurt anyone."

She turned on her heel and, with a jerk of her head indicating he should follow, walked back to her office. She dug in her file cabinet and handed a list to Neil. He scanned it. They were all privately held companies registered in the Cayman Islands, Panama, Singapore and other tax havens where secrecy ruled. He'd get Don to do an online search for more information.

"Anything else?" Neil asked.

Tonya's eyes lost their focus, and she seemed to slump a little. "We talked about the Launchpad Fund. I thought she would understand how cool it was—economic rehabilitation as a social investment strategy."

Neil suspected Howland had conned not just clients but also his staff. "Rachel didn't see it that way?"

"She had the wrong impression," Tonya insisted. "I told her about the wonderful work it was doing in countries like Haiti and in the South Pacific islands that were hit so hard by tsunamis."

"Did she believe you?"

"I think so." But there was evasiveness in Tonya's voice.

"What?" Neil pushed.

"Nothing."

"No. There's more. Tell me."

"I've said enough."

"Listen, you can tell me, or you can tell the cops."

She shook her head.

"I'm going to find out why someone killed Rachel." He jerked his thumb over his shoulder. "You think the cops will do a better job?"

She gazed through the door to the reception area crowded with NYPD investigators. She was a black woman. Her people had a history with the police. She looked at Neil.

"I gave her some Launchpad Fund files. On a thumb drive."

"Why?"

"I wanted to show her that we were really helping people."

"Let me take her place. Give me copies of the same files."

"You won't tell anyone?"

"Not unless I have to," he promised.

Tonya nodded. Neil followed as she walked back into her office, sat down and began dumping files onto a clean thumb drive. As she was doing that, Neil texted Carole. *We need to talk. Where are you?*

Tonya handed him the thumb drive. Before letting it go, she said, "Rachel was one of the special ones, you know? She had a lot to give."

"She would have wanted you to do this," Neil assured her, pocketing the drive.

Moments later, he was back in reception. Forensic technicians were still photographing, measuring and taking samples from every surface. Howland's driver was giving a statement to an NYPD detective.

Neil caught Ali's eye and drifted over to where she

stood with Adler. Neil nodded towards the driver. "He probably works for a service. Did anyone catch the company name?"

Detective Adler checked his notebook. "Echelon Security Systems."

Neil and Ali exchanged looks. The same company provided security at Santiago's Hamptons beach party.

30

Carole appreciated the art of simultaneously gritting one's teeth and smiling graciously. Jessica, the front-of-house manager for Landry's Bistro, had definitely mastered it.

Allowing customers into the elegant Gramercy Park brownstone before six o'clock threw a major curve into the pre-dinner prep schedule. Carole knew Isabelle didn't give the intrusion a passing thought. She realized Isabelle's sense of entitlement had started to bug her, although she wasn't sure why.

Jessica showed her to Isabelle's table in the otherwise-empty dining room, handed her a menu.

"Scrambled eggs with smoked salmon?" Isabelle suggested.

Carole nodded. She had learned long ago never to go to a dinner function on an empty stomach. Eating got in the way of doing business.

"And Perrier with lime."

Jessica retrieved the menu and backed away.

A text message popped up on Carole's phone from Walker. She replied *Meeting with Isabelle. Join us* and added the address for Landry's. She slipped the phone back into her purse.

Carole cut straight to the point. "What was Lattimer doing anywhere near Grupo Muxia?"

"It was a harmless fundraiser, for God's sake."

"Are you kidding? From what I've seen, they're corporate gangsters."

"Someone's been feeding you lies," Isabelle said with a *you should know better* look on her face. She brushed a crumb off the table. "So the real question becomes, What's their agenda?"

Carole shifted focus. "You don't want to talk about Grupo Muxia? Fine. What about Hudson Ventures? Rachel met with its CEO on the day she died. Have you heard of it?"

"Has someone implied a connection between this meeting and Rachel's death?"

"Are you saying they're wrong?"

"With Rachel and that gang of street people she hung out with, who knows? She was no angel."

"Meaning?"

"Rachel's save-the-poor-people shtick fooled a lot of people but not me."

"What are you talking about?"

"That wonderfully analytical mind of hers? She pimped it to Janos for fat paycheques. She was no better than she had to be."

"Are you suggesting Rachel was somehow involved in the Hudson Ventures Ponzi scheme?"

Isabelle shrugged. "Who knows what she was really up to? I certainly don't. Do you?"

Their food arrived, saving her from having to respond. While the server laid out the plates, Carole rallied her thoughts. Isabelle's attack on Rachel puzzled her. She'd never suspected that so much disdain, even hatred, ran just below the surface. To cover her momentary confusion, she lifted a bread roll from the basket and broke off a piece.

"What about Hudson Ventures? Is it a Ponzi scheme?"

Isabelle sighed and almost rolled her eyes. "We have more important—"

"Stop dancing around the question. Do you know Stephen Howland? More importantly, do we—does Bala Bay—have anything to do with Hudson Ventures?"

"You want the truth?" Isabelle put down her cutlery and placed her hands on the table. "Yes, I know Stephen. I met him years ago. I don't remember where. Probably some industry event."

"He was a broker?"

Isabelle looked up at the ceiling momentarily as if remembering details. "We sat on an investment dealers' association audit committee. A few years later, he made a precious-metals play on the Vancouver Stock Exchange and lost everything. Typical Stephen. Always going for the big win. Anyway, some of his investors had connections to the provincial NDP government. They brought the RCMP blundering into the picture."

"They arrested him?"

"No, no. Nothing like that. But I ran into him afterwards in London. He told me he'd made a clean start in New York. That's why he started Hudson Ventures. He developed an innovative investment strategy that enabled people to earn a fair return and help Third World development. *Do well by doing good* was his pitch. Risky? Certainly. That was Stephen. But a Ponzi scheme? No way."

"The FBI says it is."

"Stephen told me Hudson Ventures was one hundred per cent legitimate. That was good enough for me."

Carole watched a small smile flit across Isabelle's face. "He was more than just a friend, wasn't he?"

"He could be quite charming," Isabelle said fondly.

Carole mulled over her aunt's explanations with growing unease. Something about them rang false, which raised an even more troubling question. *If Isabelle isn't being straight about this, what else is she hiding?*

A disturbance at the door caught their attention. Neil Walker appeared in the dining room entrance.

Jessica approached him from the hostess desk. "I'm sorry, sir. We are closed—"

"He's with us," Carole called out.

"Why didn't you tell me he was coming?" Isabelle hissed. She straightened up in her seat as Neil approached.

"I'm glad you're here," Neil said to Isabelle. He pulled out a chair and sat down. "I hope you can help me figure something out."

"What's so urgent?" Carole asked Neil, but she watched, fascinated, as he and Isabelle sized each other up.

Neil looked back at Carole. "Did you tell anyone I planned to talk with Stephen Howland this afternoon?"

"No. Why would I?" She looked him straight in the eye. She found herself wanting him to believe her. "Did you learn anything new?"

"He told me some interesting things," Neil lied. His glance flicked to Isabelle. "Just in time, too. He was killed this afternoon."

"What?" Shocked, Carole almost spilled her water glass.

"Oh, no," Isabelle whispered, a hand rising to cover her mouth.

"In his office," Neil continued. "Someone wanted to shut him up. Probably hoped it would stop the investigation." He checked their reactions. "It doesn't work that way.

Now the NYPD is involved. The FBI is more interested than ever."

Isabelle stood up. "You must excuse me," she said to Carole.

"You knew Howland, didn't you?" Neil asked. "When was the last time you saw him?"

"There is a lot to be done before the dinner," Isabelle said pointedly to Carole, ignoring Neil. "What time will you be arriving?"

"There's a pre-dinner meet-and-greet in the green room."

"I will see you there." She nodded to Neil. "Carole has a lot on her plate. Try not to waste too much of her time."

"Identifying Rachel's murderer is a waste of time?" Neil called out to Isabelle's back as she walked away. She didn't flinch, didn't say a word. In a moment, she was out the door.

"Is it true?" Carole asked Neil. "Do you think Howland's murder is connected to Rachel's death?"

"The chances of it being a coincidence are pretty thin."

"If this brings in more investigators, that's a good thing, right?"

"Yes and no," Neil said. "The main problem is still jurisdiction. The FBI and NYPD will investigate Howland's murder, and the Toronto cops are investigating Rachel's murder, but they are two separate processes. Officially, there is no connection between them."

"Except you. Unofficially."

"Except me," Neil agreed. He laughed shortly. "No pressure."

"And you are going to stick with this, right?"

"That's my plan."

"Good, because I asked the Toronto Police to connect with you."

"You talked to Danny Relf?"

Carole nodded. "Let me ask you this. Why would there suddenly be two murders? What's changed?"

"It's looking like this is about a lot more than a simple investment fraud."

"What do you mean?"

"I think Hudson Ventures is just one piece of a much bigger operation. Think about it. Through the Launchpad Fund, it supposedly invests millions of dollars in jurisdictions with weak financial controls at a time when those countries are desperate for help. Howland positioned Hudson Ventures perfectly as a vehicle to launder money for organizations like Grupo Muxia."

"Money laundering? Isabelle told me she was a friend of Howland. Do you think she knows anything about it?"

"During the past few years, almost every major financial institution in the world has admitted to money laundering activities. What makes Bala Bay so different?"

"That's crazy," Carole said. "Bala Bay Financial has won a raft of awards for the quality of its anti–money laundering programs. Why would she risk that?"

"I'm not saying she did," Neil countered, "but it's one of the reasons I wanted to talk with her. At the very least, with her connections, she might have access to information that could help us."

"Let me talk to her."

Neil softly drummed his fingers on the table. "She's quite a piece of work, isn't she?"

"You don't know the half of it."

"Really? What else can you tell me?"

She was silent for a moment, weighing how she should respond. Despite her uncertainties, the next step felt a little like a betrayal. She took a deep breath and let it go.

"You should talk with Paul Collacchi. He's been around for years."

"Yeah?" Neil looked interested.

"Paul knows Isabelle, maybe better than anyone."

"And he'd talk to me?"

"He will if I ask him to."

"Okay. Set it up."

"I think it's best if I'm not there. Paul may be able to tell you something about Isabelle that he would not want to confess if I was in the room."

"How soon can we do this?"

"Tonight. He'll be at the awards dinner. Can you make it?"

"Just tell me where and when."

31

Neil grabbed a cab back to his hotel, stopping to pick up a couple of takeout sandwiches before going up to his room. More than once he checked his pocket to make sure he still had Tonya's flash drive with the files that had likely got Rachel killed.

He fired up his laptop and clicked through the folders. The Launchpad file listed dozens of investments linked to either a natural disaster or war. He scanned a few of them. Each investment showed a return of between seventeen and thirty-two per cent within the first nine months.

And that was impossible.

It would be like winning the lottery every time you bought a ticket. Nice but...a fantasy.

Neil sat back and thought about it.

The Launchpad premise was simple. When a major disaster struck, money was needed immediately for medicine, food and shelter. Governments and international aid organizations pledged funding, but everyone knew how long it took for bureaucrats to actually send the cheque. Launchpad investors were told that, because the fund was agile, efficient and committed to saving lives, they could move quickly.

Money could be delivered within twenty-four hours of the disaster, when it was needed most, then repaid a few months later once aid funding flowed from the big, established organizations such as the UN or the World Bank. Launchpad funds served, essentially, as bridge financing deployed on a first-in, first-out basis.

It was a great story to sell well-intentioned but naive investors but, as an investment strategy, it was laughable.

In disaster zones, conditions on the ground are chaotic. Day-to-day services collapse. People are desperate. Looting is rampant. Too many people in positions of power have greedy hands grabbing everything they can. There are lots of ways for money to disappear.

Every Launchpad investment would have been ridiculously high-risk. The odds against success were astronomical.

No question about it. The financial records were pure fiction. But did they include any facts that could be backtracked?

There were records of deposits into Launchpad accounts, some in the millions of dollars, received from banks in Iraq, Afghanistan, Haiti and other countries. All of them were credited as repayments against previous investments.

The total of these deposits vastly exceeded the original investments. That made no sense because the investments should have been total writeoffs. So…what was the real reason for the so-called repayments?

He took another bite of his sandwich and continued scanning the transaction statements.

Money deposited into the Launchpad accounts was in turn dispersed mainly to investment accounts held by anonymous shell companies. He quickly searched the files for any mention of Santiago or Grupo Muxia. There was nothing.

The only thing that made sense was that this was dirty money funnelled from offshore banks, laundered through Hudson Ventures and reported as clean investment returns. But, to prove it, he needed more information. Names attached to these shell corporations. Maybe Don could dig out something useful online.

He leaned back.

For someone like Rachel, these sleazy transactions would leap off the screen. He could imagine her on the plane flying back to Toronto, laptop open, working through the data, connecting it with reports from other sources, getting more and more pissed off.

Would she have made notes? Probably. He wished he had her laptop. It was long gone. Stolen by her killer.

Unless…

He scrolled through his phone contacts and tapped on a number.

"Da Silva." Her voice was crisp. From the background noise, he could picture her striding across the atrium of the university math building, towering over students milling near the escalators.

"It's Neil Walker. It's about the Rachel Lisgar investigation. I could use your help."

"What do you need?"

"I was thinking about Rachel's stolen laptop. You mentioned everything is automatically backed up on the university servers."

"So?"

"While she was in New York, Rachel received a package of files. I think she might have reviewed them and made notes on her laptop. Is there a chance the university servers have backup copies?"

"It's possible."

"Could you get me access to them?"

She paused. He heard the muted bell of a nearby elevator door opening. "Sorry, no."

"But they might contain—"

Da Silva's tone was abrupt. "There are legal issues—university liability, employee privacy—"

"Rachel may have stumbled across a major money laundering operation," he pushed. "You don't want to help them get away with her murder."

"Laying on the guilt. That's pretty devious."

"All in a good cause." He tried another route. "What if we kick it upstairs? What if Janos Pach called the dean? Or the university president?"

"It wouldn't matter," she said. "They would be worried about setting a precedent. You'll need to get a court order."

Neil tapped his fist on the hotel desk. Court orders took time. There must be another way. "Have the Toronto cops asked for access?"

"Not so far."

"What if they did?"

"Sure, that would do it."

"Okay. Would you talk to whoever you need to at the university? I'll get the Toronto cops to make a formal request."

"You're confident they'll go along?"

"How could they resist my charm?"

"Right." She sounded skeptical. "Call me when you've charmed them."

She cut the connection. Neil opened his wallet and dug out the card Danny Relf had handed him on the waterfront.

Relf answered on the second ring. "Hey, Walker. First

you warn me to be careful about Carole Lisgar. Next thing I know, she's asking me to be nice to you. How do you do it?"

"Intelligence and sheer hard work would be my guess."

"You're probably right." Relf loudly stifled a yawn. "Any other bullshit you want to peddle?"

"I wanted to give you a heads-up. You may be getting a call from either the FBI or the NYPD."

"And what did I do to deserve this?"

"Stephen Howland, the con man Rachel met with in New York? He was killed this afternoon."

"Interesting," the detective said, his tone turning professional. "Who's primary down there?"

Neil filled him in and gave him phone numbers for both the FBI and NYPD lead investigators.

"Okay," Relf said. "Thanks for the tip."

Before he could hang up, Neil said, "Wait. There's something else."

"Of course there is," Relf sighed. "What do you want?"

Neil explained about the university having digital backups of files on Rachel's stolen laptop.

"Good catch," Relf said. "I suppose you'll want access."

"*Quid pro quo*. I'm working with the FBI. You need anything, maybe I can get it. Save you from the official rigmarole that will drive you nuts."

"I don't know if I can risk doing that," Relf countered, his tone suddenly hushed and confidential. "The RCMP is whispering that you're a problem."

"Seriously?"

"The word is, don't give Walker any cooperation."

Neil took a moment to refocus. Someone was playing games. Was Isabelle pulling strings? "Since when did the RCMP tell Toronto cops what to do?"

Relf laughed. "I was just messing with you. Fuck the

RCMP. As soon as I get access to the account, I'll send you a link."

"Could you send me her phone logs as well?"

"Typical," Relf snorted, "Give 'em an inch, they'll take a fuckin' mile."

"Hey, think of me as an additional resource for your crack team."

"Yeah, yeah. And this is more bullshit than I need at the moment. I'll call you. Now, leave me alone."

Neil tossed his phone on the bed and stretched. He was convinced that connecting the two investigations would make everything move a lot faster.

The problem was, not everyone thought it was a good idea.

32

Heavy hitters from finance, big business and politics converged in a last-minute flurry of bookings at the Canada–US Chamber of Commerce Innovation Awards. They didn't give a shit about new ideas, but they had an uneasy feeling something was about to happen.

Political pressure was building in Washington to increase transparency on international capital flows. It needed to be managed, defused, sidetracked. The pre-dinner reception, with its glad-handing and bullshitting, provided cover for quiet conversations about the important stuff.

Carole caught sight of Paul Collacchi. "I need a quick word with this guy," she said, extricating herself from a trio of Wall Street brokers. She didn't know who they were trying to impress more, her or each other.

She touched Paul's arm and led him off to the corner.

"You look fabulous," he said. Her silk Armani suit draped perfectly, which she hoped would camouflage the stress that was making her feel brittle and jumpy. He looked at her more closely. "As soon as we get back, you have to take some time off."

"I can't—"

"Yes, you can. You need to. You look terrible."

"Fabulous to terrible in less than ten seconds," she said with forced lightness. "You make a girl's head spin."

"Seriously. Take a break. No one would blame you. I realize you and Rachel weren't talking, but still, her death—"

"Her murder."

"Okay, her *murder* by some junkie—"

"That's what I wanted to talk to you about."

"Huh?"

Carole glanced over her shoulder. No one was within hearing distance. Nevertheless, she lowered her voice. "I need a favour."

"Sure. Name it."

"And I need you to be discreet."

He dropped his voice, a playful glint in his eye. "Is it legal?"

Confused, then annoyed, she said, "Yes. Absolutely."

"Okay. What's up?"

"Talk to Neil Walker. Answer his questions. Be honest."

"About what?"

"He has questions about Isabelle and her business connections."

He put a big, phony smile on his face and looked around, casually checking if anyone could overhear them. "Are you serious?"

"I wouldn't ask if it wasn't important."

"Speaking of Walker, you asked me to do a little digging."

"What did you find?"

"I talked to a guy who's written a few books on biker gangs. When Walker was with the Mounties, he worked undercover during the biker wars in Quebec and Ontario."

"And?"

"The rumour is that, in one case, his key witness received death threats. The threats stopped after two bikers disappeared."

"What are you saying? He killed them?"

"Maybe he did. Maybe they went to Mexico. Maybe it's bullshit."

"Do you believe it?"

Collacchi shrugged. "The point is, he never denied it. But, after that, the Mounties pulled him out of undercover work."

Carole took a moment to digest the information. She was surprised to realize, even if it was true, she wasn't horrified. What did that mean? No time to think about it now. "Okay. Thanks for looking into that. Neil's—"

"So, now it's *Neil*? After what he did to you?"

"He's not who I thought he was," Carole said firmly. "He's been looking into Rachel's murder—"

Collacchi reared back. "And he thinks Isabelle was involved?"

"No, of course not." She moved closer, dropping her voice. "A guy was killed this afternoon—"

"Another one?"

Carole nodded. "Isabelle's somehow got herself tangled up in this thing. I need to understand what's going on. Will you talk to Neil?"

"You trust him?"

There it was. The question Carole had been wrestling with. "Yeah, I guess I do."

"Okay. If you're sure."

"I'll set it up." She put her hand on his arm. "Thanks for doing this. Things are getting weird. I feel like just about anything could happen."

33

Isabelle pushed open the glass door of the limestone-clad high-rise and strode into the rush hour chaos and honking horns of Park Avenue. She snapped her purse shut. Once again, the tests had been inconclusive. Dr. Irene Georgio was supposed to be the best cardiologist in New York City. If she couldn't say for sure what was going on, what good was she?

"What the hell does she know?" Isabelle reassured herself. As she approached the limo parked at the curb, engine running, her driver opened the rear passenger door. Getting in, she silently resolved, "I've gotten this far. I'll be damned if I let it stop me now."

With a gentle acceleration, the limo merged with traffic. They were running a little late for the pre-dinner reception, but it couldn't be helped. She had briefed the driver on the destination.

Isabelle knew exactly where she wanted to go.

34

Things were moving forward, Neil thought. He emerged from the bathroom after his shower wearing the hotel's thick, white bathrobe, drying his hair with a towel, humming a no-name tune, feeling good.

Howland's death was no big loss to the world. He'd been a con man who stole money. It was a risky business. He had taken his chances.

Whoever ordered the hit had to realize it would bring more heat, especially the way it was carried out. Midtown Manhattan in the middle of a weekday afternoon? NYPD was guaranteed to be pissed off. It made the city look bad. Violent. Dangerous. All the things that made tourists stay at home and local politicians nervous. Especially once the media started pushing it. And they would.

Howland had been a media darling—handsome, successful and quick with a quotable sound bite. Every television station had lots of entertaining Howland clips, and the viewers loved him. His murder was catnip for news directors in the most competitive media market in the world.

Neil picked up the remote and clicked through until he

reached the local cable news channel. The story had already hit the news cycle. He watched a pretty blonde at an anchor desk for a while, then muted the sound. They had nothing new. The coverage would crank up the pressure on the NYPD to commit serious resources to the case. It would also bring the FBI firmly onside.

Neil needed to stay looped in to both those investigations. Since he had no official standing, he had to figure out a way to be useful so they would want him on the inside. That wouldn't be easy, but it should be doable.

A chime drew him over to his laptop. An email notification had popped up from Toronto Police Service. There was no message, just the link to Rachel's university data-storage account and an attached file holding her phone logs.

Neil was impressed. Relf not only came through, he did it quickly.

He tossed aside the towel and accessed Rachel's U of T cloud account. There were hundreds of files, most of them related to student assignments, upcoming lectures and departmental administrivia. He sorted them by date. The top two entries were the ones that interested him. The first was the stuff Rachel had got from Tonya.

The second contained notes Rachel had made for herself during the flight back to Toronto. He opened it. His heart sank a little. Some of them were just one- or two-word queries or initials designed to jog her memory. Others were longer entries. He had no clue what most of them meant.

She had done a deep dive on Grupo Muxia, accessing data banks, industry reports and other sources that wouldn't show up in a standard Google search. The origins for many entries were identified only by initials. *UNDAC?* He scanned further and found it—United Nations Disaster Assessment and Coordination. *WB* could be World Bank. *IMF* might be

International Monetary Fund. There were dozens of others. Financial Intelligence Units in several countries—Australia, the Netherlands, Denmark—suspected Grupo Muxia of laundering billions of euros annually. An unreleased report from Transparency Watch claimed Grupo Muxia had links to organized crime worldwide, from MS-13 in Central America to Russian gangsters.

She had combed through the thicket of anonymous shell corporations linked to Grupo Muxia, then compared them with companies listed in Tonya's files on Hudson Ventures.

She'd searched global business registries and the European e-Justice Portal looking for common links, whether it was law firms in Panama, accounting houses in Singapore, bank accounts in Cyprus or even street addresses in George Town, Cayman Islands.

Neil could imagine her on the early-evening flight back from New York, her fingers flying over the keyboard, her focus intense, sniffing for links, hunting hard.

Then she'd found it.

MacklinMunroe.

A privately held limited corporation originally registered in Scotland, it owned a controlling interest in both Grupo Muxia and Hudson Ventures. It was also the major shareholder in most of the shell corporations listed in Tonya's files as receiving multi-million-dollar payouts from the Launchpad Fund.

There it was. Evidence that Grupo Muxia was connected through MacklinMunroe to a Ponzi scheme operating on US soil.

That should make Chris Rader happy. It should be enough for the FBI to get search warrants for Santiago's corporate and personal files and bank accounts.

But would it be enough to convince a US district attorney

to file charges? Given the heavyweight political connections on display at the Hamptons beach party, the DA would want a slam dunk.

More evidence was needed, starting with who controlled MacklinMunroe.

Rachel must have hit a dead end.

And it evidently had driven her crazy. Her frustration had gone into the red zone.

Her last file entry was the name *MacklinMunroe*, followed by a long string of questions marks, like she'd held down the key and watched the marks zip across her screen.

Then she'd become pissed off and started typing one word again and again and again until she had filled a screen page with nothing but *fuckfuckfuckfuckfuckfuckfuck*.

She had a temper.

He could understand that.

Had she reached the end of her flight? Had the seat belt warning come on? No time to continue the search? Was she planning to redouble her digging when she got home?

Neil was out of his depth. He only knew one person with the hacking skills needed to finish what Rachel started.

He picked up his phone and called Don.

"I need you to look into a few things." He had to speak loudly to cut through the ringing guitar music.

"Let me turn this thing down," Don said, and the music faded back. He yawned. "We've been rehearsing all night, and I'm due back in less than an hour."

"I know your gig's really important, but this thing is getting a little crazy."

"We can't even agree on the song list. Did I tell you—"

Impatient, Neil let an edge slip into his voice. "There was another murder this afternoon. Somebody's cleaning house."

"Okay," Don groaned. Twenty years as a cop. Neil

counted on him understanding how that cranked up the pressure. "What do you need?"

"Rachel found evidence that links Hudson Ventures to Grupo Muxia through a shell corporation called Macklin-Munroe. I think it got her killed. I'm going to send you a link to her cloud storage account. See if you can figure out who really owns MacklinMunroe and how they are all connected. Names, dates, hard evidence."

"You got it."

"Another thing. Rachel's phone logs show that one of her last calls was to this off-the-books phone number with a three-eight-three country code—"

"That's Kosovo—"

"But the area code doesn't exist. I need you to trace it."

"That shouldn't take too long." There was the sound of keyboard clicking. "And I may have something else. You asked me to dig into Grupo Muxia."

Neil leaned back. "Tell me."

"Your victim, Rachel Lisgar, was a finance geek, right? Within the past couple of years, three other financial analysts have died in so-called accidents. All of them had been conducting due diligence investigations into Grupo Muxia projects."

"Shit. Can you send me the details? The more we can link US companies to illegal acts by Grupo Muxia, the faster the FBI will react."

"I know a guy who can probably get you everything you need. He works for one of the international aid organizations. I did some *pro bono* work for him last year. As it happens, he's based in New York."

"Can you set up a meeting for me with him?"

"Maybe, but you gotta promise me something. Too many

people are getting killed. This guy's a bureaucrat. He's an anonymous source. He needs to be protected."

"No problem. Set it up."

"You need to take this seriously," Don insisted. "Are you carrying?"

"A gun? No."

"You want me to fix you up? There's a cop I met in Jersey—"

"No, I'll be fine. Listen, I appreciate what you're doing for me. Now, about your gig Thursday night. What time's the first set?"

"Schedule says eight thirty. Probably actually start around nine. You think you'll make it?"

Neil heard the nervousness in Don's voice. "Are you kidding? It's going to be a blast." He glanced at the bedside clock. "I have to go. I'm meeting a guy who I'm told can answer a bunch of questions."

He threw on some clothes—black jeans, open-collared shirt and a blazer—and raced out the door.

Questions tumbled through his mind, all of them circling tighter and tighter around Paolo Santiago. Did he have Howland killed to stop the investigation? Did he have Rachel killed?

As the elevator doors opened, Neil decided it was time to question Santiago. Face-to-face. He would rent a car and drive out to the Hamptons first thing in the morning.

Tonight, he'd focus on Collacchi.

35

Across Park Avenue from the Grand Palace Hotel, protestors pushed against the barrier NYPD had stationed to mark the no-go line. The mood was tense but still under control. A few demonstrators waved placards. One of them, a slender figure in a black hoodie with a scar that started under her left eye, seemed to pay special attention to Neil as he climbed out of a cab at the hotel's opulent entrance.

Inside, he followed the signs to the Canada–US Chamber of Commerce Innovation Awards reception. A knot of business-types, mostly middle-aged men, all of them wearing dark suits and professional smiles, milled around the ballroom entrance, as they waited to have their names checked by one of the harried young women at the registration desk. Neil's name was on the list. He nodded to the burly security team flanking the door and entered the noisy hall filled with the babble of a thousand voices.

He scanned the crowded room. Servers in white shirts and bow ties carried trays laden with hors d'oeuvres, circulating deftly among the continually shifting groups. The decor reeked of la belle époque. Glittering chandeliers, white walls, golden velvet curtains that hung in swags and, underfoot, wall-to-wall carpet in a dark blue floral pattern.

Neil and Paul Collacchi spotted each other at the same time and met halfway.

"Innovation awards at the Starlight Ballroom?" Neil almost had to yell to be heard over the room noise. "A joke, right? I bet nothing has changed here in a hundred years."

"These are business guys: they don't do irony," Collacchi shouted back. He brushed a lock of his hair back from his forehead. "How did you convince Carole to set this up? Me talking to you?"

"I didn't convince her of anything. She suggested it." Neil looked around. No one stood close enough to overhear them. "So. Isabelle Lisgar. What can you tell me? Surprise me."

"I'll surprise you, all right." Collacchi seemed anxious, constantly looking around, fidgeting with keys in his pocket. "Do you smoke?"

Neil shook his head.

"I quit last week," Collacchi said. He pointed to a door near the stage. "But for this conversation, I need a cigarette."

They wended their way through the room, Collacchi in the lead. He detoured long enough to bum a cigarette and borrow a lighter from an older woman with an improbable shade of red hair, who gave Neil the eye as they slid by.

Neil noticed a slender, blonde woman across the room who seemed to be tracking their progress. He took his eye off her for a moment when some guy in a hurry to get to the bar bumped into him. When he looked again, she had disappeared.

Collacchi pushed open the employees-only door and started down a dingy, yellow-painted service corridor lit by fluorescent ceiling fixtures. "Smokers always hang out on the receiving dock," he said. "It's where you'll hear the most interesting shit."

"I appreciate your helping me out, here," Neil said. The hallway was a relief after the ballroom, cooler and quieter. "Tell me anything that might be useful."

Collacchi paused at the metal fire door exit to the loading dock, his hand on the crash bar. "Someone really had Rachel killed?"

"It looks that way."

"Jesus, I hope not." He shoved open the door, already reaching into his shirt pocket to pull out the slightly crumpled cigarette.

Neil spotted a broken, old broomstick that workers had left leaning in a corner. Before the door could close, he dropped it in the jamb. Getting locked out was not part of the plan.

The deserted loading dock stretched about thirty feet wide and twenty feet deep. Security spotlights threw harsh shadows into the corners. A beat-up garbage bin sat against the wall by the door. The smell of sour kitchen scraps overlaid the night air already thick with humidity, leftover diesel fumes and stale cigarette smoke. Muffled traffic noise whispered down the alley from nearby streets.

"I always liked Rachel," Collacchi began, waving the cigarette. "Smart. Funny. She was one of the good ones." He lit up, took in a deep lungful and let it slowly stream out. He started coughing.

Concerned, Neil reached out to steady Collacchi. "Are you all right, there?"

"Yeah, yeah," he responded, waving Neil off. He looked around, glancing back over his shoulder. He was wound up tight, his foot tapping. "It's funny. If Rachel was here tonight, she'd be across the street demonstrating, not inside schmoozing."

Neil steered the conversation. "I understand there was no love lost between Rachel and Isabelle."

Collacchi swung around to face Neil. "That's an understate—"

He snapped up straight. He twisted, lurched into Neil. Blood blossomed on his white shirt. "Ahh!"

Neil caught more than two hundred pounds of flesh barrelling into him. He stumbled back. They almost fell.

Kerrang!

Fuck! A bullet ricocheted off the garbage bin. Neil bear-hugged Collacchi and instinctively kept moving, struggling to stay on his feet.

Nowhere to hide.

A quick glance over his shoulder. The fire door. Ten feet away. Maybe three long strides.

Locking Collacchi in his arms, he staggered backwards. One, two fast steps. He nearly tripped over the broken broomstick.

Pfftt! Pfftt!

Two more fast coughing sounds from the darkness. A silencer. A double tap. His mind registered the details even as his back slammed into the loading dock wall.

He reached around, scrabbling one-handed for the fire door. Safety lay inside the hotel.

From down the alley came the guttural whine of a motor scooter revving. A blinding white headlight ripped through the night.

Caught in the spotlight, the shooter spun. She was tall and dressed in black. She fired twice. Headlight glass shattered. The rider tumbled off. Metal screeched as the scooter slid along the pavement.

Neil ripped open the fire door and tumbled back into the hotel hallway. Sanctuary. He held Collacchi tight. He kicked the broomstick aside, yanked the door shut, and they slid down the wall.

Blood pulsed out of Collacchi's chest. Upper left quadrant. Must have nicked an artery. Neil's breath came in ragged gasps. He fumbled for his phone. He jammed his other hand against the wound.

"9-1-1. What is the emerg—"

"Ambulance." Neil's chest heaved, his voice harsh. "Need an ambulance. Grand Palace Hotel. At the back. The loading dock." Collacchi sagged, collapsing like a bag with the sand running out.

"And your name, sir?"

"Vic is male. Single GSW. Upper chest."

"Police and an ambulance are now on their way. Please stay on the line until they arrive."

Neil pushed Collacchi over onto his back and kept pressure on the wound. Collacchi's face was grey. He was barely breathing. "Tell them to hurry. This guy's hurt bad."

"Yes, sir. They're coming as fast as they can. Your name—"

"A scooter crashed in the alley. They may need help, too."

"I'll tell the paramedics. Your name. What is your name, sir?"

"Walker. Neil Walker. And get a message to the FBI's New York field office. Special Agent in Charge Chris Rader. Tell him what's happened."

"I'll do that. You hang in there. Help is on the way."

36

Neil's hand trembled, adrenalin aftershock, rattling the bourbon mini-bottle against the edge of the glass. The hotel room was dimly lit. He sank into an upholstered chair, let out a shaky breath, put his feet up on the window ledge and gazed out over the city lights.

Maybe he should take up Don's offer. Get a pistol. Back home, he always carried his 9mm SIG. Given the bad guys and bikers he'd pissed off over the years, better to have it and not need it than need it and not have it.

Down here, for the past couple of days, he had felt lighter, and it wasn't simply because he didn't have two pounds of metal strapped to his belt. Like switching from workboots to sandals, like a vacation.

Some vacation.

Truth be told, it probably wouldn't have made a difference back there in the alley, what with one hand holding Collacchi and the other reaching for the door. But there was no doubt. Right now, if the pistol was sitting on the table beside him, he'd rest a little easier. That's for damn sure. Maybe it would make the cold lump in his gut go away.

So. Should he call Don for the number of his friend in Jersey?

The question rolled around in his brain. The FBI and cops had had a different set of questions. They'd started in the alley before the ambulance pulled away. They'd continued over the next few hours in a stale interview room at the Midtown South precinct house. Just before eleven o'clock, word came from the hospital.

Collacchi would make it, barring unexpected complications. The guy on the scooter, who turned out to be delivering a pizza, got away with a few scrapes and bruises.

The attack cranked the pressure up even higher.

Was the killer targeting Neil?

Or was Collacchi shot to stop him from talking to Neil? If so, what information was so valuable?

And who had known they were meeting?

The questions kept flashing through his mind like a read-o-graph on speed.

He had no answers.

The cops weren't happy. Neither was he. He'd given them the best description of the shooter he could, painfully aware that it was based on an adrenalin-pumped glimpse he got in the scooter headlight.

After wrangling back and forth with a parade of detectives, Neil had signed a statement that stuck reasonably close to the facts. They'd let him go a little after midnight, and he'd returned to his hotel to change out of his bloodstained clothes.

At least there was less paperwork for him to fill out than when he wore a badge. He felt bad for thinking it, but it was a relief.

Now, with his feet up and a drink in his hand, he was drained but restless. Collacchi nearly died as a result of this investigation. His investigation. There was no way to get around it.

And that hard fact changed everything. It made him angry, and that was a problem. He had to cool down. Emotion screwed with good judgement.

Who had sent the shooter? A professional, no question about it. Just like the shooter in Toronto.

Someone banged on his door. Fast, loud, demanding.

He approached it cautiously, braced for anything. Before opening, he checked the door latch. Not that it would stop a cop with a warrant.

More pounding, this time with a fist.

"Open up, Neil. We need to talk."

Carole.

He flipped the latch, turned the handle and backed up. She pushed her way in. Her face was drawn, her eyes red, but she held herself straight, her shoulders back. He was impressed.

She rounded on him. "Tell me what happened."

"The cops—"

"I'm sorry. I should have asked. You're okay?"

"Yeah, I'm—"

"What did he tell you? What was so goddamn important?"

"Nothing."

"Are you trying to shut me out? Don't you dare. I—"

"Stop. He didn't tell me anything."

She tossed her purse on the bed. "The police say the killer targeted either Paul or you. What do you think?"

"How did you find out—"

"Our security guys are liaising with NYPD. Was Paul the target? Or you?"

"My guess? Me."

"So, Paul was—what?—an accident?" She sat down on the bed, her shoulders slumped.

"More like collateral damage. Someone ordered that attack. They are willing to kill to stop what Rachel started."

"Which was?"

"Using evidence of Hudson Ventures' Ponzi scheme and money laundering to bring down Grupo Muxia."

"How could she hope to do that?"

"She had a flash drive filled with confidential files from Hudson Ventures. I've seen the files. They show direct ownership links between Hudson Ventures, Grupo Muxia and a company called MacklinMunroe—"

Carole's eyes sharpened. "What's it called?"

"MacklinMunroe. It's registered in Scotland. Why?"

"I don't know. For a moment, it sounded familiar." She stood up, walked over to stand beside Neil and looked out the window. With one hand, she opened the curtains wider.

"There's something else," he said, watching her carefully. "Just before she died, Rachel called someone. I think it might have been Isabelle."

She looked down. "Why would she do that? They hadn't talked in years."

Neil opened his laptop and pulled up the phone logs from Rachel's mobile. He pointed to the number with the weird area code. "Do you recognize the number?"

She leaned over, then reared back. "No," she said, a touch of defensiveness creeping into her voice. She stepped away and crossed her arms. "Earlier today, you said Santiago could have been the one who ordered Rachel's murder. Are you saying Isabelle was somehow involved?"

"It's a possibility. She has some connection to Santiago. She was able to get Lattimer's name on the party guest list."

"But you have no real proof." She ran her hands through

her hair, then looked at him squarely. "You could have been killed tonight."

He raised his glass as a toast. "I'd say *luck of the Irish*, but I'm more of a Czech–Scots mongrel."

"NYPD, FBI and the Toronto cops are investigating this thing. No one would blame you if you called it quits."

Neil answered, his tone flat, "Official investigations can get sidetracked. I'm going to stay with it."

She studied him closely. "You're sure?"

"After tonight, I have a dog in the fight."

She nodded. "So, what's next? Where do you go from here?"

"Santiago. His name keeps popping up. If he's not at the centre of all this, he knows who is."

"Do you think he'll talk to you?"

Neil shrugged. "I'll go to the Hamptons in the morning and find out."

Immediately, Carole said, "I'll go with you."

He looked at her as if she was nuts. "This guy's no backbench MP you can threaten."

"Why should he talk to you at all?" she countered. "How do you expect to get past his guards?"

"I'm still working on that," Neil admitted.

"I can get us both in," she said with confidence.

"How?"

"My connections to the minister will get us a meeting."

"But—"

"We can take a helicopter in the morning," she said, standing up.

"Putting yourself on Santiago's radar could get you killed."

"My sister is dead, and my friend is in the hospital. If Santiago's responsible, I want to look him in the eye."

She turned and walked towards the door, stopping when Neil called out.

"You're tougher than I thought." He let slip a little grin, surprising himself that he was looking forward to the morning.

"I'm angry," she said, her eyes cold. "Whoever did this is going to burn in hell."

37

When Carole stepped out into the hotel lobby, a jumble of thoughts went tumbling through her mind: strategies on how to approach Santiago, whether Neil could be right about Rachel and Isabelle, and guilt over Paul getting shot.

She pushed all that turmoil aside and pulled out her phone. She needed to check in with Rae, find out how she was doing, let her know what was happening.

Once they were connected, she paused near one of the couches in the lobby, halfway to the revolving doors that led to the street. "How are you holding up?"

Rae exploded. "A cigarette? He was out there smoking a fucking cigarette? He told me he'd quit. I don't know whether to laugh or cry." Her voice was rough, her words slightly slurred. Carole could hear voices in the background. Good. People were looking after her.

"You can tear a strip off him when he gets home," she said. "He's going to be okay. I've arranged for private nurses 'round the clock. I'll send you their contact info. Call them anytime."

There was a long pause. Carole could picture Rae in the

condo, her back to whoever was there with her, leaning against the wall, her mouth tight, maintaining self-control through sheer will. There must have been a million scary things going through her mind.

Rae finally spoke. "Did the cops catch who did it?"

"No, but tomorrow—I guess later today—we're going to see someone who might be able to help."

"*We*? Who's *we*? You're not—"

"I need to find out what's going on, that's all."

Concern in her voice, Rae protested, "Don't do anything stupid—"

"It'll be fine."

"I'm starting to worry, here."

"Don't. Right now, what's important is for you to take care of yourself and little Charlie. As soon as Paul's able to travel, I'll get him on an air ambulance back to Ottawa."

"Thanks for that, and the nurses. But promise me you'll be careful."

"I will. You take care, too. I'll call you later." She slid the phone into her purse and took stock. She had dreaded that conversation, but it'd turned out better than she had hoped. It was a relief to hear some strength in Rae's voice.

Looking through the lobby doors, she spotted an empty cab parked right in front of the hotel canopy. She gathered herself, pushed through the revolving doors, waved off the doorman and climbed into the back seat of the cab.

Before the cab took off, a bag lady in a floppy old hat leaning against the wall near the hotel entrance surreptitiously snapped Carole's picture with her phone.

Karin Reichelt was watching for Neil Walker, waiting for an opportunity to complete the assignment.

Now she had ID'd Carole.

38

The helicopter cabin noise made quiet, private conversations difficult, which was frustrating. As they flew across Long Island Sound towards the Hamptons, it left Neil alone with his thoughts. Despite the bright morning sun, those thoughts were dark with uncertainty and after-effects of last night's shooting. He'd asked Carole how she'd convinced Santiago to meet with them, but all she would say was that it hadn't been a problem. He did not like confronting a major player like Santiago without a solid game plan.

And he was not fond of heights. Travelling by helicopter always reminded him of carnival rides designed to make people disoriented. Maybe it was a fitting way to start this particular day.

On their approach, they spotted Santiago on the lawn just beyond the beach. He was in conversation with a tanned, casually dressed man of about forty with longish hair that ruffled in the sea breeze. As the helicopter hovered momentarily before final descent, Santiago nodded and the other guy walked away. He looked familiar. It took Neil a minute to make the connection. He wasn't a hundred per cent sure, but he could swear it was Pol Luuckser, the Eurotrash money shark who had been circling the Waterloo tech firm with the encryption software. Was that only three days ago?

Santiago stood patiently, hands clasped behind his back, ignoring how the helicopter's rotor wash buffeted his loose linen shirt and trousers. Neil and Carole did that awkward, hunched-over walk until they cleared the spinning blades.

"I'm so happy to finally meet you," Santiago greeted Carole, kissing her first on the left cheek, then the right before looking into her eyes with friendly curiosity. "Your aunt speaks highly of you. A *protégée*, one might say."

"Thank you for seeing us, especially on such short notice," Carole replied with a warmth that went beyond mere courtesy.

"*De nada*," he said softly, still holding on to her hand. "My deepest condolences on the death of your sister."

"Thank you. And this is Neil Walker."

"We're hoping you could help us with some information," Neil said, his expression neutral as he and Santiago shook hands.

"I understand you had a dramatic night," Santiago responded, his expression equally cool.

Neil caught Carole's eye. She shook her head. She hadn't mentioned it to him. "You're well-informed," Neil responded.

"I do what I can."

Santiago gently turned Carole towards a courtyard seating area near the house. "Come. There is coffee and some pastries that you might enjoy. My chef is a magician."

As they strolled up to the house, Santiago glanced at Neil. "I confess I took an interest when you showed up with our friends across the bay. You have an impressive record."

"As do you," Neil replied graciously. "That is, if the FBI files are accurate."

Santiago laughed. "Accurate? The FBI? I doubt that."

Arriving at the courtyard, they settled on antique, white wicker couches under a large shade umbrella. A young housemaid poured coffee and departed silently.

"It's lovely here," Carole observed, and Neil had to admit she was right.

The house was a striking combination of stone, sand-coloured stucco and weathered grey cedar. Sunlight sparkled off the freshly cleaned windows. It was quiet. The soft morning breeze carried a warm hint of salt.

"I find it restorative, and perhaps you will, too," Santiago said. "You have had a horrible week."

"It's been challenging," Carole acknowledged, "in no small part because it has raised some disturbing questions."

"Yes, you mentioned that on the telephone. Could you elaborate?"

"Of course. Before I do, I want to assure you that I will fully appreciate any help or information you give us. In my world, such considerations are highly valued—"

"As they are in mine," Santiago assured her, a spark of amusement in his eye.

Carole acknowledged it with a slight tip of her head. "They can provide the foundation for an ongoing, mutually beneficial relationship."

Neil kept his jaw from dropping. It sounded like she was opening the door to a long-term connection. What was she doing?

Carole pulled a business card from her pocket and placed it on the table in front of Santiago. "Whether you are able to help us this morning or not, please do not hesitate to call me if there is anything I can do for you. My private number is on the back."

Santiago picked up the card and flipped it over to check the back before slipping it into his pocket. He flashed a conspiratorial smile. "I can see why Isabelle is so proud of you."

Neil seized on that as an opening. "Have you known Isabelle for long?"

"That's difficult to say," Santiago replied, settling back with his coffee.

"Would you say she's a friend? A business associate?"

"Excuse me?" He looked to Carole, then back to Neil. "This sounds less like a conversation and more like an interrogation."

"Not at all," Carole assured him with a pleasant smile. When she looked at Neil, her eyes held a warning.

"I'm sorry, old habits die hard." Neil changed focus. "What we're really interested in is Hudson Ventures and the Launchpad Fund." He sat forward. "We believe Rachel's death is somehow connected to her meeting with Stephen Howland."

"Go on."

"Hudson Ventures, through the Launchpad Fund, appears to be providing money laundering services to various organizations."

"Really?"

"Rachel uncovered evidence, and that led to her murder."

"And what was the nature of this evidence?"

"Business relationships linking certain shell corporations. We were hoping that you might be able to help us."

"I don't understand. How?"

"Since Hudson Ventures and Grupo Muxia are both subsidiaries of MacklinMunroe—"

"No, not at all. We may have some investors in common, nothing more."

"There are records of financial transactions."

"We occasionally did business together, that is all."

"The files suggest otherwise."

"I can't help that." Santiago shrugged. "Perhaps the files are...how do you say it...*bogus*?"

"Which is why we are reaching out to you," Carole said quietly, inching forward in her chair. "Any...insights...you could share would be helpful."

Santiago thought for a moment and glanced at Carole. "I will tell you what I know." He cleared his throat. "Stephen Howland was a truly larger-than-life character."

Neil asked, "How did you meet him?"

"I don't remember." Santiago shook his head. "You must understand, when one is building a business, one leverages what you have and who you know." He glanced knowingly in Carole's direction.

"That's the way the world works," she responded with a polite smile.

"Stephen was available," Santiago continued. "Was he perfect? No. Was he worth the trouble? Most of the time."

Neil couldn't believe it. "You're saying Howland was a supplier and a bit of a cowboy, but he delivered results?"

"He provided certain services to Grupo Muxia, mainly contacts and connections here in NYC. It is, after all, one of the biggest financial and human capital markets in the world. What he did beyond that was his business. I knew nothing about it."

"And MacklinMunroe?" Neil asked.

"An early investor. We have long since parted ways," Santiago assured them. "If you like, I could have someone look into the files. Who knows what they might find?"

Before Neil could press Santiago any further, Carole stood up. "Thank you for your time, Señor Santiago—"

Neil, taken by surprise, scrambled to join them.

"Call me Paolo, please," Santiago responded, getting to his feet.

"Paolo, then," Carole continued. They began to stroll back across the lawn to the helicopter. "You have been most helpful. I won't forget it."

"We must stay in touch," he replied. "If I can be of further assistance, call me anytime."

Neil and Carole climbed aboard the helicopter. The rotors spooled up. They buckled in for the forty-minute ride back to the heliport at East Thirty-Fourth Street. Neil was just as happy that the helicopter noise would make conversation impossible. He had a lot to think about.

Before the rotors got too loud, he leaned towards her. "You looked like you were getting cozy with Santiago. Is that smart?"

"I'm not an idiot," she retorted sharply. "He's a predator. I recognized the type."

"You don't—"

"I probably met more of them around the Sunday dinner table than you did during all your years with the RCMP."

"He's more dangerous than you think."

"I can handle him."

"He's not a guy you want to fuck with."

"He has information he knows is valuable to us. He won't tell us until we meet his price."

"What price?"

"That's the question. What does Santiago really want?"

"Just be careful. In this game, it's not political points at stake. It's your life." Neil grabbed a pair of ear-protecting headphones. "And since we're now working together, you're also risking mine. Excuse me if I'm a little cautious."

As he slipped on the ear protectors, he considered the wisdom of trusting his life to a woman who, until twenty-four hours ago, hated his guts.

39

Isabelle watched CNN's latest business news reports as her black Bentley rolled through the late morning traffic along Fifty-Second Street towards Fifth Avenue.

Russia announced full support for the proposed OECD anti–money laundering rules. As usual, the pundits in pinstriped suits were bickering over what that actually meant. Everybody accepted that Russian oligarchs were among the world's top money launderers. Among CNN's serious thinkers, there must be something diabolically wrong with the OECD proposal if Russia backed it.

Tina Smarland, sitting beside Isabelle, was on her phone with a cable news editor. "That's right," she said. "It's like the goddamn fox endorsing the new security plans for the henhouse." She paused to listen, then broke in. "I tell you, if this OECD disaster goes through, what's to stop the Russians from seeing all our private financial data? Yeah, yeah. Call me back." She cut the connection. "Jesus. That Jerry. Sometimes, he's got his head up his ass."

Isabelle muted the television. "They'll run with it?"

"Oh, sure. He owes me. They'll get it into heavy rotation all afternoon."

"Good. And congratulations on bringing Petr Arakelova on board."

"He promised the official statement would stand for a few days."

"That will be enough. Was he expensive?"

"Five million."

Isabelle smiled. "It's nice to see another convert to capitalism."

Tina changed the subject. "We'll need to feed the conspiracy blogs something provocative by four thirty. That'll freshen the story for the evening news cycle."

Isabelle nodded. "Work up a few options. Nothing too extreme. We may need to escalate later."

"No problem. Give me an hour."

The limo pulled to the curb outside Lucien's, a classic French restaurant with a blue and yellow awning shading a half-dozen bistro tables that had colonized a roped-off stretch of sidewalk.

"This is me," Isabelle said, gathering her purse. "Keep the car."

She strode past a lineup of waiting customers that snaked patiently through the door. Bernard, the diplomatic front-of-house manager, greeted her warmly.

"You look wonderful," he said, ushering her upstairs to an intimate dining room, each table covered by snow-white linen and sparkling glassware. Tapestries and oil paintings hung on the walls. Hand-knotted carpets lay underfoot. Large, voluptuous flower arrangements provided informal privacy screens between the tables.

Waiting for her was Ambassador Jean-Robert Soromon, the permanent representative to the United Nations from the tiny Pacific island of Vanuatu. Cyclone Isko, the latest in a long line of destructive tropical storms, had recently devastated most of Vanuatu. That combined with frequent earthquakes earned the tiny country the UN's top ranking for vulnerability in natural disasters.

Soromon stood as Isabelle approached their table. He was tall, and his elegant suit almost disguised the thug underneath.

"Did you hear the news?" he asked her, his voice pitched low. "Why would the Russians support the OECD initiative? They have much to lose."

"Who knows?" Isabelle said innocently as she sat down. "I heard it has more to do with internal Russian politics than anything else."

"What if the OECD gets even more support—"

"My sources tell me it is as good as dead."

"Is this true?"

"It will not affect our arrangements," she assured him.

The conversation paused while Isabelle surveyed the other tables. A young Asian couple, loaded down with shopping bags from Barneys, Saks and Bergdorf Goodman sat nearby. It reminded Isabelle she needed to order gifts for her upcoming meetings in Beijing and Singapore.

"I trust the discussions with your countrymen were successful?"

"They questioned why we should sign a tax treaty with Haiti," he replied. "We do no business with them at all."

"Did you explain that your two countries have much to gain by working together?" For Isabelle, these explanations were tedious enough the first time, let alone the second or third. "Like Vanuatu, Haiti is a member in good standing of La Francophonie and, like Vanuatu, Haiti has received hundreds of millions of dollars in disaster relief funding."

She knew Soromon and the other Vanuatu kleptocrats had siphoned tens of millions of that money into personal Swiss bank accounts. Unfortunately, Swiss bankers no longer delivered the same privacy they once did, especially for Third World despots.

"What differentiates your two countries is that Haiti now has corporate and financial privacy laws that are second to none. A tax treaty would give you access to that regulatory environment."

"Are you saying that Haiti is no longer a tax haven? How does that help us?"

"Over the past three years, my company worked with the Haitian central bank, providing it with anti–money laundering training, regulatory frameworks and compliance reporting systems." Isabelle leaned over the table to bring Jean-Robert into her confidence. "For World Bank and IMF purposes, my company certifies Haiti's total AML compliance. Today, Haiti is a full participant in the global financial payments and transfers system."

"You are confusing me," Soromon charged.

Isabelle smiled politely while she gritted her teeth. The stupidity of some clients was unbelievable. "For high value clients such as yourself and your colleagues, we can provide, via Haiti, the secure untraceable conduits for any funds you want to deposit outside Vanuatu and invest anywhere in the world."

"And what is the nature of your company's relationship with Haiti? What do you get in return?"

"We have a ninety-nine-year contract to manage Haiti's financial system."

"And what would you want from Vanuatu?"

"To make transactions as seamless, secure and cost-efficient as possible for clients, we would need unrestricted access to both ends of the conduit."

"You want the keys to our banking system," Soromon grumbled.

"It could be structured as a simple, consulting contract giving us the access needed to run systems analytics and upgrades."

Soromon made a show of mulling it over, a crafty look creeping into his eyes.

"Yours is not the only company offering—shall we say—confidential offshore investment services. Many of your competitors are much larger."

"Our smaller size means we are more flexible and less likely to turn up in tomorrow's embarrassing headlines," she responded smoothly. "We also provide encryption and disbursement systems that set the gold standard worldwide. The IMF, World Bank and virtually every other major player licenses their encryption technology from us. Because we control root access to the algorithm, our special clients are always one step ahead."

"I will convey all this to my colleagues," Soromon said, smiling sweetly. "I hope it will be enough."

Isabelle masked her amusement. Hundreds of millions of dollars, possibly billions, were on the table, and this backwater gangster demanded a little extra taste for himself. The greed was breathtaking.

"Jean-Robert, my friend, I appreciate all the work you have undertaken to make this arrangement possible. In recognition of your efforts, once a long-term contract is signed, I would be prepared to waive any transaction fees for you personally for a generous period. Say, ten years?"

"For the rest of my life," Soromon bargained, an arrogant smile of victory tugging at his lips.

"That's what I meant," she conceded.

"And this arrangement would remain confidential between you and me?"

"Absolutely."

Isabelle swallowed the urge to laugh in his face and raised her wineglass instead. She had learned, in dozens of countries across the global south, few thugs like Soromon had a life expectancy longer than ten years. "*À votre santé*—and to our success."

40

Throughout the flight back to the city, Carole deliberately ignored Neil. She answered emails from Ottawa, read issue notes from the policy wonks and checked online feeds from CBC News, CNN and BBC World News.

Her thoughts kept shifting back to Rae and the baby. And Paul, lying in the hospital. And Rachel, gone forever.

She had to get her head back in the game. The last twenty-four hours had taken a toll, but she was a pro. She had to deliver solid intel and advice on time. She shoved the whole mess—Neil, Santiago, and Paul lying in a hospital bed—onto the back burner.

At the East River heliport, they split up. Carole took a cab back to the Four Seasons, concentrating during the ride on facts and arguments to brief the minister. She had to be cool, focused. Two issues topped the agenda: the current status of the OECD AML initiative and, far more importantly, Wall Street's spin on the upcoming Canadian election.

How many briefings had she done over the years? Hundreds, certainly. Maybe thousands. There was a format to them, a logical structure.

Carole paused outside the minister's suite. Every briefing was also a performance. Confidence. Energy. She squared her shoulders and knocked.

Cal Sturman opened the door and let her in without a greeting, not even a nod.

Uh-oh. Not a good sign. She walked into the sitting area.

"There you are," Lattimer growled.

"What's the problem?" She looked around. Cindy kept her head turned to her laptop screen. Jack O'Connell lounged in the corner, a smirk showing how much he was going to enjoy this.

"Why the hell did you meet with Santiago?" Lattimer stood in front of her. "He has nothing to do with this mission."

Her face froze. How did he find out? Why would he even care? Her eyes narrowed.

"I was doing my job." Carole, thinking fast, looked him straight in the eye. "I cleaned up your mess."

"What mess?"

"That FBI video? The one with Canada's minister of finance—that would be you—meeting with a suspected money launderer the night before publicly opposing the OECD's new anti–money laundering directive. Have you forgotten?"

"I told you to drop that. Besides, I don't see how your little adventure this morning changes anything."

"Simple. It creates a different narrative. A set of facts that supports an alternative interpretation to explain away the FBI video."

"This will be a good one," he said, his voice laden with sarcasm.

"We spin it that you attended the party to intercede on my behalf. I wanted to meet with Santiago. It was personal, not political, part of the search for my sister's killer."

"So, now you're an amateur detective?" He jabbed at her

with his finger. "Leave the investigation to people who know what they're doing."

"I need—"

"You need to do your job. Because of your meddling, Paul nearly died."

"That's not fair!"

"You're a loose cannon," he snarled. "No wonder the Party didn't want you on the campaign committee."

"You don't know what you're talking about," Carole spat. "As usual."

"Enough! You're fired."

Incredulous, she stepped back. "You can't be serious."

"Do I look like I'm joking?"

She stared at him coolly. "You don't have the authority."

"You report to me—"

She almost laughed. "I report to you? Give me a break."

"Get out!"

"You're a salesman," she sneered, her pent-up frustrations rushing out. "Your job is to sell whatever shit the Party hands you. My job is to keep you from fucking it up."

"Go! Get out of my sight. Make sure Paul gets back to Ottawa. Can you at least handle that?"

Carole backed away. She was angry, and a little embarrassed at losing control. But overriding it all, in the cooler part of her brain, she was puzzled.

This attack—and it was an attack—came out of the blue. Where had Lattimer got the balls to do this to her?

No one said a word. The minister stood with his fists on his hips. Jack O'Connell gloated in the corner. Cindy looked stricken.

Behind her, she heard Cal open the door.

Carole stiffened her back. Damned if she would run. She

slowly counted to five. Silently, she turned from the room and walked out.

She knew it was petty, but being fired from a job she didn't like still stung. Especially by some jumped-up lightweight like Lattimer.

This was definitely not over.

41

The Worldwide Alliance of Red Cross and Red Crescent Societies had offices in an anonymous seventies-era office building a few blocks from the United Nations.

Neil checked the ninth-floor directory and turned left. The hallway, with its worn industrial carpeting under dim fluorescent lights, was a world away from the luxury and soft breezes of the Hamptons. The reception area held modest furnishings, bland geometric paintings on the walls and a smiling, overweight middle-aged woman wearing glasses and a pale blue hijab. It gave off the vibe of a chronically underfunded operation that was always on the brink of being overwhelmed.

Within minutes, Neil was sitting across the desk from Selim Junkaya, Associate Regional Director for the Americas. Junkaya was a thin man with intelligent eyes and a cautious manner.

"Thank you for meeting with me," Neil began. "Don Cale mentioned—"

"I'm sorry. Who? I do not know anyone by that name."

Neil paused. Something was going on here. "My mistake."

"It's not a problem. How can I help?"

"I'm trying to understand how the whole disaster recovery process works," Neil said. "I've seen video clips on television, of course, and all the fundraising appeals. But what happens after the TV crews leave? I'm interested in the private–public sector aspects."

"Well, as you can appreciate, it is a complex collaboration that brings together humanity worldwide to help families and children who find themselves—through no fault of their own—in desperate, life-threatening situations." With practised ease, Junkaya slipped into what Neil recognized as a standard pitch. "It involves organizations like ourselves, nations, private citizens and companies of all sizes—"

"Let me be more specific," Neil interrupted. "Have you heard of Grupo Muxia?"

Junkaya paused and nodded guardedly.

"And Hudson Ventures?" Neil asked. "The Launchpad Fund?"

The bureaucrat said nothing. Neil sensed the force of Junkaya's intelligence. The moments stretched in silence. Junkaya looked at his watch and stood up.

"Where are my manners?" he said. "It is lunchtime. Will you join me?"

"Thank you," Neil said, without missing a beat. "What a good idea."

"I will just get my coat and meet you at reception," Junkaya said, ushering Neil to the door. "I know a nice place quite close by."

42

Times Square was at its carnival best. Steamy, sticky, full of wide-eyed tourists, buskers and hustlers. A fat Midwestern couple in sensible shoes grinned hugely as they posed for a picture with the famous Naked Cowboy. They were having a ball in the hot afternoon sun.

Isabelle watched it all through the tinted glass of her air-conditioned Bentley. She was headed for Teterboro Airport. The plane's takeoff slot was booked. She needed to wrap up her phone call before hitting the Lincoln Tunnel and losing the signal.

"I'm not a micromanager," she said. "When I put someone in a job, as long as they deliver, I give them a lot of leeway. Perhaps with him I should have known better. Like that old story about the scorpion that stung the frog halfway across the river. You know the one?"

She paused, listening. "Yes, I know. In the story, they both died. We would both prefer a different ending."

Another pause. Her grip tightened on the phone. "What did you do?"

A double beep sounded from the phone. Isabelle checked

the screen, recognized the number, then put the phone back to her ear.

"I have to go. There's another call. But you should have checked with me first."

The limo eased into the Ninth Avenue intersection. The tunnel was just a few blocks away.

"Leave it with me. I'll take care of it," she said, her lips tightening. "I'm beginning to suspect I need a whole new management team."

Isabelle ended the call. She stared at the phone, gathering her thoughts before answering the other call. What was the play here?

She leaned forward and gave her driver new instructions.

43

The tall trees of Bryant Park shaded a scattering of small round tables with metal bistro chairs. It was an urban oasis where people could eat takeout food or just sit as long as they wanted. When Neil and Junkaya arrived, it was crowded with the usual lunchtime mix of office workers and tourists. There were enough uniformed cops circulating to keep the street people on their best behaviour.

They scored a table where they could talk without fear of being overheard. They opened the Styrofoam clamshells and paper-wrapped lunches they had bought from a food truck on Forty-Second Street.

"Mr. Junkaya—" Neil began.

"Please call me Selim."

"Why are we here? Are you afraid your office is bugged?"

He shrugged. "Before I say anything, I need to know—why did you ask about those companies?"

"A woman was killed a few nights ago, and yesterday a man was murdered. Both were connected to Hudson Ventures and possibly Grupo Muxia."

"I see." Selim studied Neil's face as if carefully weighing

how much he should say. After a moment, he nodded to himself. He had agreed to meet Neil. He had a story to tell.

He hunched over, rested his elbows on his knees and leaned closer. "Grupo Muxia wins contracts for post-disaster reconstruction projects all over the world. Their proposals always stress the number of local jobs they will create. Their practice, however, is to provide generous consulting contracts to a handful of local advisors, many of whom are close relatives of government officials. We have concluded that is the situation right now in Haiti. Just this morning, I received word that our project engineer was murdered."

"And why do you suspect Grupo Muxia was involved?"

"Zhang Jie discovered that Grupo Muxia had received millions of dollars as payment for rebuilding a neighbourhood destroyed by earthquakes. They had done no work. Zhang told people in the office he was meeting with company representatives at the project site. He never returned. We found his body lying in a ditch by the side of the road. A pack of feral dogs had already gotten to it."

"You reported this to the police?"

"They say Zhang was robbed and killed by thieves."

"So, the case is closed already? That was fast."

Selim flashed a brief, cynical smile. "At least this time they bothered to show up."

"And the Grupo Muxia representatives?"

"Long gone. A private jet."

"Do you know their names?"

Selim nodded. "They were in Zhang's meeting calendar. Louis Brisbane, Grupo Muxia's VP for the Caribbean, flew in just for the meeting. He brought a female assistant with him, but we do not know her name."

Neil made notes on his phone. "Do you have descriptions?"

"I can get them for you."

"Good." Neil slipped his phone back into his pocket. "I'm sorry for your loss. The engineer—did you know him?"

Selim nodded. "I interviewed him for the post. He came from a wealthy and respected family. I informed them myself. They are devastated. He was the oldest son."

Selim finished his lunch and scrunched up the paper.

Neil looked around, considering the options. "This is not your first run-in with Grupo Muxia. If the local police won't do anything, what about Interpol? Or the UN?"

"They claim they don't have the jurisdiction, but the truth is they lack the political will to get involved," Selim said. "They simply have other priorities." He looked weary, as if he had seen this same scenario play out too many times. Beneath Selim's bone-deep fatigue, Neil could sense the man's anger, and it was growing.

"Some corporations are getting rich off the suffering of people caught up in bad situations. They loot smaller countries, gain control of the politicians, then impose everything from unfair trade agreements to rigged compliance certifications and exorbitant insurance rates. They are like criminal gangs that terrorize a community, then charge protection fees. They are economic gangsters."

Selim stopped himself and looked slightly embarrassed. "Sorry for the rant. You seem to be a good man. I'm afraid you opened a floodgate."

"So—what can be done about Grupo Muxia? Are they vulnerable?"

His glance measured Neil. "There might be a way."

"How?"

Selim reached into his pocket and pulled out a flash drive. He held it in the palm of his hand.

"Follow the money. Isn't that what they say on television?

A few months ago, we...*acquired*...these Grupo Muxia files and have been holding on to them for the right moment."

Neil looked at the flash drive. So small. So much power.

Selim continued. "All project financing and payments, including the bribes, were processed through a network of banks, all controlled by a single company, that stretches throughout La Francophonie."

"I understood La Francophonie focused on cultural and scientific exchanges."

"That's true, but it provides Grupo Muxia with cover for a corrupt network spanning North and South America, the Caribbean, Europe, Africa, the Middle East and Southeast Asia."

"You're describing a massive financial conspiracy."

Selim nodded.

"And no one knows about this?"

"These are small, Third World countries. Who cares?"

Neil looked at the flash drive. This was more than he'd hoped for. "You have bank records that link Grupo Muxia to all this?"

"Even more. Copies of the corporate registries behind the shell companies. It shows who controls Grupo Muxia."

"You mean MacklinMunroe."

Selim shook his head. "MacklinMunroe is owned by Bala Bay Financial."

Neil was stunned.

Selim dropped the flash drive in Neil's hand. "I don't need to tell you to be careful with this information. Enough people have died."

Neil watched him walk away, a thousand thoughts pinballing across his mind.

Isabelle?

The implications were enormous. A global cyberlaundry

controlled by a woman with prime ministers and presidents on speed dial.

A woman who now owned the encryption software used by police, intelligence services, banks and major corporations worldwide.

If Selim was right, Isabelle Lisgar ruled a criminal network, with tentacles reaching into secret areas, that put entire countries at risk.

And Rachel had stumbled across this.

That explained the extraordinary reaction in her notes when she uncovered the name *MacklinMunroe*, the string of *fuckfuckfuckfuckfuck* that filled the screen.

He kinda felt the same way.

44

Carole looked down from her hotel room window, not seeing the people on the sidewalks or the yellow cabs jammed up in traffic. She was concentrating, keeping her anger shoved down into a box.

At first, she focused on how to destroy Peter Lattimer. The trick was to do it without creating any blowback on the Party. It had to be quiet, private. Delicious.

But a cool warning whispered up from the ancient lizard brain lurking at the back of the neck where the hairs rise for no good reason except...

What had made Lattimer overreact? Was it a petty impulse? Or calculated? Was he testing his strength? In every political party, factions wax and wane. Lattimer's brand of buccaneering, highly partisan, dog-whistle politics gained traction with every poll. The fight would be down and dirty. Maybe it was time to let it go.

Walk away, but not with her tail between her legs.

On her own terms. Her reputation intact.

And the countdown had started. The first one to get their side of the story to the right people usually won. She needed to act fast. But she needed to be strategic.

Where the hell was Isabelle when she needed her? All her life, Isabelle had been her mentor, her advisor, the one person she could rely on to watch her back.

Was that still the case? The fact that she was asking herself the question was in itself disquieting. She sensed hidden agendas, like people in distant rooms preparing threatening moves against her.

It sounded foolish, even to her, but she couldn't shake the unease.

Her phone buzzed. She checked the caller ID. Finally.

"Did you hear what Lattimer is trying to pull?" Carole began to pace. "We can't let him get away with it. We need to—"

"What you need is to calm down." Isabelle's cold, clipped voice was like a slap in the face. "Get packed. I'm in the car, on my way to the airport. I'll swing by and pick you up."

Surprised, Carole stopped pacing. "No, no. I've got calls to make. I need to control the narrative. I need you to—"

"Your job was to keep an eye on Lattimer. You disappeared for three hours."

"What are you talking about? There were no meetings scheduled. Lattimer reserved it as personal time. He was supposed to be picking out new suits at Barneys. Santiago might have had information about Rachel's—"

"Enough! Whatever your sister got herself mixed up with, you don't want any part of it. It got her killed. And it put Paul in the hospital."

"What are you saying? I can't—"

"Ten minutes. Be in the lobby. Don't let me down."

Confused, Carole stared at the now-silent phone.

What was going on? Could Isabelle be right? Had she really fucked up?

45

Neil hunched over his laptop at a back table in a coffee shop across from Bryant Park. His coffee grew cold as he scrolled through Selim's flash drive.

It was all there. Just as promised.

Fractured, split up into dozens of folders. Fragments from sources around the world. Files hacked from lawyers in Panama and bankers in Lichtenstein, the Caymans, Singapore and beyond.

If these files were accurate, if they had not been doctored, then the facts were clear.

One: Isabelle Lisgar, through Bala Bay Financial, controlled both Grupo Muxia and Hudson Ventures.

Two: Paolo Santiago would not have ordered the death of Rachel, his boss's niece, without Isabelle's okay.

Three: Rachel's death, coming as it did after she identified the link between Hudson Ventures and Grupo Muxia, could be laid at the feet of Isabelle Lisgar.

The big problem was the files' sketchy provenance made them inadmissible in any courtroom.

An email notification popped up from Don. The content

added one more piece of evidence. He had traced the mysterious phone call Rachel had placed after her meeting with Howland through Bosnia to a mobile phone registered to a Waterloo tech company that had been acquired last year by Bala Bay Financial.

What were the chances the phone belonged to Isabelle?

If so, it proved that Rachel had called Isabelle. Would she have declared her intention to take down both Hudson Ventures and Grupo Muxia?

Given what he'd discovered about Rachel, Neil could see her doing just that.

Isabelle would be disgraced and possibly end up in jail or broke or both. She would never stand for that.

Anyone who threatened to crack the veneer of respectability around Bala Bay took their life in their hands.

Neil suddenly thought of Carole. How much did she know? How much had he told her? What had she mentioned to Isabelle?

What if Carole became a threat?

Neil snatched up his phone. The call went straight to voice mail. He left her a message. "I have some files you need to look at. There's information you need to see for yourself. Call me. It's important."

He had barely put the phone down when it rang again.

"Carole?"

"Sorry, it's your friendly neighbourhood FBI." Ali Gorka's raspy voice snapped him back to the present reality.

"Hey, Gorka. What's up?"

"We may have a lead on last night's shooter. I just sent you a photo array. Take a look and give me a call."

He caught her before she could break the connection.

"Hold on. We were asking who really controls Grupo Muxia. I might have some info—"

"You might? What—"

"The source is...questionable. Probably wouldn't stand up in court."

"Who cares? We'll deal with the legal shit later." Excitement caused her voice to speed up. "Can you send it to me? Like, right now?"

Neil hesitated. He didn't want to hand Selim's files directly to the FBI. Who knows what their computer nerds would be able to track back through the metadata and other bits of code? He needed to buy enough time to check it with Don. "The file's too big to email," he lied. "I'll make a copy and get it to you this afternoon."

"I can send someone—"

"Your photo array just arrived." The perfect distraction. "Let me open it."

The photo lineup filled his screen. Headshots of eight females, a mix of passport and DMV photos, all white, mid- to late thirties, slender builds. But there were differences. Three he ruled out immediately. The faces were too round. Another two looked like junkies. Another two were just wrong.

"And we have a winner. Number six. Who is she?"

"Number six? You're sure?"

"Not a hundred per cent. I was scrambling there, trying to drag Collacchi out of the way."

"But you're pretty sure? On a scale of one to ten, what would you say?"

"Eight and a half?"

"That's close enough."

"Who is she?"

"Karin Reichelt, Norwegian, ex–special forces. Now in private security."

"Any idea who she's working for?"

"One of the big contractors included her in a bunch of security clearance requests. We'll follow up."

"You have an address for her?"

"That would be too easy. We also spotted her outside Howland's office building."

"Weren't the security cameras down?"

"We got lucky with a traffic cam," Ali said, practically bursting with happiness. "This is great. It's real progress. And you'll get those files to me?"

"Absolutely. By the end of the day."

"As soon as you can. God! I don't want to jinx anything, but we may finally be getting momentum on this thing. Stay in touch." And she was gone.

Neil emailed Selim's files to Don and asked him to scrub the metadata, then return the files asap. All the while, he was growing restless.

What was happening with Carole?

He checked his voice mail. Nothing. That wasn't good. Neil signalled a server for his bill. While they got it together, he had time for one more fast call.

From his contacts, he pulled up the number for Joanne Reynolds.

"So, how's New York treating you?" She sounded stressed. He was sorry he had to add to it.

"A little rough. Stephen Howland's dead—"

"What? When?"

"Yesterday. That's not all."

Neil quickly filled her in on Howland's murder, Collacchi's near death and the mounting evidence that Isabelle Lisgar controlled Grupo Muxia. She had a ton of questions, but he overrode them all.

"Isabelle's playing both sides of the street. She uses her AML consulting business as a Trojan horse to gain behind-the-firewall access to the computer systems of banks, insurance companies, development agencies, you name it. Through these connections, she gets credibility and connections with financial intelligence networks at the OECD, the World Bank, among the G7—basically, anywhere she wants it."

Joanne was silent as she worked through the implications. "This is not good."

Neil grunted in agreement. "Basically, her reputation as an AML champion masks a banker for the bad guys."

Joanne made the intuitive leap. "And she now owns the ICE cybersecurity suite." Unconsciously, she whistled. "The security services are not going to be happy."

"Sorry to be the bearer of bad news."

"Thanks," Joanne said dryly. "Speaking of bad news, you must be stepping on someone's toes."

"Why? What's happening?"

"I heard that the RCMP is being pressured to trash your reputation with the FBI."

Neil grunted. "I can guess who's behind it."

"It's political, coming straight from the Langevin Block."

"What a surprise."

"You watch out."

"Always. I gotta go."

"Wait! One more thing. After our conversation the other day about Isabelle Lisgar, something rang a bell. It took me a while to remember. The death of her brother Thomas. There were some questions about it. One of the investigators floated the idea that Isabelle needed a closer look."

"Interesting. And...?"

"Nothing came of it, but I thought you should know."

"To tell you the truth, nothing would surprise me. You stay safe. Who knows where this will end."

He cut the connection and sat back.

Carole—what was happening to her? And why did he care so much?

He tried her phone one last time.

Again, it went straight to voice mail. He left a message.

"I'm only a few blocks from your hotel. I'm going to take a chance that you're there. If you are, stay put. I'll be over in less than ten minutes."

46

Carole pushed through the revolving doors of the Four Seasons Hotel into a scene of traffic chaos that fit her frame of mind.

As she stopped under the canopy with her carry-on bag, a tour bus unloaded a gaggle of white-haired seniors, all wearing matching red T-shirts. Hotel porters descended on their luggage, whisking it inside. Across the street, an armoured truck blocked the lane, one rear door open, a uniformed guard standing watch, his hand gripping a holstered pistol.

Outwardly, she looked like a polished executive in chic sunglasses with everything under control. Inside, a hurricane raged. Through sheer tenacity, she held her position in the calm eye of the storm. Anger with Lattimer, worry about Paul, mistrust of Santiago and, yes, stirrings of grief over Rachel. All took a back seat to her frustration with Isabelle. What game was she playing?

Isabelle's Bentley edged around the bus and pulled to the curb. Carole crossed the sidewalk as the rear door opened.

"What the hell is going on?" she asked, her voice low and urgent.

Isabelle's glare was cold. "If we move quickly, we might be able to save a shred of your reputation."

Carole stopped as if she'd run into a wall. "What? Are you saying I should let Lattimer get away with this?"

Isabelle scoffed. "Grow up. You think the Party owes you something? Now it's your turn to collect?"

"You're damn right."

"Even when no one will return your calls? Lattimer will be prime minister within the year. People are lining up to jump on his bandwagon. You don't stand a chance. Get in the car."

Carole stood rooted to the sidewalk. The sense of betrayal left her at a loss for words.

Isabelle beckoned her from the back seat with a wave of her hand. "Come. It may be too late, but I'll see what I can do."

Carole didn't move.

She heard someone in the distance yell "Wait!"

She looked up. It was Neil. He was waving from across the street. For some reason, her heart lifted.

He dodged between the armoured car and a yellow cab.

"Get in," Isabelle repeated. "The plane is waiting."

"Don't go," Neil called, holding up his laptop bag. "There's something you need to see."

He stopped at the car, breathing heavily from his race to the hotel. "New evidence. Corporate registries. Isabelle controls both Grupo Muxia and Hudson Ventures through MacklinMunroe."

Carole took an involuntary step back from the limo. "Is that true?"

"No," Isabelle said coldly. "Not a word of it."

Dazed, Carole looked from Isabelle to Neil.

"Rachel discovered the connection just before she died."

"He's lying," Isabelle stated, looking directly at Carole. "Remember, this is the guy who planted those phony emails. He's doing it again."

Neil ignored the jibe. "Before exposing everything, Rachel wanted to make sure she was right. That's why she called Isabelle."

"That's idiotic," Isabelle said dismissively. "I haven't talked to Rachel in years."

"She recognized the company name, MacklinMunroe, in Howland's files. As soon as her plane landed, she called a number. Why don't I try it?" Neil held out his phone so Carole could watch him tap in the number.

"You're wasting our time." Isabelle was growing exasperated. "Come, Carole, let's—"

Isabelle's phone rang.

"Are you going to answer that?"

"My phone rings all the time," Isabelle explained impatiently. "That's why God invented voice mail."

"Prove me wrong," Neil said. "Answer the phone."

"I'm not playing games with you."

"Sure you are," said Neil. "It's what you do best."

"You had one close call," Isabelle said softly to Neil, the threat clear. "Don't risk another."

"Call your smartest lawyer. Cut a deal while you still can," Neil countered. "Don't go down the drain with Santiago and his friends."

"Speaking of friends, what about your friend Joanne Reynolds? It would be a shame if she lost her job, what with her daughter needing such expensive, special care."

Neil stepped forward, towering over her. "That's a line you don't want to cross."

Carole watched Isabelle's face harden. Dead eyes. Set jaw. Not a hint of emotion.

"The plane is waiting. Get in the car," Isabelle commanded. "Now."

"Don't do it," Neil warned.

Carole suddenly realized with crystal clarity that Isabelle was here not to help her but to clean up a problem. And she was the problem. Never had she felt more alone.

She watched as Neil leaned in closer to Isabelle. "What are you going to do? Send Santiago's thugs after me? After us? Just like you did with Rachel? Maybe just like you did all those years ago with Thomas?"

Shocked, Carole could barely get her mind around it. What was he talking about? Her father? Isabelle was involved in her father's death?

"I don't have time for this." Isabelle closed the car door with a solid, uncompromising *thunk* that resonated in Carole's soul like a body blow. Only by tightly clutching the upright handle of her luggage did Carole save herself from falling to her knees.

The black Bentley pulled away from the curb, merging smoothly with midtown traffic, heading for the airport.

Everything was suddenly bright and brittle. The gritty New York sidewalk tilted. The doorman pushed a trolley stacked with more luggage. Nearby, Chinese tourists took selfies of themselves in front of the hotel. A homeless old woman pulled a bundle buggy overflowing with everything she owned.

Carole's world had been ripped apart. Isabelle had been her mentor, her protector, her closest confidante. It was a heartbreakingly immense betrayal. *And what happens now?*

"Let's get out of here."

She saw concern in Neil's eyes.

"What you said about my dad. Was that true?"

"Yeah, there was some suspicion at the time."

"But no proof? No real evidence?" She searched his face for the truth.

"Not enough to act on."

Disjointedly, Carole watched the street swirl in front of her eyes—the well-dressed tourists, the impressive buildings and the limos inching along Fifty-Seventh Street. Without looking at him, she spoke softly, almost to herself.

"What the hell just happened? Why do I feel, all of a sudden, like everything is gone?"

"It's the shock," Neil said. "It will pass." For a moment, he watched her wrestle with the enormity of the revelations, then cleared his throat. "By telling you about the new evidence, I'm afraid I've put you in danger."

"Sooner or later, I might have figured it out on my own."

"I couldn't let you get into that car. You wouldn't have been safe."

"You believe she was responsible for Rachel's murder, don't you?" She straightened her shoulders.

"Yeah," he said. "Even though we may never be able to prove it."

"We have to try." She looked at him bleakly. "I will not live the rest of my life thinking that Isabelle was responsible for my sister's murder and knowing that I did nothing about it."

"You know her better than most. She will come after you."

"Do I have a choice? The cost of doing nothing would be unbearable."

"Then, let's get back to Toronto," Neil said. "We'll figure out something."

47

They came together in the conference room of Janos Pach's townhouse offices on Charles Street East.

It had been a long day. On the way to the meeting, Neil detoured by his house to drop off his suitcase and pick up a pistol. Carole booked into a hotel. Tomorrow or the next day, she would return to her Ottawa condo and piece together whatever remained of her life.

"Isabelle Lisgar needs to be stopped, and I'm fresh out of ideas," Neil stated, looking around the table.

Janos seemed more reserved than usual but still quietly in command. Ali Gorka had flown up to represent the FBI's interests. She sat beside Danny Relf and compared case notes. A few minutes earlier, Joanne Reynolds had sailed in with a big, old-friends smile for Janos. A tall guy, at least six foot four, slipped in behind her. He was bald, with a broad forehead, thin lips and deep-set, watchful eyes that scanned the room before settling on Neil.

Tom Llewelyn had risen in the RCMP ranks since Neil had left the force. Over the years, their paths had crossed. They had never worked together directly, never had any major conflicts, but a mutually wary uneasiness tainted the air whenever they met. Llewelyn was a bit of a cipher, occasionally spotted at the back of the room during high level anti-terrorism conferences or at parliamentary committee hearings whispering in the ear of the minister of public safety. Now, according to Joanne, he was RCMP liaison with the Five Eyes security alliance.

Neil summarized how Rachel's discovery of a global cyberlaundry had led to her murder, the killing of Stephen Howland and the shooting of Paul Collacchi. Through it all, Janos maintained a stoic expression.

"Isabelle Lisgar's got pit-bull lawyers, the PM on speed dial and a private jet," Danny Relf said with a helpless gesture. "We have no witnesses, no physical evidence and no legally acquired digital files—nothing I can take to the crown attorney."

He opened a file folder. "Canadian Border Services used the FBI photo of Reichelt to search their records. She landed at Billy Bishop Airport in a private jet two hours before Rachel Lisgar's flight arrived. She was travelling with Louis Brisbane, a consultant, former US Army Rangers. Both work for Echelon Security Systems."

"Echelon provided security for both Hudson Ventures and Grupo Muxia," Neil said, glancing over at Ali, who nodded in confirmation.

"Why am I not surprised?" Relf made a note. "Canadian Border Services has them flying out later that evening—"

"They cleared US Customs at Teterboro Airport at eight twenty-seven that evening," Ali Gorka confirmed.

"That puts them in Toronto at the time Rachel was killed," Relf said, "but it's not enough."

Janos said, "Did not a witness identify Karin Reichelt as the Serbian's killer—"

"She was wearing a bike helmet and sunglasses," Relf interrupted. "Any good defence lawyer would tear that apart. Besides, we have no proof of a connection between Reichelt and Lisgar. What else do we have? Some hacked corporate files that allegedly link Isabelle Lisgar to offshore companies suspected of money laundering and other criminal activities."

"What if I—" Neil stopped, then started again. "Hypothetically, what if those files were anonymously posted online? Possibly through something like WikiLeaks?"

"Could we use that to get search warrants? Not without hard evidence to back them up."

"There must be a loose thread we can pull," Joanne said, concern in her eyes. "She'll soon control the encryption algorithms used by banks, blue-chip companies and security services."

"And next week, she'll be appointed Canada's representative on the International Financial Intelligence Alliance," Llewelyn added. "We can't allow her to hold a digital key to the national secrets of Canada, the US, the UK, Australia and New Zealand. That would be a disaster."

"If we're going to stop her, there's not much time," Carole warned. "She's in town tonight, but Isabelle has meetings in Beijing and Singapore. She's flying out tomorrow."

A gloomy silence settled around the table. Relf absently tapped his pen. Joanne stared at the ceiling, lost in thought. Carole had her eyes locked on Llewelyn.

Janos turned to Carole. "You understand Isabelle better than any of us. Is there anything you think we should be aware of?"

She cleared her throat. "Isabelle must be stopped. No question about it. But we need to be careful. When she's arrested, there will be market impacts, particularly on the legitimate businesses that make up the bulk of Bala Bay operations. Many of the subsidiaries are publicly held companies. Share prices are fragile, especially these days. If there are messy, public headlines, hundreds, possibly thousands of people will be thrown out of work."

"She is right," Janos said. "The value of pension investments in Bala Bay Financial would be gutted."

"The trick will be to take down Isabelle Lisgar but keep the money laundering angle out of the story," Joanne added. "Canadian financial services have a global reputation for integrity."

"Whether or not they deserve it," Neil muttered.

"Like it or not, that reputation is a hugely valuable business asset," Joanne snapped. "It's worth billions. Bala Bay Financial sets the global gold standard for providing AML compliance services. Its exposure as a cyberlaundry would do irreparable harm to the international reputation of all Canadian financial services—"

"Including your own Northern Bank?"

"We are partners with Bala Bay Financial in several ventures," Joanne admitted, "but that's not my point."

"No?"

"This is about strategy," she said patiently, her backroom savvy showing through. "What happens to Isabelle, ultimately, will not be decided by the handful of us in this room. We all have bosses."

Neil snapped. "I don't—"

"Sure you do," Relf countered, nodding at Janos.

"You want important people to support you," Joanne continued, "you need to show them you're protecting their interests. Otherwise, you're screwed."

Silence descended on the room but was broken by Ali Gorka. "If you could connect her directly to Grupo Muxia, I could try for a material witness warrant." She didn't sound optimistic.

Neil's frustration was growing. "Do I smell one of those *nolo contendere* deals cooking here? You know, *We didn't do anything but promise to never do it again*? Pay a fine, and all is forgiven?"

Joanne leaned back. "Nobody's suggesting that."

"Yet," Neil scoffed.

"Let us focus on items on which we agree," Janos broke in, his calm tone cooling down the emotions. "We all agree Isabelle cannot be allowed to walk away from this."

"We need more intel, and we need it fast," Llewelyn said. "Let's put her under the microscope."

"What do you have in mind?" Relf asked.

"Bala Bay's acquisition of ICE Technology should be enough to trigger a national security review, which we can leverage to get warrants for wiretaps and start surveillance. I suggest a coordinated blitz. I can bring specialists on board—digital forensics, international liaison—whatever we need. Meanwhile, we leave her in place."

"We don't have time," Neil protested. "She already knows we're after her. She'll burn files and create smokescreens."

He looked around for support. Relf had nothing to add. Joanne shook her head. Ali Gorka shrugged sympathetically.

"I'm only talking about a few days," Llewelyn said.

Neil checked with Janos. "Is this really what you want?"

Janos nodded. "Thanks to you, we are closer to the truth than we were four days ago."

"But—"

Carole touched Neil's arm, a gesture that didn't escape Joanne.

"Let them go ahead," Carole whispered. "Who knows? They might find evidence that can stand up in court."

"Neil has brought us this far," Janos stated. "He should be part of the conclusion. That is, if he wants it."

"Yeah, I want to see it through, no matter how it turns out." He gestured to Carole. "Just by sitting at this table, she's put her life at risk. She needs protection."

Carole shook her head. "No, I'll be fine. From here, I'm heading straight back to my hotel."

"Isabelle's a killer. You being family doesn't matter. She can still get to you."

"No police," she stated flatly. There was no give in her voice. "I haven't had a moment alone for days. The last thing I need is to be babysat by a couple of big guys in body armour." She looked across the table. "No offence, Danny."

"None taken, but you really should reconsider. At least for the next twenty-four hours. Then see where things stand."

"How about private security?" Janos offered. "I can have Securitec personal protection for you whenever you want it. They can be discreet."

Reluctantly, she agreed. "They can meet me at the hotel."

Neil was relieved. He worried that Carole, in her heart, might not be willing to believe Isabelle was capable of murder.

In his world, not facing reality could get you killed.

48

The hot, sticky night air on Charles Street East offered little relief from the tensions of the conference room.

"It's not enough to know why Rachel died and who ordered it," Neil said. He stretched his back muscles. "That old saying? *The truth shall set you free*? Well, I'm not feeling it."

"Let's walk," Carole replied. "I need to clear my head."

Side by side, they made their way towards Church Street. Labour Day weekend was coming up, marking the end of summer. A turning point in the year.

"She'll run rings around them," Carole said. "I'd say she was laughing at them, but I doubt she's paying much attention at all."

"I brought the wrong people to the table," he said. "Everybody played it safe."

Following her own train of thoughts, Carole said, "I can't believe I let Isabelle make such a fool of me."

"What do you mean?"

"I thought her opposition to the EU directive was PR bullshit to attract rich clients. I was wrong. She was afraid the capital reporting requirements would expose her cyber-laundry."

Neil glanced at her, curiosity in his eyes. "She was grooming you to take over?"

"That's what she told people. Was it true? Who knows? One thing's for sure. It's not going to happen now. If she survives this, Isabelle will lock me out."

"I'm worried she'll do more than that."

She stopped abruptly and turned to him. "We need to attack, put her on the defensive. Let's leak it to the media. We'll throw her into the public spotlight. Paul Collacchi has a lot of journalist friends. I could reach out to them and plant the story."

"What about the need to tread cautiously?" Neil objected, discouraged. "Besides, with that private jet, she could be out of our reach within a few hours."

"Okay, how about this?" Carole responded. "I've got a lot of contacts and allies within both the PC Party and Bala Bay Financial. I can ask questions, start a few rumours. There's a chance someone would turn on her."

"It's risky." He rubbed both hands across his face. "My brain is mush."

"You and me both," she said. They reached the corner of Church Street. Traffic was steady, some cars heading south to the bars in the gay village, others north to Bloor Street shopping. "I think I'll go back to my hotel."

"Hold on." Neil looked around. There was no one nearby. He pulled out his pistol. "You know how to use one of these?"

"Are you kidding?" She took it from him and cradled it in her hand. It was warm from his body and lighter than she expected. She could smell a slight tang of gun oil. "You're looking at the Camp Madawaska Olympics gold medal winner, three summers in a row."

"Aren't you just full of surprises."

"Target shooting, .22 calibre." She passed it back to him. "If you're thinking of lending it to me, no thanks."

"You need to take this seriously."

"I do," Carole insisted. "That's what bodyguards are for." She shook her head wearily. "I can't believe things are so screwed up that I need to be surrounded by people with guns."

She spotted a cab, raised her hand and flagged it down. The cab rolled to a stop. She opened the rear door and paused. "Listen, no matter what happens, I appreciate what you've done. Because of you, I learned some truths. So, thanks."

He tilted his head. "What's that all about?"

She slid into the cab.

He held on to the door. "A friend of mine's got this gig tonight. Want to come along? Guaranteed to take your mind off all this."

"It's been a long day," she said gently. "I've been going back and forth with the with lawyers about Rachel's estate and I'm meeting with them in the morning to sign some papers. I have things to do tonight. How about breakfast?"

"You got it." He watched the cab roll into the night, feeling he should do more, not knowing what it could be.

He needed a drink.

49

The Round Room at The Carlu glittered with art deco elegance, from the domed ceiling and massive Lalique chandelier down to the intricate mosaic floor, all of which reassured the two hundred carefully selected dinner guests that they were part of the right crowd.

Each guest had been personally invited by Conservative Party bagmen. They were here to mix, mingle and cough up a minimum of ten thousand dollars each to fund the election campaign of Peter Lattimer, minister of finance and—rumour had it—future prime minister of Canada.

Isabelle swept in, radiating genteel charisma and velvet-gloved power. She greeted a Calgary oil baron with a conspiratorial smile, congratulating him on a deal he had just closed in Senegal. An aging senator from New Brunswick got a whispered compliment about his new young wife. It made him blush and beam. She sailed through the crowd, measuring the players, seeing no real A-listers but a lot of hungry B-listers and a few ambitious in-betweeners. Lattimer should make out okay, as she'd planned.

The room buzzed. Servers proffered trays of exquisite

hors d'oeuvres. The smoked Arctic char tartlets were a big hit. A Grammy-winning jazz trio played on the small bandstand. This was her playing field. By God, she loved the game!

Her glow dimmed fractionally when Jack O'Connell, the minister's wingman, sidled up. "He wants to see you."

"Of course. Shall we say ten min—"

"Now." Behind a barely disguised smirk, his tone pre-empted any excuse.

"Where is he?" she asked evenly. O'Connell had just unwittingly changed category from Unimportant Hanger-on to Future Roadkill. She would remember.

"The Clipper Room." He gestured to an unassuming door, which led to one of the private meeting rooms. "He's on a tight schedule. I suggest you don't make the minister wait."

Isabelle brushed by O'Connell. Standing just outside the door, Cal Sturman nodded to her as she passed.

Inside the room, the minister was going over speaking notes prepared by his constituency assistants, mainly shout-outs to major donors in the crowd. He looked up when Isabelle entered. The party hubbub died as she closed the door behind her.

"Excellent media coverage of your trip in both the *Globe* and the *National Post*," she said. "Congratulations."

"That's the last time I'll be your hatchetman," he growled. "You want somebody fired, do it yourself."

"Don't worry about Carole," she counselled him. "I'll make sure she behaves."

"And what the fuck have you got me into with this guy Santiago? She was right, wasn't she? I'm on some FBI surveillance video?"

"So are a number of ambassadors and Fortune 500 CEOs," she countered. "What's the problem? You wanted to meet people, you said. Real movers and shakers."

"He's a fucking criminal!"

"Some of the best people are under indictment in one country or another," she said sharply. "You want to play with the big boys, you play by big-boy rules."

"And that means what, exactly?"

"Peter, you're good with people. You could be useful to me. You could make a lot of money, but you have to learn to roll with things."

"We can't afford a scandal this close to the election." He stepped closer and loomed over her. "If this thing breaks—"

"Don't embarrass yourself," she retorted. "You think the FBI video is a problem? Did you realize that Paolo has security cams in every room of that house?"

He stared at her, his lips thinning.

"I guess not." She laughed. "You look good. In fact, you look, well, ecstatic. And no wonder!" The smile stayed fixed, but her voice hardened. "There's a little bit of coke on your upper lip and two blondes taking turns sucking your dick."

"You wouldn't dare—"

"He sent me a link," she replied. "Would you like me to forward it to you? Or anyone else?"

His fists clenched, but he said nothing. Isabelle saw the defeat in his eyes.

She smiled sweetly. "You will make a wonderful prime minister for the country—and for me."

She straightened his tie, patted him on the chest and walked out. As she closed the door behind her, she nodded to Cal Sturman.

"Lovely event, isn't it, Cal?" She wondered how much, if anything, he had overheard.

Something to think about.

50

Neil walked the back streets, ending up on St. Patrick, so tired he was dragging his ass every step. Even though he'd made a promise to Don and Moni, he wasn't sure he would make it to the gig until he walked through the side door of the old Ace Hotel.

The building showed every one of its hundred-plus years. The so-called dining room was two notches above a dive bar.

Tonight, the place was jammed, hot and sweaty, smelling of stale beer and fried food. The band was blasting a slow blues shuffle with a nasty, dirty slide guitar solo in full flight and a thudding bass line that walked right up his spine.

It was fucking wonderful.

He craned his neck, found a spot at the bar and wedged himself in. Miracle of miracles, the bartender appeared as if by magic. She was middle-aged, with spiky black hair, tattoos and a vintage T-shirt.

"Jameson, straight up. Make it a double. And a Blue."

She executed a perfect five-second ballet. Grabbed an old-fashioned glass, snagged the bottle from the back bar, *glug-glug*, a half-turn and opened the cooler, popped the top off the beer, kicked shut the cooler door, plopped the glass and beer in front of Neil.

"Thanks," he marvelled, but she was already gone.

The crowd was swaying, eyes glued to the stage. He recognized a few cops from 52 Division around the corner and lawyers from the courthouse down the street. No big surprise, given it was a benefit for the family of a cop killed on the job.

He spotted Don behind his Hammond organ, sweat rolling down his face, eyes focused on the guitar player, lost in the music. Off to one side, Moni ran the soundboard. He caught her eye, waved, and she responded with a huge grin.

He tilted his head back, drank deep and felt relief bathe the marrow of his bones. He savoured the moment, noticed his shoulders ease down and his centre drop from his throat to the middle of his chest. He reached for his beer.

"Helluva band," said a voice in his ear.

It was Danny Relf, holding a Creemore lager in his hand. They saluted by clinking bottle necks.

"And a great turnout," Neil said, leaning in so he could be heard.

The crowd burst into whistles and applause as the band kicked it up a notch and segued seamlessly from "Stormy Monday Blues" into "Further On Up the Road."

"That guy Llewelyn moves fast," Relf said with an approving nod.

"What do you mean?"

"He's brought in analysts from FINTRAC. They've already uncovered hundreds of bank accounts belonging to tech start-ups acquired by Bala Bay that were supposed to be dormant."

"Let me guess. Offshore wire transfers. Lots of them."

"Most of them traced to a back-office operation in the Philippines."

So what? Neil thought but didn't want to say. "Every little bit helps."

"Hey, things are moving in the right direction. A few days ago, we didn't have a clue. Now we're closing in on her."

"A cop and an optimist. My friend, you're a rare bird." Neil drained his beer. "And, on that positive note, I'm outta here."

"What's the rush? You saved us from screwing up that case. Let me buy you a drink."

"Thanks, but I'm totally beat, and tomorrow looks like a long day."

He edged through the crowd, managing to snag Don's attention along the way. He gave him a thumbs-up and got a big, snappy salute in return that kept him laughing until he was out the door and onto the street.

51

Carole sipped a takeout coffee from Tim Hortons as she stood in a doorway of College Park. It gave her something to focus on other than the jumble of anger and disbelief fighting round and round in her brain. Upstairs in The Carlu, Lattimer's fundraiser was in full swing. Isabelle would exit through the revolving door behind her. She still wasn't sure what she would say.

How had it come to this? Money laundering? Murder? How had she missed the signs? Somehow, Isabelle had slid past the grey zone of what's acceptable to a place where the only goal is to win. Nothing else counts. Anything goes.

She watched a black Bentley ease to a stop on Yonge Street. The four-way flashers came on. Cars piled up behind it, horns blaring, as if that would make a difference.

"Asshole," a voice called out.

She turned. It was an old street guy, raggedy clothes, greasy hair, missing teeth. A baseball cap at his feet held a few coins.

"Just 'cos they're rich, they think they can do whatever the fuck they want," he said this in a conversational voice, knowing Carole could hear him. He glanced at her.

She said nothing. *It's not only the wealth,* she thought, *it's the sense of unlimited entitlement. Take whatever you want. Dare anyone to stop you.*

The driver climbed out of the Bentley. She had never seen this one before, but she recognized the type. Mid-thirties, cropped blond hair, a bodybuilder squeezed into a dark suit. When he came around to stand by the rear passenger door, Carole guessed Isabelle was on her way down.

The revolving door turned slowly.

Carole stepped up. "Did you know it would happen?"

Startled, Isabelle stopped on the sidewalk. "What are you—"

"I assume it was Santiago, right? He's the one who ordered Rachel's—"

Isabelle tried to step around Carole. "I'm not going to—"

Carole blocked her. "What's the matter? There's only the two of us here. Tell me."

Across the sidewalk, Isabelle's driver reacted. She held up one hand, stopping him, her eyes never leaving Carole's face.

"This is not the time—"

"And Dad's death? Did you have a hand in that?"

"Don't be stupid."

Carole's tone grew scornful. "You don't have the guts to tell me to my face."

"You want to do this here? Fine!" Isabelle snapped, her voice taut. "Pay attention. Let's see what you're made of."

Isabelle looked down at the homeless guy, knowing he was close enough to overhear, her stone-cold eyes ordering him to move away.

He stared at her defiantly, but only for a moment. His

gaze faltered, then he gathered his stuff and shuffled down the street.

Isabelle watched him go. "Dear Tommy," she said disdainfully before returning her full attention to Carole. "Your father nearly bankrupted us. He wouldn't listen to anyone. When it was my turn, you saw what happened. I rebuilt the company bigger and better than ever before. Along the way, I learned what it took to be the best in the business."

"And what was that?" Carole watched Isabelle's face. For the first time, she glimpsed a cold, remote, calculating soul and realized that was all there was. The humour, the lavish affection, the quick witticisms were merely a shell.

"My epiphany came in a hotel room in Davos. The eleventh commandment. *Thou shalt not get caught.*"

"And Rachel?"

"I put her in that ivory tower. She should have stayed there. She threatened to wreck everything."

Carole was stunned. "Did you even talk with her? Try to make a deal?"

"With Rachel? She always had that holier-than-thou attitude. It would've been a waste of my time."

"And the others? Paul? He's my friend!"

"This is our future. Ours! Yours and mine!"

"Oh, no." Carole backed away. "You're not putting this on me. I had no idea—"

"You always had did have a squeamish streak," Isabelle said, her tone belittling. "I'd hoped you would learn to be tough. I was wrong. You're weak. Just like Tommy."

And there it lay with shocking clarity.

Isabelle had the blood of family and friends on her hands, and it meant nothing.

Zero.

And in that same moment, Carole accepted something

else. In the end, this was family. The police had no chance of convicting Isabelle. The responsibility was hers.

"I guess we'll see if I'm tough enough," she said, pulling herself up straight. "With Rachel's death, I inherit her shares. I now control Bala Bay Financial."

She brushed past Isabelle and on the way said simply, "You're fired."

52

Who knew you could be grateful for the familiar smells of old wood and dust and trapped summer air?

Neil shut his front door and took in a deep breath. Home at last.

He almost stumbled as he kicked off his shoes. He paused and closed his eyes for a moment. A helluva week. Two murders, a shooting and too much time spent in airports and taxis.

He ignored the suitcase he had dropped in the living room, tossed his jacket on a chair, put his gun on the coffee table and made his way back to the kitchen.

He grabbed a beer from the fridge and took a long swallow. He rolled the icy bottle across his forehead and contemplated the biggest problem in his immediate future: what to eat. Or rather, which takeout joint to call. Thai? Italian? Given the temperature, Indian?

The doorbell rang, interrupting his thoughts.

At this time of night? Not likely a friend. Less likely a Jehovah's Witness. Maybe just ignore it?

It rang again.

Neil padded to the front door and looked through the peephole. He retreated to the living room, picked up the pistol, checked the magazine and slapped it back in place.

Rack in a round. Index finger on the trigger guard. Deep breath.

He opened the door halfway, the gun held down behind his leg.

An Asian guy stood calmly under the porch light. He was maybe sixty and slender, a hundred and forty pounds. Dark suit, short grey hair.

"Mr. Walker? I believe our interests overlap. I would like to discuss it with you."

"Could you be a little more specific?"

"I mean you no harm. You do not need the pistol."

"Glad to hear it." Neil didn't move. The old man was sharp. "It's late. What's up?"

"You are investigating a certain individual who has holdings in many countries. I have an interest in the outcome of your efforts."

"How do you know what I'm working on?"

"You came to our attention in New York, shortly after the party at the estate in the Hamptons."

Neil said nothing, prodding his visitor to say more.

"We knew of the FBI task force. After you met with them, we followed you."

Neil studied him for a minute. "And you are?"

He held out a business card. "My name is Zhang Chao."

Neil glanced at the card. Zhang was chairman and CEO of Sino Dayun.

"And what exactly does Sino Dayun do?"

"We supply seventy-three per cent of all the assault

weapons and body armour used by the Chinese army and national police force."

"An arms dealer?"

He nodded. "But that is not why I am here."

Neil opened the door wider. "You'd better come in."

They stood in the foyer.

"Thank you," Zhang said. He paused, listening for a moment, and took a quick look around to confirm they were alone. "Is it true you are continuing to investigate Isabelle Lisgar and her relationship to Grupo Muxia?"

"How do you know that?"

"Are you aware that Ms. Lisgar has meetings scheduled in Beijing?"

"What of it?"

"Your investigation might interfere with her ability to attend those meetings."

"I certainly hope so."

"That would be a mistake. I am prepared to compensate you—"

"Not interested." Neil handed the business card back.

"Please hear me out."

"You were about to offer me a bribe, right? Tell Isabelle I want to see her ass in jail." He opened the front door.

Zhang didn't move. "We want the same thing."

"Say again?"

"Would you agree it's unlikely that Isabelle Lisgar will ever be convicted in a Canadian court?"

"What are you getting at?"

"I am here with an alternative."

He studied Zhang. Was the guy trying to hustle him? He had nothing to lose by listening. "Go on."

"If you allow her to leave Canada, the moment she lands

in Beijing, she will be arrested. She will be charged with murder, fraud and corruption. She will confess to these crimes and be imprisoned. Given her age and the state of our prisons, I doubt she will last long."

Zhang stated all this as if it was a set of facts, like gravity. His absolute certainty surprised Neil. And it made him curious. "And why would the Chinese police do that? I'm sure she's guilty of all that and more, but why—"

"You showed us the way."

"How so?"

"We had begun an investigation into Grupo Muxia, specifically about a project in Haiti—"

"Zhang Jie," Neil broke in. "The engineer who was murdered."

"My son." The Asian man's face was impassive, but behind his eyes Neil saw a dangerous anger. "It was through monitoring your efforts that we came to understand that Isabelle Lisgar held ultimate responsibility for the murder of Jie."

"I'm sorry for your loss."

Zhang nodded curtly. "I ask you to step aside. Allow her to depart for Beijing. Let us take care of it. Could you do that?"

Neil thought about the slow, grinding process of surveillance and wiretaps followed by—best case scenario—long, drawn-out court proceedings. Then he pictured Isabelle, the rapacious Western businesswoman, trapped as a nameless prisoner in a communist re-education camp.

"Isabelle Lisgar has powerful friends. Possibly even in your country."

"I know how these things work," Zhang said with a confidence that spoke volumes.

Neil flicked the edge of the Sino Dayun business card. As a key weapons supplier to the Chinese government, Zhang would have powerful connections within the inner sanctums of political decision-makers.

He reached out and shook Zhang's hand.

"No promises, but I'll keep in touch."

53

The hotel room's air conditioner generated soothing white noise. The remains of a late-night snack cluttered a room-service tray on the side table. An empty courier package and legal files lay scattered over half the bed.

Carole hung up the phone, sank into a deep upholstered chair and kicked off her shoes. The conversation with Rae had gone as well as could be expected. Paul's condition was improving rapidly. An air ambulance from New York would deliver him directly to the Ottawa hospital tomorrow afternoon. At least there was that bit of good news.

She played with a business card, slowly flipping it over between her fingers as she collected her thoughts. She put it aside and picked up her cellphone, knowing he would recognize her number on his call display.

"*Buenas noches*, Señor Santiago," she said when the phone was answered. "I trust I am not calling too late."

"Not at all, señorita. I am delighted to hear from you." She heard ice cubes rattle in a glass and, in the distance, waves rolling onto the beach. "How was your flight?"

She was momentarily surprised that he knew she had left

New York, then pleased. It meant he thought there was value in having his cyberwonks track her. That was good.

"I hope we will have more time to socialize soon," Carole said, "but a business situation has come up that I wanted to discuss. Do you have a few minutes?"

"Of course. How can I be of assistance?"

"With the death of my sister, I have inherited her estate, which gives me control of Bala Bay Financial."

"I see," he said, his friendly tone becoming more businesslike.

"I have recently learned that some subsidiaries of MacklinMunroe—Hudson Ventures, Grupo Muxia, possibly others—may be involved in activities that are...shall we say...*problematic*."

"That must have come as a shock," Santiago said. She could feel him relax slightly and picture his sly grin. He would know there was a good chance the FBI was listening.

She played along. "Often, one person's problem can become another person's opportunity. I am restructuring Bala Bay Financial. Those companies no longer fit. MacklinMunroe will be spun off and sold, ideally as soon as possible. One option I'd like to explore is a management buyout."

"It's an interesting concept," Santiago responded slowly. "These assets—would they include the ICE algorithm? In today's world, estimating the market value of such advanced technology can be difficult."

"My field of expertise is Canadian politics, not computer programming," she admitted. "When it comes to technology, I must rely on others to assess the market potential."

"Another question for you. These changes you plan. How do you think existing management will respond?"

"Within Bala Bay Financial, MacklinMunroe and its subsidiaries operated as a completely separate division." She had confirmed this during earlier discussions with the lawyers. Isabelle had maintained strict silos. Executives of the mainstream businesses were not aware of the money laundering operations. "The only potential issue will be with a certain C-suite executive."

"And may I ask what your strategy is for dealing with that issue?"

"I would expect the new owners to deal with it promptly."

"Could you be more explicit?"

"It would be a condition of sale that the new owners respond effectively at the earliest possible instance."

"Respond how?"

She knew he was testing her resolve. Could she say the words? She cleared her throat.

"In the last few days, previous management executed an extreme response to resolving business issues. It would only be fitting that they now receive the same treatment."

Santiago burst into laughter.

She was silent, mystified. "Did I say something—"

"Forgive me, señorita, but you Canadians are supposed to be so nice. This whole drama falls somewhere between a Shakespearean tragedy and an afternoon telenovela."

"What do you mean?"

"Not two hours ago, I received a phone call from current management to discuss a similar initiative. The only difference was the subject. In that case, the problem to be resolved was you."

"What? She wanted—"

He laughed in delight. "All I can say is you must have royalty in your bloodline. No one else could be this treacherous."

Stunned, she simply asked, "What do you intend to do?"

"Have your lawyers send me the contracts," he answered,

still laughing. "As soon as everything's signed, I'll deal with any staffing issues."

Carole disconnected the call and powered down her phone. On the darkened screen, she caught a shadowy reflection of her face. It looked harder, her eyes a little more hollow, the lines around her mouth a little deeper.

With that one deal, no matter what happened next, her world and who she thought she was had just changed forever.

So be it.

54

The Modern Diner on Richmond near York Street specialized in all-day breakfasts. It was all you'd expect from a local mini-chain. Booth seating, lots of eggs on the menu and the smell of coffee in the air. Neil picked up someone's discarded *Globe and Mail* and slid into a booth to wait for Carole. The headline story in the business section was "US Pulls Support for EU AML Directive."

"Chalk up another one for the lobbyists," Neil said as Carole sat down opposite him.

"Let's agree to disagree, and let's change the topic," she said. "I need your help."

Neil scanned the room. "Where's your security?"

"Outside," Carole said.

"But—"

"I insisted."

The waitress arrived with a coffee pot and menus. They both knew what they wanted—omelettes, toast, black coffee—and waited for the server to leave before speaking, both at the same time.

"Last night—"

They stopped.

"Go," Carole said. He couldn't read her expression, but he had a feeling she didn't want to be first to reveal her thoughts.

"I had a visitor," Neil began. He recapped Zhang Chao's story and the Chinese government's plans to arrest Isabelle as soon as she landed in Beijing. "Not my first choice, but it's a fallback."

"She's bribed officials in half the countries in the world," she scoffed. "Why would China be any different?"

He shrugged and spread his hands. "Give me another option."

"I did a lot of thinking last night." She cleared her throat. "A press release will go out after the markets close today. I'm assuming control of Bala Bay Financial."

He sat back. "What does that mean exactly?"

"Isabelle is out. By five o'clock, her access to corporate accounts, resources, assets, records—everything—will be cut off."

"You're taking over a global criminal network? Why the hell would you want to do that?"

She shook her head. "Bala Bay will be a clean, totally legitimate company once again."

"You think you can just walk away from the money laundering operation? You honestly believe your customers will let you?"

"I'm spinning that off as a separate entity." Her voice was businesslike, but her face was pale. "I've sold it to Paolo Santiago."

"The whole thing?"

She nodded.

"What about the RCMP? The FBI? You expect they won't come after you for Bala Bay's past sins?"

"My lawyers have had a busy night," she said. "As the new

CEO, I receive total immunity for any past misdeeds of Bala Bay. All will be forgiven. In return, the RCMP gets backdoor access to Grupo Muxia, ICE Technology—the entire operation."

"Won't Santiago's techies go over the system line by line?"

"That's not my problem," she responded tightly. "*Caveat emptor*."

"And the money laundering? You're okay if it continues?"

She shrugged. "People will always try to hide assets, maybe from a husband or wife, maybe from the taxman, maybe from the courts or maybe simply because they're paranoid. It's the nature of the beast."

"That's cold," Neil said.

"Somebody will provide those services," she countered. "It's just that I don't want to be in that business."

"You talk about money laundering as if these people are dealing a little weed on the side. They're not. They're helping bad guys get away with serious crimes worth billions of dollars."

"For a moment there, you sounded just like Rachel," Carole said, a wistful sadness in her voice.

"I've been accused of worse."

They sat silently for a moment.

"I could use your help," Carole said tentatively.

"You're crazy to think you can trust any deal you do with Santiago. Or the RCMP, for that matter."

She reached across the table and placed her hand on his. "In the future, when I look back on all this, I don't want to be haunted by the thought that I let Isabelle get away with what she did to Rachel and Dad and Paul. I have to make sure she's stopped—"

"What does that mean? Goes to prison? Dies?"

"Either one works for me."

"For Santiago to take over, he'll have to kill her."

"I can live with that."

He drummed his fingers on the table. She withdrew her hand.

He leaned forward, dropping his voice. "What do you bet Isabelle has already caught wind of your plans? You're putting yourself right in her sights."

"It's a chance I have to take," she said bleakly. "I have a responsibility to fix this thing."

Neil knew he shouldn't agree, but he understood exactly what she meant.

"Okay. What do you need?"

And as the words left his mouth, an expression flashed through his mind: *the road to hell is paved with good intentions.*

55

At Toronto Police headquarters, the room jangled with people, phones and the click of laptop keyboards. Display monitors and bulletin boards hung from cinder block walls. Danny Relf directed the blitz—organizing surveillance, digging into files and identifying potential interview subjects, mainly pissed-off former business partners.

The hunt was laser-focused: find enough admissible evidence to justify the next round of warrants.

An assistant crown attorney sat in a corner reviewing thousands of documents mysteriously leaked overnight via an anti-corruption blog based in Iceland.

"Move fast, but be careful," Neil warned them all. "Isabelle's attorneys will put everything we do under the microscope. No mistakes. We won't get a second chance."

"We could focus on catching Reichelt and Brisbane. Get them to flip on Lisgar and Santiago," Relf said. "Old school, but it works."

"No time."

Relf called out to the assistant crown attorney. "Do we have enough for warrants on the shooters?"

"Not based on what I can see here," Beth Ryland answered. She was short, with big glasses and thin lips. For an assistant crown attorney, she was good, Neil thought, but possibly a little too intense. "We would need documented proof that Reichelt and Brisbane work for Santiago's security forces and that Isabelle controls Grupo Muxia."

"Let me see what I can do," offered Ali Gorka, picking up the phone to call the FBI field office in New York.

Llewelyn pulled Neil aside. "In case no one says it, thanks."

Neil looked at him suspiciously. "What for?"

"You put Isabelle Lisgar on our radar. If it wasn't for you, we would be looking at a security nightmare."

"Rachel started it. I'm just trying to do right by her."

Llewelyn leaned forward. "I know we never hit it off, but there's no reason we can't work together."

"Like now?"

"Now, the future. Who knows?"

Neil was wary. "What did you have in mind?"

Llewelyn shrugged. "We both work on cases that stray into grey areas. Things can become murky. You have a certain latitude for action that I don't have. I have access you might find useful. From time to time, our paths may cross."

Neil's phone buzzed. He glanced at the caller ID. This gave him a minute to think about Llewelyn's proposal.

"I gotta take this," he said. "What's—"

"Help!" Carole's panicked voice electrified him. "She's been shot!"

56

The private elevator chimed softly as the doors opened on the forty-third floor of the TD Centre North Tower. Carole entered the empty car, followed by Tracy Cosgrain, a mid-forties Securitec bodyguard in a dark pantsuit, who leaned over and hit the button for the underground parking level.

"I want to stop at the shopping concourse," Carole said, rubbing her forehead. "I need something before my brain melts. There was no air in that room."

"No problem." Tracy pushed the concourse button. The two women fell silent.

It had been a long morning in the offices of Arles Thompson, the law firm that had handled the Lisgar family's legal business for decades. Jeff Arles, grandson of one of the founders, walked her through the complex web of Ontario Securities Commission forms, submissions and contracts she needed to sign. Some were related to Rachel's estate, others enabled her to assume control of Bala Bay Financial. The board of directors would vote on it, of course, but Carole controlled enough shares to make their approval little more than a rubber stamp.

She had known Jeff for most of her life, so she was not surprised he protested the speed with which things were moving. She negotiated a simple agreement in principle with Paolo Santiago to buy the MacklinMunroe money laundering operation for twenty-seven million dollars, one-third of which was due on signing. A bargain price she knew he couldn't resist.

Now it was early afternoon, the contracts executed, the money transferred, and Carole had a screaming headache.

She begged off a celebratory lunch offer from Jeff but gave him a rain check. Her days in Ottawa were over, at least for a while. He would be a useful guy to have around as she figured out how to run the restructured Bala Bay Financial.

Once she dealt with Isabelle.

But that was a problem for later.

First, get rid of the headache.

The elevator doors opened onto the underground PATH concourse. It was a maze of interconnected shops, restaurants and subway stations that lay beneath dozens of office towers clustered in the downtown core.

There was a familiar semi-controlled chaos of office workers hurrying to grab quick lunches and squeeze in a bit of shopping. For Carole, the TD Centre had been part of her life forever. Her dad's office had been here. As a kid, after every visit, she and Rachel always insisted on visiting the WH Smith bookstore before climbing into the limo for the drive home. Today, those memories made her feel more alone than ever. She pushed them aside.

Carole glanced around, with Tracy a half-step behind her. A Shoppers Drug Mart caught her eye, and she headed that way.

She had taken two, three steps when it happened.

She was shoved hard from behind. Startled, she stumbled, almost going to her knees.

She turned around. "What the f—"

Tracy, her eyes stretched wide open with stunned incomprehension, fell to her knees, a bloody hole in her forehead.

Carole instinctively reached for her. She looked up.

A woman. Straw fedora. Tinted glasses. Scar on her cheek. Their gaze locked for a moment.

Carole reeled back. *Oh my God. From the photos. The woman who shot Paul.*

She scrambled to her feet, backing away, abandoning Tracy, her attention riveted on Reichelt.

She was peripherally aware that somebody screamed, a woman. A man bent down over Tracy, cellphone to his ear. In one of those funny tricks of sound, she could hear him shouting to the 9-1-1 operator. In one of those odd connections the brain makes in the shock of sudden stress, Carole hoped the call went through okay. Cell coverage was always spotty in the PATH.

She snatched her own phone from her pocket and hit redial, all the while keeping her eye on the killer who was calmly stalking her.

"Help!" She heard her words tumbling out, panicking, a rope of fear choking her. "She's been shot!"

"Slow down," Neil responded at once, his voice calm. "Who's been shot?"

"Tracy. The bodyguard." Carole was panting. She turned and pushed her way through the gathering crowd, looking over her shoulder, moving fast towards the next corridor of shops. "I saw her! It's Reichelt."

"Where are you?"

"The TD Centre. North Tower."

Her breath was coming in ragged gasps.

And she was terrified.

She looked around and panicked. She was lost.

She scanned the overhead signs. Arrows pointed in every direction. So much had changed. Royal Bank Plaza. Commerce Court. First Canadian Place. The Exchange Tower. Union Station. Confusion snarled her thoughts. She pressed her phone harder to her ear.

"Get outside, fast as you can," Neil said slowly, clearly. "Those towers all have bank branches at street level. Find one. Go inside. Tell security you need help."

"What if she finds me?" Her voice was low, a whisper almost. She was breathing even faster. She skirted around a pair of old men lugging wide legal briefcases. She looked back. She spotted a straw fedora in the distance.

"I'm on my way," she heard Neil say. "Stay on the line. We'll meet—"

Carole staggered, blindsided.

"Hey! Watch it!"

A young couple with a baby, loaded down with suitcases and backpacks, had stopped to consult a map. She had run smack into them.

"Sorry," she called back as she recovered her footing. She spied an exit sign and raced for it.

She reached the crowded escalator and looked up. There was sunlight at the top. She dodged around passengers and zigzagged her way up the slow-moving stairs.

At the top, she spilled out onto the plaza. Frantically, she looked around. Knots of people filled the sidewalks. Bumper to bumper traffic and red lights snarled the street.

On her left, sunlight flashed off the revolving doors to a Royal Bank branch.

Walking fast, slipping between people, Carole crossed to the glassed-in lobby, entered the bank, spotted the security desk and headed straight for it.

Her heart was pounding. Her throat was raw. Relief poured in.

57

Isabelle's three-storey townhouse had a small flagstone front courtyard surrounded by a wrought-iron fence with spear-point finials that seemed dangerously sharp.

Neil pushed open the gate and held it for Carole. In her hand was a front door key, one she had used routinely for years. Tonight, it was clenched in her fist. Her knuckles were white.

He knew she was furious, and that worried him. The TD Centre had been locked down, but Reichelt had escaped. They'd spent the afternoon at police headquarters providing statements. His pistol was tucked under his jacket at the small of his back next to a pair of flexi-cuffs borrowed from Relf. He felt better having them, but they might not be enough. If they wanted to get out alive, they needed to be smart and ice cold.

The stately front door opened silently on to a marble foyer. Neil checked the parlour on the left and the dining room on the right. Both were empty. Carole absently touched the microphone taped under her blouse.

She looked at him, a silent question in her eyes. He nodded in reassurance. She let out a slow breath, then pointed to the back of the house where Isabelle had her office. He gently closed the front door and followed her down the hallway.

They caught Isabelle at her desk. She was packing a slim briefcase. Something alerted her. She stood and closed the case. Calmly, she studied the two of them.

Her voice was carefully controlled. "How did you get in here?"

"I still have a key," Carole said. "Since it's now my house, I must remember to change the locks."

"You really expect to be around that long?"

"You sent Karin Reichelt after me this afternoon, yet here I am."

"You were lucky, and no one's luck holds forever."

Neil stepped forward.

"You're her protection?" Isabelle scoffed.

"You had me fooled," he admitted. "I knew you were a greedy bitch. I didn't think you were a killer."

"I don't kill people. I hire specialists for that."

Would that be a clear enough confession for the cops listening on the other end of the wire? Neil caught a ghostly shadow in the corner of his eye. He spun.

Karin Reichelt appeared in the doorway from the kitchen, a pistol in her hand, a silencer screwed onto the barrel.

Carole sucked in her breath. "You tried to kill me."

Reichelt tilted her head in acknowledgement. There was almost an apology in her gesture. "Communication issues. Apparently, the world has changed since this morning."

"What do you mean?" Isabelle asked calmly. "And how did you get in?"

Reichelt lifted her gun casually. "Echelon Security installed your system. Your codes were on file."

"No matter, I'm glad to see you," Isabelle said, satisfaction spreading across her face. "Your timing is perfect."

Neil stepped in front of Carole. He stood tall and spread his arms, screening her protectively.

His expression froze when he felt Carole reach under his jacket and tug the gun free.

"Karin Reichelt, right?" Neil wanted to focus the killer's attention on him, his voice loud enough to be picked up on the wire.

"And you're the private detective from New York." She grinned. "You move pretty fast." She flicked the gun barrel at them. He noticed she was wearing thin latex gloves. They shuffled uneasily to one side of the office.

"You're probably better prepared than at our last meeting," Reichelt said. "Open your jacket."

Slowly, he parted the front of his jacket to show her there was no shoulder holster or gun in his waistband.

Reichelt glided around behind Isabelle. "Should I be impressed by your confidence or insulted by your stupidity?"

"What shall we do with them?" Isabelle asked rhetorically.

"I wouldn't know," Reichelt said. "I am still getting used to how things are done in the private sector." Her left hand slipped into her jacket pocket.

"They broke in here," Isabelle mused aloud. She obviously was enjoying toying with Carole and Neil. "Is this a solution disguised as a problem?"

"No, it's a complication," Reichelt said. She shifted her aim. She put the barrel at the back of Isabelle's head.

"What—" Isabelle started to twist her head.

"Don't move!"

Isabelle froze.

Reichelt pulled a syringe from her jacket pocket and, one-handed, flicked off the point guard.

"In my old job," Reichelt said, glancing at Carole, "we called this *regime change*."

She plunged the needle into the back of Isabelle's neck.

"No!" Carole yelled.

Isabelle, with nothing to lose, threw herself on Reichelt. The killer, taken by surprise, staggered momentarily.

Neil was on top of her instantly. He grabbed for her gun hand. She twisted away. Isabelle still clinging to her shoulder.

Reichelt crashed backwards into the bookcase, dislodging Isabelle, who collapsed. Carole rushed to her.

Neil again leapt for Reichelt. He had more than fifty pounds and a six-inch reach advantage. But she was tough and trained and ten years younger.

He smashed her gun hand against the bookcase. The pistol clattered to the floor. He threw a solid punch at her throat. She tucked her head down, and the blow bounced off her shoulder.

She retaliated with an incredibly fast palm strike to his solar plexus. He turned just in time. Lightning quick, he grabbed for her hand and locked onto it before she could pull it back. He yanked her towards him.

He expected her to resist.

But when he pulled, she flowed with it.

In a flash, she was in his face. She snapped her head forward. She smashed her forehead into his nose, breaking it.

The pain was enormous. His eyes streamed tears, blinding him. He held her and squeezed tight, trapping her arms at her sides.

He sensed her rearing back for another head-butt. He set his feet and beat her to it, slamming his rock-hard forehead into her face.

Her eyes shot open wide, stunned, disoriented. He crashed them to the floor. He pinned her and reached under his jacket for the flexi-cuffs.

A mistake.

The instant she felt his weight shift, Reichelt erupted from the floor scrambling for the gun. He lunged after her, tackling her legs. Before she could reach the pistol, he was climbing up her body.

She squirmed away, gaining a few inches of freedom. It was enough. From beneath her jacket, she pulled her black stiletto. She flipped around to face Neil.

Desperately, he reached for her knife hand, every fibre focused on this new threat.

Fast as a snake, she struck but not with the blade. The side of her fist hammered into his broken nose.

For a split second, white sheets of pain paralyzed him.

She drove the blade down towards his unprotected back.

Gunshots exploded in the room.

Two, three, four, five explosions.

Carole, shooting wild.

Reichelt's shoulder jerked as a bullet smashed into it. The blade dropped to the floor.

Nearly blind, blood smeared across the bottom half of his face, Neil grabbed the knife. He clamped one arm around her. He shoved the stiletto deep into Reichelt's side. Her back arched. She roared with rage.

He held her tight and feverishly stabbed again and again. She twisted, spasmed, then went limp.

He rolled off her and looked over at Carole, who was holding Isabelle in her arms. His gun was still clenched in her fist. Her face was chalk-white, her expression blank, her eyes staring at the floor.

"We need an ambulance!" he yelled.

Between ragged gasps for air, his voice shaky from adrenalin, he reached out to her. "Are you okay?"

She locked eyes with him. She nodded.

His gaze settled on Isabelle. Lifeless eyes, mouth sagging open, wrinkled flesh. The undignified smell of piss and shit as her body had let everything go. The witch was dead.

He heard the front door slam open.

The cavalry. At last.

It was over.

58

Rachel's eyes flashed with intelligence in the video projected against the white cinder block wall of the U of T Goodman Centre atrium. It was a clip lifted from her final online seminar in social entrepreneurship.

"While academic life can be enormously satisfying, knowledge carries with it the weight of responsibility. Sir Isaac Newton said it best. *If I have seen further, it is by standing on the shoulders of giants.* The facts in your head, the truths you discover, were made possible by the work of others. You, too, have an obligation to engage with the world. Your expertise, your insights, could be the keys needed to unlock problems and open doors to better lives for millions of people. And you know what? It can be fun. By my calculation, that's a pretty good reason for getting out of bed in the morning."

The video froze as a big grin lit up Rachel's face and the crowd broke into applause. More than three hundred students and faculty members had gathered for a special celebration of the department's research achievements. The high point was the announcement of a new graduate scholarship in Rachel's memory. Annie Da Silva, the centre's executive director, had introduced Carole and now stood on stage behind her.

Carole looked up from the podium, her eyes sweeping the crowd, resting for a moment on Neil's face before she continued.

"Rachel challenged the status quo and that often made people uncomfortable. In fact, she took a devil's delight in other people's discomfort. As her sister, I speak from personal experience when I say I know how much that could sting."

An appreciative chuckle echoed through the glass-and-steel atrium.

"She's got them eating out of the palm of her hand," Neil murmured to Janos Pach. They stood together at the back of the crowd. There were students in fashionably odd clothes, professors of both sexes in tweeds and chinos, and a comfortable atmosphere of academic celebration.

"Rachel used her mathematical gifts and passion for justice as a lever and fulcrum to change the world. To help that spirit inspire the dreams of future mathematicians, I am pleased to announce today a new scholarship. The annual Rachel Lisgar Award will support groundbreaking work in advanced mathematics and social justice research. The amount will be $1,123,581.32."

Applause broke out, then laughter rippled through the crowd as people got the joke.

Neil looked at Janos, an eyebrow raised in question.

"It is the Fibonacci sequence," Janos explained. "It is a mathematical formula that is found everywhere, from the golden mean to computer algorithms to genetic codes."

"Nice touch," Neil said, watching Carole step down.

Summer had turned to fall. She had waited long enough. Memories of the townhouse debacle had faded.

Forensic tests had shown Reichelt's syringe contained a

lethal dose of potassium chloride, a natural bio-chemical virtually undetectable in an autopsy but one that causes cardiac arrest in anyone with Isabelle's medical history. It was quietly agreed that *heart attack* was the best cover story for the published obituary. Karin Reichelt's body was never claimed. She ended up buried by the city in a cemetery on the outskirts of town where the plots are cheap.

Carole worked her way through the crowd and joined Neil and Janos for a glass of champagne.

"A lovely speech," Janos said, raising his glass in salute.

"You're a natural," Neil added. "Maybe you should give away huge sums of money more often."

"I can't see that happening, but I must admit it was fun."

"Get used to it," Janos advised. "As CEO, corporate philanthropy is part of your job description."

"We'll see," she laughed, then turned to Neil. "But speaking of jobs, have you given any more thought to coming to work for me? I could use your help cleaning up whatever dodgy stuff Isabelle left behind."

"You'd be better off with auditors and forensic accountants."

"Possibly," she responded. "What are you doing this weekend?"

He glanced at Janos before looking back at her. "Why?"

"I'm closing down the cottage on Lake Rosseau. We could talk it over."

He was torn. The idea of a weekend alone with her up north started a buzz in his gut. It was dangerously tempting.

"That could be a very bad idea," he said regretfully. He could tell by her grin that she knew exactly what he was thinking.

Janos intervened. "May I make a suggestion? This research award. There will be come kind of vetting, I assume?

A peer group, certainly, but you will want outside perspectives as well."

"That's true," she said, looking at Neil playfully. "You could be part of the selection committee—"

"God save me from committees."

She rolled her eyes. "A panel, then. Could you accept *panel?*"

"A panel. Sure, okay."

"Excellent," she said with a wink to Janos. She glanced at an incoming message of her phone. "I have to go." She leaned over and gave Janos a kiss on the cheek. "Thanks for everything."

Neil opened his arms, and they hugged. There was a slightly awkward moment when they broke free. Was the hug too long? Too tight? Too revealing?

Carole stepped back. With a final wave, she turned and walked through the atrium to where her car sat, waiting at the curb.

And then she was gone, leaving a void. He hadn't expected it would mean so much.

"I also want to thank you," Janos said, placing his hand lightly on Neil's shoulder.

"For what?"

The ceremony was over. The crowd was breaking up. Neil and Janos strolled towards the atrium's exit onto St. George Street.

"Because you found out what really happened to Rachel, I sleep better."

"I'd say that calls for a bonus."

"In your dreams," Janos said with a quick smile. "I will, however, pay for lunch."

"Deal," said Neil as he stepped through the revolving door and back onto the city street.

IF YOU ENJOYED THIS STORY...

... please leave a review on Amazon, Kobo, your favourite online bookstore, Goodreads or any other website where like-minded readers are searching for their next book. They are interested in your opinion, and I'd really appreciate your support.

ACKNOWLEDGMENTS

While my name stands alone on the cover, this book might never have been published without the help of many people.

Novelist Barbara Kyle provided invaluable insights and advice that enriched the final story. A big thanks goes out to copy editor Vanessa Wells and proofreader Kelly Lamb who did their best to sharpen my prose. Any and all remaining mistakes are mine and mine alone. Big thanks also to my family and friends who read earlier drafts. Their comments, criticisms and enthusiasm kept me going.

And finally, at times when I was most discouraged and did not know if I would ever finish the story, my wife Sandra would look at me as if I was crazy and simply say, "Of course you will, and it will be great."

How could I be so lucky?

ABOUT THE AUTHOR

Bill Prentice is a crime-fiction author and freelance writer specializing in international trade and investment marketing, economic development and public-private sector partnerships. *Why was Rachel Murdered?* is his debut novel. An earlier story was shortlisted by the Crime Writers of Canada as one of the best unpublished crime novels of 2015. Bill lives in Toronto, Canada.

CPSIA information can be obtained
at www.ICGtesting.com
Printed in the USA
LVHW042255040319
609514LV00001B/159/P